BROKEN GLASS

A Pittsburgh Murder Mystery

BROKEN GLASS

A Pittsburgh Murder Mystery

REBECCA A. MILES

Durham, NC

Broken Glass: A Pittsburgh Murder Mystery
(The Pittsburgh Murder Mysteries #2)
Rebecca A. Miles
rebeccaamystery@msn.com

Published 2022, by Torchflame Books
an Imprint of Light Messages
www.lightmessages.com
Durham, NC 27713 USA
SAN: 920-9298

Paperback ISBN: 978-1-61153-499-3
E-book ISBN: 978-1-61153-500-6
Library of Congress Control Number: 2022922709

To the hard-working glass artists of Pittsburgh
and those around the world.

CHAPTER 1

KATE CHAMBERS PLACED THE BLOWPIPE into the opening of the oven. The temperature was around two thousand degrees Fahrenheit, so she had pinned her luxuriant black hair into a bun. Like all the other glass-blowing students, she wore a bandana to capture the sweat running down her face and neck. The physicality of the hot shop suited her—blowing glass was athletic and artistic, and when a piece hit the floor, also heartbreaking—as of late, the totality of the experience suited her mood.

She often used a blow hose to puff air into the gather of hot glass, but today Kate's best friend, professor Johnny McCarthy, was her assistant and held the blowpipe. "Give me a light puff," requested Kate. Johnny breathed lightly into the hollow rod, causing the bubble at the other end to expand. Kate returned the rod to the oven to keep the glass malleable, then swung the rod like a clock pendulum until the hot glass grew to the size she wanted. Puffing air into the hollow rod and then placing it into what is, unfortunately, called the glory hole, was the rinse-and-repeat process of hot glass work.

Kate transferred the glass to the punty rod, where Johnny used wooden paddles to help form a flat vase bottom. Finally, she firmly tapped off the glass piece at the end of the rod, dropping it into a box lined with a fire blanket. Johnny rushed it to the annealing oven, where the glass would slowly cool down.

"All right, then!" Kate high-fived Johnny while they both drank deeply from their cold water bottles. She looked around at the other stations watching fellow students create their pieces. Everyone was from a different background—some were wannabe glass artists, some were art students, and some were people who simply wanted to learn about the craft of hot glass. Kate fell into the latter group.

Two ovens down from hers, she noticed that Eugene Rose, one of Johnny's graduate students, looked unstable on his feet. He seemed to be losing strength in his legs and arms; Eugene Rose's knees buckled, and he collapsed onto the concrete floor. The glass at the end of his punty rod shattered as it hit the ground.

"Someone call an ambulance," shouted Kate as she rapidly crossed the short distance to the young man. Kneeling beside him, she felt for a pulse. Johnny crouched close to her, also putting his fingers on the young student's carotid; their eyes locked, and Kate whispered, "He's dead."

The glass instructor, Andy Ormsby, who had been standing behind the two friends, heard her declaration and immediately took control of the hot shop. "Everyone! We must wait for the paramedics to arrive to take care of Eugene. Get your pieces into the annealing ovens." He conveniently avoided mentioning that Eugene Rose might be dead.

Kate turned to Andy, advising, "No one should leave. Police might be called, and they will want to interview everyone." All the participants had gathered close together. Some turned so as not to look at their fellow student. Others held hands or quietly wept in shock.

Within minutes, the city paramedics arrived and began to assess Eugene Rose's condition. They asked Andy, "Has everyone in this class been vaccinated for COVID?"

Andy nodded in the affirmative. "What about Eugene?"

Looking straight at Ormsby, the paramedic responded, "Unfortunately, this young man is dead."

Johnny blurted out, "How can that be? He's my graduate student. He's only in his early twenties! He was vaccinated and was able to get the booster shot. What could he possibly die from?"

"I'm afraid that is a question for Dr. Patel, the medical examiner. Sorry for your loss, professor."

Kate placed her hand on Johnny's back. "You know how good Dr. Patel is. She will give us answers." Just as the words were out of her mouth, everyone turned and, like the parting of the Red Sea, made a pathway for a tall, broad-shouldered man who moved into the room with confident strides and an unmistakable air of authority.

"Chief Jablonsky," said Kate. Pittsburgh's Chief Detective Stefan Jablonsky stopped, clearly surprised to see the sometimes amateur sleuth at this scene. Jablonsky had permitted Kate and her university friends to help on several murder cases. Still, he liked civilians to stay on their side of the thin blue line, something the smart and inquisitive Kate had a hard time doing.

"Dr. Kate Chambers. Oh, and I see Professor McCarthy is also here. Taking a class? I can always count on something happening when you are together."

Jablonsky grinned at Kate and Johnny, then turned to speak with the paramedics. The chief was of middle European descent, his physique was still strong and muscular, but his brown hair had thinned. Now in his sixties, he had enjoyed a long, successful career in Pittsburgh, the city in which he was born, raised his daughter, and in which he probably would die. He knew where all the small-time and big-time criminals operated—a glass-blowing hot shop was not one of them. He addressed the members of the class.

"No one is allowed to leave until we have taken your statements about what happened here. This is detective Antoine DeVille—he will organize all of you. We will use Andy Ormsby's office for the interviews. Let's get started."

Jablonsky interviewed Kate and Johnny himself. As they sat down to talk, he couldn't get over how hot it was in the furnace area; to himself, he quoted a line from the movie *Birdcage*, "*I'm sweating like some kind of farm animal*," and wondered if the young man might have died from heat stroke. Stefan took out his small paper notebook and a pen and flipped to a clean page.

"Johnny McCarthy. How do you know Eugene Rose?"

"Well, Eugene is, or was, a graduate student of mine. Really smart guy almost finished with his dissertation. Easy going. His area of study was the history of classic Venetian glass techniques, so he decided to take this class to deepen his understanding of how hot glass is made." Johnny unconsciously ran his hands over his thick red-gold hair, then wiped his freckled face with a starched old-fashioned handkerchief. In his late thirties, Johnny was still an attractive and athletic man, but that aside, Jablonsky recognized the symptoms of shock distress in his interviewee.

"Do you know if there is anyone who might have wanted to hurt him?"

"No—as far as I can tell, he was liked by everyone. I mean, he's a graduate student in art history. Who would want to hurt him?" Johnny turned to look at Kate, who indicated she had something to add.

"One of Eugene's close friends was referred to me by the chair of the Fine Arts department, Dr. Robert Morelli. The chair felt he needed some academic advising. You know him, Johnny—Zane Davies. He sometimes referenced Eugene in our advising sessions." Johnny was surprised that Kate knew one of his graduate students—but then, she was closed-mouthed about her young advisees.

Jablonsky said, "Kate, this is a police inquiry. You weren't Mr. Davies' psychologist, so you aren't bound by confidentiality. What kinds of things did he say about Eugene Rose?"

"Well, he wanted to be closer to Eugene, I mean, romantically, but Eugene wasn't interested. I also think Zane was jealous of Eugene's standing in the department. All of the graduate students are smart; some have a more pleasing personality than others. Unlike Eugene, Zane frequently challenged his professors to the point of causing out-and-out arguments—he had a hard time controlling his temper."

Jablonsky noted the name Dr. Morelli and the student Zane Davies. "Did he mention any other close friends?"

"Yes. There was a girl named Sarah Braithwaite; her parents are from South Africa, but Sarah was born here. She is, was, Eugene's roommate." Kate looked to Johnny to add what he knew.

"Sarah is a master's student in the music department. She studies the development of the fifteenth and sixteenth-century violin. She has cross-registered for a few of my classes. Sarah just returned from a semester abroad—she studied in Cremona and Venice, looking at the Amati and Stradivari violins."

"Did Eugene Rose visit her there?"

"Yes. Zane Davies and Eugene spent time in Florence and Venice with her."

Kate jumped in. "That's right! They just made it out before the country locked down over COVID-19. Around the time they returned to the States, all my university appointments went to virtual meetings—my department colleagues are just now seeing advisees in our offices again."

"Have you seen Zane Davies since he got back from Italy?"

"Yes. I saw him this week." Kate hesitated. She hated talking about her advisees.

"Did he mention Eugene Rose?"

"No. He didn't mention him in this particular session." Kate didn't offer any more information.

"If Eugene Rose wasn't interested in Zane Davies, did he have a romantic partner?" The chief had turned to Johnny, who laughed.

"Chief, not all gay people know every other gay person in the city. I can say that the gay graduate student community is tight and gossipy; Eugene might have had another partner or several." The chief looked to Kate for confirmation.

She shrugged. "I don't know. I just know that Zane Davies carried a torch for Eugene."

"John. Do you have Zane Davies' and Sarah Braithwaite's contact details? Give them to Coupe, please."

Antoine DeVille, a handsome light-skinned black man in his early thirties, had been raised in New Orleans but educated in Pittsburgh. After finishing his degree, he began to build a reputation for smart police work, and Jablonsky took notice. Since most groups of men assign nicknames, DeVille's last name begged for his to be Coupe, and it stuck. Antoine, with his easy-going Creole genes, found the moniker amusing. DeVille informed the chief that all the students' statements had been taken.

Andy Ormsby spoke up. "What do you intend to do with all of the glass pieces that are cooling?"

"I want them as evidence. Mr. Ormsby, I'm afraid we are going to take the glass and have forensics look at it."

"Chief Jablonsky, that might be impossible. All the glass pieces are still hot and in the annealing ovens to cool slowly—if you take the objects out of the ovens, they will crack. Those pieces belong to hard-working students. Is it possible for the forensic team to examine them here at the shop, say tomorrow when they are cooled?" Andy Ormsby was clearly upset; his tone was almost pleading.

"Let me see what I can do," replied the chief. "In the meantime, however, no one goes in or out until forensics has released the scene. That includes you and all your students, cleaning people, and the like. Are we clear?"

"Understood." Ormsby looked to Kate and Johnny for sympathy. One of the best student pieces cooling was her tall wine decanter. Kate shrugged her shoulders in a gesture of, "What can you do?"

Jablonsky explained to the students that all of their creations were now possible evidence and must remain in the hot shop. Amidst much grumbling, the students, including Johnny and Kate, were finally allowed to leave. They headed to her Fifth Avenue condominium in the university area while Jablonsky left for the medical examiner's office to view the body and talk about the cause and manner of death.

CHAPTER 2

THE GUEST ROOM at Kate's condominium was Johnny's home away from home. Since his recent break-up, he preferred the cozy atmosphere at Kate's to his very modern house on the South Side Slopes. Tonight, Kate wanted to pick Johnny's brain about Eugene Rose.

Bourbon Ball, her chocolate Labrador, wiggled around his dog mom and Johnny, then stood in front of the pantry door where his food was kept. "Hello, my beautiful boy. Hungry?" As she poured the kibble into his dish, she asked Johnny what he knew about Eugene's life.

"Not a whole lot—I try not to get too close to my graduate students. It can complicate things. I know that he was local. Grew up in Squirrel Hill—Sam, his father, and Ada, his mother, own several men's high-end clothing stores. I'm not sure about siblings. I liked Eugene as a person and because he was becoming such a good art historian."

"So, his area of academic interest was Venetian glass? I bet it would be interesting to read his writings. What did his dissertation focus on?" Kate offered Bourbon Ball fresh water, which he immediately slopped all over the floor as he drank.

"He focused on the development of the Murrine technique in Venetian glass. You know, how the glass cane is cut and then manipulated into different shapes or patterns—like the famous millefiori. It was strictly an academic topic—

he would have gotten several publications out of it." As he talked, Johnny massaged BB's silky ears, clearly attached to the block-headed lab. "Kate, do you know anything relevant about the girl, Sarah?"

The coffee Kate was brewing perfumed the air with a sweet and acrid fragrance. She paused before answering to enjoy the scent while putting out cups and saucers; Johnny hadn't known that, along with Zane, Sarah was also one of her academic advisees. She finally responded to his question.

"Well, Zane Davies mentioned that Sarah and Eugene were two peas in a pod—same dry wit and interest in very specialized academic inquiry—like her study of the origins of the four-string violin. He spoke about her as if she were the female version of Eugene—he was jealous. Zane doesn't strike me as much of an academic. I'm not sure what he is doing in your program. I think he views the world more like a businessman."

Johnny sipped the hot coffee, murmuring an appreciative *ah.* "Zane Davies comes from money. His father is in the tool and dye industry—big factories here and in South America. He's indicated to me that his family buys art—paintings, sculpture, other handmade objects—and that his father relies on him to say which artist will appreciate in value. So, in a way, he's already a businessman."

"That's interesting. He procures art as an investment for his family. Well, nothing wrong with that—it just strikes me that someone like Eugene Rose wouldn't think in those terms. No wonder there wasn't an attraction between them." Kate questioned Johnny further. "Were there any other graduate students with whom Eugene Rose hung out? If he didn't die from natural causes, then it was foul play. For an academic only in his twenties, what could he have possibly done to provoke someone to kill him? And how was he murdered?"

Johnny gave her the universal sign that he didn't have any answers—palms up with a lift of the shoulders.

"Just an aside, Kate, you look lovely. Your skin is glowing; your dark eyes are shining—you are animated! You love talking murder," observed a grinning Johnny. Since her fiancé, and husband of only several hours, Eddie Fitzroy, unexpectedly died from injuries sustained in a tractor-trailer accident, Kate had been living in a state of mourning. Then came the COVID-19 lockdown—it had been a tough year for the usually irrepressible Dr. Chambers.

It was very early the next morning when the chief leaned over Eugene Rose's lifeless body listening to Dr. Aashi Patel deliver her findings.

"My students may never see this again. This young man was poisoned by a plant called Atropa Belladonna, or Deadly Nightshade. It was a popular method of poisoning people in European courts because you could put the black berries in food and wine. It was said that the Borgias got rid of many of their enemies that way—including bishops and monseigneurs." Dr. Patel's lilting Indian-American accent became more pronounced, and to Jablonsky's ear, endearing, as she warmed to her subject.

"Observe the extremely dry tissues of his mouth and throat and the rash. His vision would have blurred, and he would have lost his balance. The normal activities of the parasympathetic nervous system, like breathing and heart rate, would have been compromised." Patel paused, waiting for her colleague and special friend to comment.

"I take it that you are pronouncing the cause of this young man's death to be poison and the manner of his death to be murder. Okay, that is clear enough. Did the poisoning take place over time or all at once?" Jablonsky knew about the Deadly Nightshade plant, but in twenty-first-century America, there were so many other ways to poison someone that it was rarely used.

"The science tells me it was all at once. It was delivered through the mouth, so either he drank something containing the berry juice, or the root of the plant could have been ground up and put in something that he ate. I would like to see the crime scene." Patel covered young Eugene Rose's body. There was always respect in how she approached the dead; he often heard her teach her students that the Medical Examiner speaks for the dead. Jablonsky admired that quality in her.

"The forensic team is there now. I can take you right away." Jablonsky could be quite mannerly, almost courtly—he was the grandson of a stern 'Studda Bubba,' his mother's mother. He held the morgue door for Dr. Patel and carried her black bag. It was only a short drive to the glass shop.

After one of their mutual cases, the two colleagues started having breakfast together at Sophia's Café in the Strip District. At first, it was all business, but as time passed, they spoke about personal things—divorce, children (her son, Sai, his daughter, Carly,) and ex-spouses. It was a sweet, later-life romance underpinned by friendship, similar interests, and mutual attraction.

When they got there, Dr. Patel slowly walked around the hot shop, saying hello to the forensic team members and observing how they handled the cooled glass pieces. "I've never been to a murder scene in a place where art glass is made. Look at all this equipment." Tools from Eugene Rose's section of the hot shop had been tagged and bagged—a steel blowpipe, a punty rod, jacks that would hold glass, paddles, and torches used for shaping hot glass. Eugene Rose's glass pieces were comprised of several wine glasses, in which he attempted a glass roundel on either side. The pieces of glass that shattered when he fell had also been bagged.

Andy Ormsby stood sentry. Along with being the center's director, he was also an expert in glassblowing. The chief introduced Andy to Dr. Patel, who requested that his students' DNA and fingerprints be gathered and sent to her office. Jablonsky mentioned to her that Kate and Johnny were part of the class. "We already have their DNA from the attack on John's mother," he remarked.

"That Kate Chambers is always up to something interesting. Where is her glass piece?" Andy Ormsby pointed to a tall clear wine decanter that had green vines winding around it. "Very beautiful," Dr. Patel remarked.

Ormsby replied, "It's a type of decanter called *stangenglas,* or tall thin glass. This was Kate's station. Over here was Eugene Rose's. She got to him quickly when she saw he was losing his balance."

"What exactly was he doing when he fell?" questioned Jablonsky.

Andy lifted a steel blow rod and demonstrated how it was used in gathering and forming glass. "He would have puffed into this rod; then it would be placed in the hot oven to keep it malleable, then he would roll it on this steel marver table, and then back into the oven. I've heard Kate refer to it as a tedious process of 'rinse and repeat' work." The chief noticed that Andy smiled when he mentioned Kate.

Dr. Patel addressed herself to the forensic team. "Please make sure every single one of Mr. Rose's tools is taken to the forensics lab." The chief was interested in something she had said about Belladonna when they were at the morgue.

"Is there a deli or coffee shop here on the premises? Some place where they serve drinks and sandwiches?" Since

Eugene Rose had ingested the poison, he might have bought a sandwich and then brought it into the hot shop."

"Yes, there is a coffee shop on the main floor as you enter the building. They sell sandwiches, wraps, salads, fruit, cold and hot drinks—that kind of thing."

The chief grabbed one of the forensic techs. "I want your team to examine any empty water bottles or sandwich wrappings around Eugene's station or in his garbage can. Then, fan out to everyone else's drink containers and garbage can. Make sure you have samples from the deli, particularly food that remains from yesterday that Eugene Rose might have eaten."

He thought to himself, *the murderer either brought poisoned food or drink into the hot shop, or mixed poison into what was already here. This murder was carefully planned by someone who knew Eugene Rose's habits. This perpetrator is a meticulous person.*

CHAPTER 3

"WHY KILL SOMEONE AT THE HOT SHOP? Is there some meaning to it—for instance, is there something about the glassmaking process itself, or was it just a place where the murderer knew Eugene would be?" Kate paddled close to Johnny's kayak to hear his response.

"On the surface, it seems to me that it was merely convenient. The killer knew when Eugene would be in class."

The two friends often kayaked on the Allegheny River before heading to work. During the pandemic, it was one of the few activities they could safely do for exercise; it provided a connection to the natural world and relief from the unnatural situation of sitting in front of the computer screen for Zoom meetings.

This morning the river was so calm that one of Pittsburgh's ubiquitous bridges was perfectly mirrored in the clear blue-green water—it was like a scene from a Turner landscape. Kate smiled with pleasure; there simply was something magical about being on the water; it evoked a state of being that was ambiguously relaxing and invigorating. As she watched groups of ducks bob for food along the shores, she quieted her mind and let her thoughts unspool.

"Sarah Braithwaite called for an appointment. I'm seeing her today. The last time I spoke with her, she was considering going back to Italy to study for another year. I'm not sure the department chair is thrilled about the situation—I'm sure he told her how he feels."

"Do you think that's what she really wants to talk about? She and Eugene were roommates and friends." Sarah cross-registered from the music department, so Johnny didn't know her very well. He was, of course, curious about her and Eugene's relationship.

"I can't speculate on what she wants to talk about. I'm just so happy to be back in the office seeing my advisees face to face.

"Kate. Why are you so interested in getting involved in this case?" Johnny asked. "You didn't know Eugene, except as a fellow student in the glassblowing class."

Kate stopped paddling, letting her kayak drift in the current before she answered. "He was the same age as my parents when the drunk driver killed them. Eugene's whole life was ahead of him, just as theirs was. Every adult rite of passage awaited Eugene—love, commitment, getting his doctorate, starting a career—all of that was taken from him, just as it had been taken from my parents. I can only say that I don't want his death to just be a terrible twist of fate. I want to know the reason, the motivation for denying him a full future."

Johnny reached up and squeezed Kate's shoulder, his voice thick with emotion. "I'll help in any way I can, my dear friend. You can count on me."

Kate was shy when it came to sharing her inner life. She brusquely responded, "We'd better get going—I don't want to be late. Will you take Bourbon Ball for a walk before you leave?" The two friends easily picked-up their pace, and since the current was with them, they arrived at the landing in just a few minutes.

After spending so much time at home during the pandemic lockdown, mostly outfitted in sweats and tee shirts, Kate enjoyed dressing for work again. Today she wore a heather-gray skirt, an oversized gray silk blouse, and hand-crafted turquoise jewelry. On the middle finger of her left hand was the large emerald ring that Eddie Fitzroy had intended as an engagement gift, but which ended up being substituted for a wedding ring. Kate liked that it was nontraditional; she considered most of her life to be nontraditional.

"Good to see you again, Sarah," she said warmly as she opened her office door. They settled down to talk. Kate sat in front of her desk rather than behind it, and Sarah sat opposite the desk on a small leather couch.

Sarah was twenty-five and in the final year of her master's program. Her father was a physician; her mother was an epidemiologist; both were Afrikaners from the Cape of Good Hope who emigrated years ago to make their careers at the university. Kate found Sarah easy to be with—she was a serious graduate student with a playful, humorous side to her. Her appearance reflected her South African Dutch genes—straight blonde hair, creamy white skin, and shining green eyes.

Sarah took a deep breath before beginning. "You know I'd like to return to Italy for another year abroad. I'm finished with my coursework; I just have to write my final paper, which I can do while I'm there. I'm not sure why the chairman objects to me writing there instead of here. Could you talk to him?" Kate liked that Sarah always came directly to the point.

"I can certainly call him on your behalf and see what we can negotiate; remember, each department has its own rules. When did you want to leave?"

"Well, I've already spoken to the professor with whom I worked in Italy, and she has agreed that I could come at the end of the semester." Sarah looked down at her hands and sighed.

Kate knew that people needed to warm up to talking about death. Like Sarah, a person would start out focusing on some practicality, then slowly would enter into describing their grief over a loss. Kate waited for that transition to happen.

"You heard about Eugene?"

"Yes, I did. I'm so sorry, Sarah. Is his death part of the reason you want to go back to Italy so quickly?" Kate asked, keeping a neutral tone.

"Yes." Tears spilled over onto Sarah's cheeks. "My parents think it would do me good to get away—especially to leave our shared house. The police were already there going through Eugene's stuff. I'm supposed to meet with a detective to give a statement." Sarah's speech became more urgent. "This is all so strange. I'm just a regular person, a regular graduate student. What do I know about giving a formal statement to a detective? And who would want to murder Eugene Rose? Maybe he just died of some underlying medical problem."

Kate spoke calmly to Sarah, describing what she could expect from the meeting with Chief Detective Jablonsky.

"They took Eugene's computer, but I kept this." Sarah reached into her purse and pulled out a well-worn notebook. She handled it as if it were a very precious item. "This is his 'idea book.' This is where he kept all his thoughts about design, Venetian patterns, early glass-making—if I have this, I feel like he is still with me." Through Sarah's heartbroken expression, Kate saw something else, a streak of defiance toward authority.

"I understand your feelings, but you must tell the Chief Detective you have it. They will take the notebook for a while, but you will get it back. It could provide a clue to Eugene's death." Kate's tone was warm, but she remained firm in telling Sarah that she was in possession of possible evidence. Kate took a few minutes to leaf through Eugene's drawings and designs, finding several notes that were quite interesting.

"I know. I know I shouldn't have taken it, but...."

"You were in the grip of an important loss. You wanted something of his to keep close to you." Sarah nodded and then excused herself from the meeting to go to the lavatory. While she was gone, Kate grabbed the idea book and made copies of as many of the pages as she could before her advisee returned.

When Sarah came back into the office, Kate assured her that she would speak with the department chairman on her behalf. She also gave her the name of a clinical psychologist to call if she wanted to talk more in-depth about Eugene's death.

After Sarah Braithwaite left, Kate decided she would tell Jablonsky about the notebook because she wasn't confident that her advisee would. She wasn't going to mention that she had copied most of it for her own use—the contents of the notebook were the most interesting clue so far.

CHAPTER 4

"DR. CHAMBERS! I wondered how long it would take before I heard from you." Jablonsky made some lame broken glass jokes before asking why Kate had called. As he listened to her explanation, he unwrapped a piece of cinnamon chewing gum, rolled it into a small cylinder, then placed it against one side of his cheek. The cinnamon flavor always helped him think better—he listened intently as Kate reported her discovery of Eugene Rose's notebook.

"Thanks for the heads-up, Kate. You did the right thing. Ms. Braithwaite is on our list for an interview, along with Mr. Rose's other friend, Zane Davies. We asked Andy Ormsby to also stop around—he might be able to add something to his original statement. What can you tell me about him?"

Jablonsky noted that Kate paused before giving any details about the glass instructor. Being the father of a young woman and a detective that had interviewed many women, he suspected that Kate's hesitancy was due to having been the recipient of unwanted flirtatious gestures from the instructor.

"Andy Ormsby is a master glass artist. Many of his pieces are in private collections. In addition to being the glass center's director, he offers classes at well-known glass centers, like here in Pittsburgh or at the center in Seattle. He's originally from New Zealand but has lived in Pittsburgh for a long time. I don't think that he knew Eugene Rose other than as a student. Eugene wasn't a glass apprentice; he just was an art history doctoral student wanting to know more about the glass-blowing process."

"Have you known Ormsby long?" Jablonsky valued Kate Chambers' perspective on people. And, since he knew the tragic story of her relationship with Eddie Fitzroy, he also was just snooping around in her life in the same way he did with his daughter Carly.

"I only met him when the course started. I'd see him in class—that's it. He is always very encouraging and helpful to me. Judging from his reaction to Eugene Rose's death, I'd say he was as shocked as the rest of us. I don't know anything about his personal life—I'm not sure if he is gay, straight, bi, or even dating anyone." Kate grew quiet.

Jablonsky knew from having watched Ormsby at the glass center that he was, no pun intended, hot for Kate. "We will follow up on Eugene's journal. Talk with you soon." Jablonsky abruptly ended the telephone call when Antoine DeVille came into his office, announcing that Mr. Ormsby had arrived at the station and was waiting in one of the interview rooms; DeVille would watch the interview from behind the one-way glass window.

"Thanks for coming in, Andy. Have a seat. There are just a few things I want to go over with you concerning Eugene Rose's death, particularly about your relationship with him." Jablonsky opened his small paper notebook and took out a pen.

Ormsby jumped right into the conversation. "I didn't have a relationship with Eugene—he was a student in my glassblowing class. I met him a couple of months ago. As you already know, he was a graduate student of Professor McCarthy's and was interested in Venetian glass. That's it."

Andy sat upright in his chair, his brown hair swept back at the ears, his eye contact direct. To the chief, unlike most people who had sat in that chair, Ormsby didn't seem at all anxious over being questioned by the police.

"Did you ever see Eugene Rose in an argument with any of the other students?"

"No. He was an amiable guy, really focused on learning glass technique." Ormsby paused, looking as if he was trying to remember something. "But, now that I think about it, there was a guy who originally registered for the class, came in a couple of times, but then dropped it. I think they were friends. He had an unusual name; it was Blaine, no, it was Zane—something. There seemed to be tension between the two of them."

Jablonsky watched Ormsby's face closely. "Did you hear what they argued about?"

"I didn't know what the tension was, but I did ask this Zane person to dial it back—the hot shop is a very dangerous place. I can't allow any heat there except what comes from the ovens. Oh, I remember now; his last name was Davies, Zane Davies."

"Do you remember Mr. Davies ever waiting for Eugene after class?"

"No. I'm usually busy at the end of a class checking to see that each glass piece is in one of the annealing ovens." Andy's demeanor remained neutral; he leaned back, his long legs casually crossed while he waited for Jablonsky's next question.

"Did you ever notice Eugene writing or drawing in a paper notebook?"

"Why yes, now that you mention it. He would draw a design or write some notes to himself. I always thought it was odd that he didn't use a design program on a tablet. Come to think of it, I didn't see him writing in the notebook at the last class, nor did I see your detectives take it." Jablonsky didn't mention that he knew about the notebook.

"Mr. Ormsby, what happens to all the tools at the end of the classes?"

"Each student is responsible for cleaning all of their equipment. Since the pandemic, cleaning measures for the blow rods, punty sticks, marver tables, and so forth, are stringent. Everything is locked up at night and only taken out when either I use them, an artist in residence uses them, or students in a class use them. It sounds like you think Eugene was killed at the hot shop?" For the first time, Andy Ormsby looked unnerved.

"It is just a line of inquiry we are pursuing. Did you see anyone else approach Eugene Rose to borrow or use his equipment?" The chief never disclosed information to an interviewee without a purpose.

"Not that I can remember. As the instructor, I'm focused on helping the individual student learn and not suffer a burn. When I work with one student, I'm only peripherally aware of what's going on with the others. You know, Kate Chambers might know if anyone borrowed Eugene's tools. She is friendly with everyone and is usually the first to finish her piece." This was the second time the chief noticed that Mr. Ormsby's posture and tone of voice became more animated when he spoke about Kate—the first was the evening of the murder. He made a note of it.

"Mr. Ormsby. We are releasing the hot shop back to you. You are free to hold your classes again, and everyone's glass pieces can be returned. Dr. Patel and forensics still retain a few of the tools."

"Will you be keeping Eugene's wine glasses?" Ormsby asked. "I mention them because I think they should be returned to his parents. I wasn't sure if they are important evidence."

"You may return them to his parents; we've processed them," was Jablonsky's only response.

The chief remained in the interview room, completing his notes. *Mr. Ormsby did a good job of teeing-up Zane as a primary suspect. Takes the spotlight off of him,* thought Jablonsky.

Right after Ormsby left, Antoine delivered Zane Davies; Jablonsky waved him toward a chair, not offering his hand. He wanted to create an undertone of tension with Eugene's so-called friend.

Jablonsky immediately understood why people didn't like this young man. Zane had the unmistakable looks of a rich prep schoolboy—all that was lacking was the school blazer and a British accent. Mr. Davies was of normal height and weight, with thick blond hair that fell across his forehead and shiny dark eyes, watchful, like those of a blackbird. He was handsome, but something in his comportment struck Jablonsky as slack. The chief observed that Zane wasn't paying attention to him. Instead, he was watching Antoine as the detective closed the door and left. *He's* on *the make at an interview in a police station—that speaks volumes about this young man's judgment,* Jablonsky scribbled in his notebook.

"Mr. Davies. You understand that you are here to give a formal statement about your relationship with Eugene Rose. You are not under arrest."

"Yes. Detective DeVille explained that to me. What would you like to know?"

Zane finally looked directly at the chief—a slight downward turn of his lips gave the impression of disapproval—he tossed his hair like a twelve-year-old girl.

"We are trying to put together a picture of Eugene's life, his friends and family, and his graduate work. Tell me about him." Jablonsky purposely made his question open-ended to see where Zane would begin.

"Well, I've known him, that is, I knew him, for the last four or so years. We were in graduate school together, so we had similar academic interests. I was his roommate for a while, me and another friend by the name of Sarah Braithwaite. Have you talked with her?" Zane's tone was accusatory.

"Were the two of you lovers?" Like turning the flame on a stove burner from low to medium, Jablonsky began to ratchet up the tension.

Zane couldn't hide his surprise over the question. "Who told you that? No, we weren't lovers."

"Did he reject you as a lover? Did you two argue about it?" The chief's questions were asked rapidly; he was pushing to elicit that temper Ormsby had mentioned.

"What makes you think it wasn't me who rejected him? Unless you haven't noticed, I'm an attractive guy. Eugene didn't have the guts to date someone like me. There, I've said it." Like a fashion model, Zane struck a pose as if he wanted Jablonsky to appreciate his looks. The chief smothered a chuckle at the young man's audacity.

"You were seen arguing with Eugene on several occasions at the hot shop. What were those arguments about?"

"Italy. They were about Italy. Sarah Braithwaite was returning to Italy to study for another year, and I wanted to go. It would be a free place to stay and I could acquire some more art for my family while I was there. Eugene felt that I would be using Sarah, that's all. It was bull."

It seemed odd to Jablonsky that Eugene would insert himself into a situation that was between Sarah and Zane. "Wasn't it for Sarah to say whether she wanted you to stay with her?"

"Exactly. You got it in one, chief. Like I said, it was bogus. Anything else?" Zane's hands were in his lap, and he started to stroke one thumb with another as if to soothe himself. *Good,* thought the chief, h*e's getting antsy.*

"Did your arguments with Eugene ever come to blows?"

"No! Never. I don't go around hitting people. Nor do I kill them." A flush of red crept into Zane's cheeks.

"Did you originally sign-up for the glassblowing class because Eugene did?" Jablonsky asked casually.

"Yes and no. Like I said, I acquire art objects for my parents, so the more I know about all types of fine art, the better. And, since Eugene was going to be there, the class would be more fun." Zane leaned forward toward the chief, attempting to take control of the interview.

"Look, we were friends, and like all friends, we had our ups and downs. He was a good guy—honest and seriously smart. I'm attracted to men like that. I don't have any idea why someone would want to kill him—do you?" Zane answered, clearly implying that Jablonsky wasn't doing his job. Stefan remembered Kate's statement about Zane and his professors; *If this is his attitude toward authority, no wonder they didn't like him.*

"Mr. Davies, we will want to talk with you again, so please stay in town." Jablonsky ended the interview without answering Zane's question. He wanted to leave a crack in the story so anxiety could seep into Zane's mind. He took his small paper notebook and left the room.

Back in the bullpen, Jablonsky unwrapped another piece of cinnamon gum and tore off little pieces, putting them into his mouth one at a time. Antoine had begun the murder board by placing a picture of Eugene Rose in the middle. There was a small photo of Zane Davies and one of Sarah Braithwaite, who had yet to be officially interviewed, and a picture of Andy Ormsby. The chief wrote some questions on the board.

Was Eugene Rose murdered at the hot shop by Zane Davies, and if so, why there? How was the poison delivered? Eugene, Sarah, and Zane were all in Italy at the same time. Did something that is important to the murder happen between them or to them? Does Andy Ormsby know more about the murder than he is saying, and if so, why?

CHAPTER 5

"KATE! THIS IS A SURPRISE. I hope everything is okay with your health." Dr. Marco Rossetti, the world-renowned surgeon who had operated on Eddie Fitzroy, suddenly appeared beside Kate's waiting room chair.

"Marco, it's nice to see you. I could ask you the same question since I guess you are also here to see Dr. Smythe." Kate had been reading Eugene Rose's dissertation and several other of his papers while waiting for the doctor; she unobtrusively closed her laptop.

Marco sat down beside Kate, who thought he looked like a teenager wanting to talk to a girl in the cafeteria; excitement and shyness waltzed together across his face. She knew that Marco Rossetti liked her, but she also knew that he knew she was not ready for a romantic relationship. From the contact she had had with him so far, she had surmised he was inexperienced with women; Kate could say the same thing about herself and men.

"Ellen Smythe and I are colleagues on a number of university committees. I started seeing her as my primary care physician after my grandfather died. Then, after Eddie died, she wanted to see me more frequently—just to check that I'm eating and sleeping okay. As you know, my mother and father died when I was young, so since Smythe is the same generation, I look to her for medical judgment and occasional career advice. I admire her." Kate, a very private person, was always shocked at how many personal details she spontaneously would offer Marco Rossetti, and he back to her.

"Have you heard about the death at the glass shop?" Kate asked, regaining her composure.

"Yes. I remember that you mentioned you were going to try something new—I guess glassblowing is it. Were you there when it happened?" Marco leaned closer, lowering his voice.

"Actually, I was there, taking the same class as the young man who died. And so was Johnny, whom you know. The victim was one of his doctoral students. Chief Jablonsky was called, of course, and Dr. Patel did the autopsy. She has declared it to be death by poison and a murder. She did release the body to his parents—Johnny is at the funeral right now."

Kate became aware that a nurse was hovering, waiting to take her back to the exam room; *She's enjoying seeing the great Dr. Rossetti flirting with a woman,* thought Kate, amused by the situation. Marco persisted in making the connection with her.

"Since I'm finished operating for the day, I was thinking of stopping by the family bakery. They have expanded it—there are now several small tables where they serve a variety of delicious Italian coffees. Would you want to come by after your appointment? We could ask Johnny as well, and he can tell us about Eugene Rose's funeral." As he made the invitation, Marco blushed.

Marco remembered how his older sister always valued the opinion of her best friend; he knew that Johnny McCarthy held that position in Kate's life and therefore understood that he had to woo Johnny if he wanted to get to know Kate.

Kate wasn't sure she was ready for dating, so her response time to Marco's suggestion was excruciatingly long. Finally, she decided to go. It was just coffee, after all. "Why not? I'd like that. I'll text Johnny to meet us there. By the way, will your mother be at the bakery?"

Marco burst into laughter, understanding the inference about Italian mothers and their sons. "No. She rarely goes there anymore. Just the regular ladies who wouldn't dare say anything to me or you."

The Rossetti family bakery had been the subject of a murder case involving Marco's brother, sister, and Johnny McCarthy's mother, which is how Marco and Kate first met. Given that recent history, it was unnerving for Kate to walk through the door of Rosalie's Bakery. She was pleasantly surprised to see the upgrades that had been made to the historic shop on Forbes Avenue. There were new display cases, and a modern computer check-out system, and the back of the store had been expanded to include café tables and a scattering of brightly colored Italian pots with pretty plants in them.

A young woman hurried over to their table to take their order.

"Hello, Dr. Rossetti. Would you like your usual order or something new today?"

"I'll have the usual coffee and plate of pastries—bring enough for three, please. Someone else will be joining us." The waitress placed several attractive screens between the front of the bakery and their table giving them privacy. *Nice touch,* thought Kate.

As Marco ordered, she noticed how good he smelled—it was something she had taken note of before. Whatever brand of soap it was, the smell of it was refreshing and pleasant, even standing out against the fragrance of the baked goods. When the platter of pastries was set on the table, Marco began naming them in Italian, regaling her with amusing stories of his trying to bake them at home for himself. Kate couldn't remember the last time she had laughed so hard.

Just as their steaming cups of coffee arrived, so did Johnny, who looked around at the upgrades in the bakery where his mother had worked for decades. One of the ladies behind the counter recognized him and scurried over to smother him in a bosomy hug.

"The place looks great, Marco. Kudos to your family. I feel like I'm in a café in Florence!" He took a tentative sip of the coffee and murmured his appreciation of its dark richness. Johnny was a coffee aficionado.

Marco crunched on a cannoli while Kate dipped her pistachio biscotti into her coffee. "How is the glassblowing going?" Marco asked as he wiped the cream filling from his upper lip.

Kate laughed. "It is so much harder than you can imagine! I'll never look at studio glass the same way again." She paused and then jumped right into the subject of the murder. "Eugene Rose, the graduate student who died, was interested in Venetian glass techniques. Johnny said that's why he was taking the class. I've been reading his dissertation."

"Was it just the techniques that interested him?" Marco asked.

"No. He was also following the provenance of particular pieces—who owned the art pieces from generation to generation, and whether it was held privately or was in a museum." Kate began to slowly rotate her coffee cup as she considered the themes in Eugene Rose's papers. She was aware that Marco was watching her.

Johnny had placed several pastries on his plate and attacked them hungrily. Kate laughed. "Johnny, try not to be Lucy with the chocolates on the conveyer belt; slow down and eat one at a time!"

"What are we talking about?" Johnny ignored Kate and ate half of a cannoli in one go.

"We are talking about Eugene Rose's academic work, but first things first, how was the funeral?" Kate passed a napkin over to him.

"Very sad. There were plenty of people there from our department. I saw Sarah Braithwaite and Zane Davies. Sarah spent time talking with Eugene's parents, who looked, and are, devastated. Davies hovered on the edge of things; he didn't stay for the luncheon." The waitress unobtrusively refilled their cups with fresh coffee.

"Do you know if Eugene Rose's family are collectors of fine art?"

"I don't really know, Kate. He did mention that his grandmother had a particular interest in glass." Johnny pressed the few crumbs left on his plate onto one of his fingers and stuck it into his mouth, clearly feeling comfortable enough in front of Marco to ignore dining etiquette.

"Eugene's grandmother had an interest in glass? Now that's a clue to pursue if I ever saw one. I wonder if she has a collection in which she had involved Eugene? Hum, it would be interesting to know that fact—you met his parents today?" Johnny knew where Kate was headed with the question.

"Yes. I met them, but I don't know them. We can't just call them at this time of grief."

Kate pulled herself back from the brink of saying something insensitive. "I know, I get it—some organic pathway will open up vis-à-vis finding out about a potential Rose glass collection."

Johnny, who had known Marco's brother and sister, turned the conversation to the old Oakland neighborhood. Doodling on her paper napkin, Kate wrote a quick note. *Is there something about the Rose family that is important to Eugene's murder?* She began to formulate ways to meet Mr. and Mrs. Rose.

Jablonsky had ordered the red bell pepper and feta cheese omelet with a side of rye toast. Aashi Patel ordered her favorite—one lightly poached egg on a toasted English muffin with a side of fresh fruit. Since they had started meeting for breakfast at Sophia's Café in the Strip District, she had become like a general who had retreated from the field in terms of trying to change what the chief ate. He liked his cholesterol, and there was no talking him out of it. The medical examiner was a realist.

As usual, they were speaking about poison, so Jeanne, their regular waitress, refreshed their water glasses and also retreated.

"This is such an interesting case!" Dr. Patel squeezed the water out of her teabag and pointed her spoon at Stefan for emphasis. "Eugene Rose was not only poisoned by old-fashioned Belladonna, but the method of delivery was through what they call the blowpipe."

"The blowpipe. That's the hollow steel pipe the glass artist blows into to expand the hot glass? Am I close?" His omelet had arrived, so the chief busied himself with squeezing a thin line of Heinz Tomato Ketchup onto his eggs while he waited for Dr. Patel's answer.

"That's the gist of it. I found traces of deadly nightshade in the blowpipe from Eugene Rose's station, both in the pipe and on its rim. He put his lips on the rim to seal it, then would have puffed into the pipe to expand the glass bubble, and then without thinking, he would have taken a breath. The poison deposits on his lips and also is taken directly into his lungs—a one-two punch, as they say. Quite interesting, isn't it?"

Jablonsky looked pleased; he knew that Aashi delighted in having a murder case that wasn't just someone shooting someone else. She mused aloud, "But why do it in this manner? I mean, people have been poisoning each other via food and wine for centuries. There was no evidence of any poison in the food at the canteen or in his water bottle. I come back to, why poison this young man this way?"

Jablonsky paused in his attack on the plate of food to answer her question. "I don't know the why, but I know a few other things. For example, someone knew that Eugene Rose was interested in glass and had registered for this class. The person also knew what furnace station he would be at, what tools he would be using, and that he would definitely be in the class that day. And putting the poison in the pipe was effective and expedient. Right now, that only leaves a few suspects who had the opportunity to commit the murder."

"Who are?" Dr. Patel gently cut into the poached egg, allowing the rich goldenrod yolk to ooze onto the muffin.

"Of course, we must look at the instructor, Andy Ormsby, a good friend, Zane Davies, who was a rebuffed lover known to argue with Eugene, and who was supposed to have also taken the class but didn't." Jablonsky polished off the buttered rye toast.

"Anyone else?"

The chief was holding something back, something he was uncomfortable with, and he knew Aashi could see it on his face. "Well, Eugene Rose was Johnny McCarthy's doctoral student. Johnny, how do they say it, directed his dissertation.

With the exception of Zane Davies, I can't yet imagine what a motive would be for either the professor or the glass instructor. I just can't rule them out."

"What about Kate? Did she know Eugene Rose?" Patel dispassionately mentioned Dr. Chambers, even in the face of how much she liked and respected her. Aashi Patel was surprised by very little in life, so in her world, anyone could be a suspect.

"I take your point about Kate. If you are an amateur sleuth like her, you can sometimes get caught in the crosshairs. She only knew this student through the glassblowing class. Other than that, she had no relationship with him. She did mention another of Eugene Rose's roommates, Sarah Braithwaite."

"If this young woman didn't take the class, it doesn't sound like she had the same opportunity to place the poison that Ormsby, Davies, Johnny, or Kate had." Dr. Patel finished her eggy muffin and began enjoying the fruit cup.

The chief's cell phone pinged. "Talk to me," was his stark hello. "Okay. I'll be at the office in a half hour and can see Kate and Johnny then."

Since it was Jablonsky's turn to pay, Dr. Patel gathered her things and left a tip. She knew the chief would circle around and add to it; she just never mentioned that she knew he did it. As she headed toward the door, the chief walked back to the booth pretending to look for something and discreetly dropped several more dollar bills on the table; he admired Dr. Patel, but she could be cheap.

Antoine walked Kate and Johnny back to the chief's office. "Have a seat," said Jablonsky's number one. The uncomfortably full Jablonsky leaned back in his swivel chair to give his belly a little extra room. "So, Kate, what's on the agenda?" Stefan was happy to be able to question Johnny McCarthy under the guise of Kate believing she had important information.

Kate smiled sweetly as she opened her slim laptop, hoping to dispel any belief that her insights weren't important to the case. She summarized Eugene's interest in the provenance of certain glass objects, his attention to particular designs in sixteenth and seventeenth-century Italian glasswork, and that his grandmother might have a collection of glass. Kate considered these all fertile avenues of investigation.

Jablonsky looked at Kate for quite a while, then, keeping a neutral tone, asked the obvious question. "So, you think his interest in early Italian glass is a clue to his murder? Hum." The chief noted that Johnny slightly raised one eyebrow in agreement with the chief's doubt. Jablonsky knew better than to dismiss her far-out academic ideas because she had been proven right so many other times. He turned to Johnny.

"John, as his dissertation director, is there anything you have remembered since we spoke right after the incident? For example, at the funeral, did his friends or family say something that struck you as unusual?" Jablonsky continued with a nonchalant tone.

"I didn't know much about his personal life—the funeral was the first time I had met his parents. Eugene and I mostly talked art history. No one at the service or the luncheon mentioned that Eugene was depressed or in any trouble with a friend or a lover. Dr. Joan Wiesner, whom you know, was at the funeral with her parents, so you could also ask her about the family. Apparently, her parents attend the same synagogue as that of the Roses.'"

There it is; there is the natural path to meeting the Roses, thought Kate, who repressed a smile of glee. *Why didn't Johnny tell me Joan was at the funeral? That scamp!* Jablonsky noticed that Kate was disconnected from the conversation; he shot her a quizzical look, wondering where her mind was going, but he continued to question Johnny.

"I have to ask you directly—did you have a romantic relationship with Eugene Davies?" Jablonsky asked.

Coupe leaned forward in his chair, observing how the chief handled this delicate situation and because he was interested in Johnny's answer.

"I've never had a sexual relationship with a student. I did not have one with Eugene. Chief Jablonsky, it is often easy to take advantage of a student, even a graduate student in his mid-twenties; I know professors who have routinely done so. I'm not one of them." Johnny's tone gave no hint of annoyance over the question. The chief was inclined to believe him, so he ended the interview.

As Kate and Johnny walked to the elevator, she grabbed his arm. "You didn't tell me that Joan was at the funeral!"

"I forgot. Is it important?" Johnny pressed the lobby button in the elevator, and they stopped talking until arriving on the first floor. They stepped out, and Kate pulled Johnny to one side of the lobby.

"It's important because it might mean I can talk directly to Mr. and Mrs. Rose. I have to find out how well Joan knows the family. Come on!"

DeVille and Jablonsky stood before the murder board, talking through the new information. Eugene Rose, Sarah Braithwaite, and Zane Davies all studied the historical era where Belladonna was used as a common method of poisoning. This type of poison wasn't hard to acquire or make. Sarah and Zane could have worked together to poison Eugene or could have worked with Andy Ormsby. But what would be the motive? As far as anyone knew, Eugene didn't have anything worth collecting, let alone being murdered over.

"I believe we can take Kate Chambers and Professor McCarthy off our suspect list. It's an interesting perspective that his interest in early Italian glass and his being murdered at the glass center might be linked." The chief pulled out his pack of cinnamon gum, offered a stick to Antoine, and then opened one for himself.

Jablonsky wrote one word underneath Eugene Rose's photograph. *Glass.*

CHAPTER 6

SARAH BRAITHWAITE WAS SHOPPING for groceries at the local food co-op. The military alignment of the rich jewel-toned vegetables was pleasing to her eye and soothed her rattled nerves. She slowly wheeled her small cart through the aisles, picking up and sniffing some freshly baked bread, then placing it alongside her choice of butter and a few different varieties of artisan cheeses. Sarah grabbed a sleeve of cut flowers to brighten her table, helped the checker place her items in a reusable bag, and left to drive home.

It was a beautiful day—sunny with low humidity, the trees were still dressed in their fall colors, and a few potted purple and white mums greeted her on the front porch of the rented house. Sarah set down her bag of groceries, found her door keys, then paused a moment to enjoy the spicy smell of a Pennsylvania fall. For those minutes of noticing her natural surroundings, the loss of Eugene Rose was eased. She hummed the tune to Pharrell Williams' song "Happy" as she opened the door.

Sarah screamed at what she saw; then she cursed in Italian. "Cazzo!"

The house she had shared with Eugene Rose had been trashed. All of her things were strewn around the room—books, plants, her computer. Her clothes had been thrown on the floor in her bedroom, and the dresser drawers were gaping open. Shoe boxes had been gone through. The couch cushions had been sliced open, and the stuffing ripped out. Someone had even looked through the freezer, leaving the lower drawer gaping open. Eugene Rose's possessions were still with the forensic team, so the damage was to her things.

I don't know what to do. What should I do? she obsessively repeated to herself as she started to shake. Unfortunately, her parents were away at a conference. *I guess I should call the landlord.* She tapped in the owner's number on her cell phone, and luckily someone answered, advising, "Call the police right away," which she did. Then she called Zane Davies, who responded with, "Get out of the house. Wait in your car; I'm on my way."

Detective Jablonsky and Antoine DeVille, accompanied by several black and white cruisers, arrived at the same time as Zane. Sarah was still sitting in her car with the doors and windows locked, clearly afraid.

"It's okay to come out now, Ms. Braithwaite," said the chief in his most reassuring manner. "We are all here to protect you. Come into the house with me and tell me what happened."

As if she were a little child, Sarah slowly opened the car door, slid her legs out until her feet touched the ground, and took Jablonsky's outstretched hand. The minute his strong warm hands took hers, she burst into tears. "You are okay now; you are safe with us. The officers have made sure no one is in the house, so let's go talk about what happened." The chief put his arm around her slim shoulders and moved her into the house. Jablonsky had that British 'Morse-like' reassuring way with women.

"I was at the food co-op. I came home, unlocked the door, and saw all this." Sarah swept open her arms to indicate the breadth of the destruction. Zane Davies stepped onto the porch—DeVille stopped him at the threshold and kept him there, asking him what he knew about the situation and why he was there.

"Sarah. Obviously, whoever did this was searching for something. Do you know what it would be?" The chief spoke softly and deliberately, attempting to lower her anxiety so she could think more clearly. High anxiety impedes memory.

"I don't know. I don't have anything important or costly—nothing you could sell—like for drugs or such. Why is this happening?" Sarah's anxiety was morphing into hysteria, so the chief walked her into the kitchen, found a clean glass, gave her water, then distracted her with questions.

"Since the freezer was searched, and your shoe boxes, then the couch cushions, it leads me to think the burglar was looking for something relatively small. What about Eugene Rose's notebook? Do you have it?"

"Oh. The notebook. Yes, I do have it. It's in my purse, which is in the car—I'll go get it." Sarah quickly went out the front door, and Jablonsky motioned to DeVille to stay with her. Zane Davies remained on the porch, slouched against the railing like a saloon cowboy. "What are you doing here, Mr. Davies?"

Defiantly, and to indicate disrespect, the young man shoved his hands into his jean pockets and jutted out his jaw. "Sarah called me! I was the one who told her to get out of the house until you police arrived. I came to protect her."

"Did you? What a generous friend you are, Mr. Davies. Who did you believe was still in the house?" Jablonsky could throw down sarcasm with the best, and did so now, then made a slight movement toward the young man—not directly menacing, but on the verge. "Do you know something about this break-in? Do you know what someone was looking for in the house?"

The color drained from Davies' face. "Hey! Don't come any closer to me. I can have one of my father's attorneys here in a few minutes."

"Answer my question," growled the chief. "Is there something in Eugene's possession that someone wants badly enough to do this? Is that someone you?" Jablonsky wanted to create just enough intimidation that Zane would reveal something helpful before any attorney arrived.

Antoine interrupted the exchange, holding up a set of keys. We found these in Eugene's room. They don't fit the lock on the front or back door. This small one looks like it might fit a storage unit or a desk." Jablonsky moved a smidge closer to Zane.

"Did Eugene Rose have an office or a storage unit?"

"He didn't have an office. I don't know about storage. His parents live close by. Why would he pay to store something?" Zane dropped his sneer and looked puzzled. He turned away from the chief and made a phone call. Stefan overhead him say, "Dad."

The chief and Antoine exchanged grins over the fact that his first call was to Daddy. Stefan thought, *Now we are getting somewhere.*

The forensics team arrived. "Get Mr. Davies' and Ms. Braithwaite's DNA," Jablonsky directed them. "If Mr. Davies resists, wait until his attorney gets here, then take it. He is a person of interest."

Kate sat staring out of her office window. The afternoon sun made interesting patterns that stretched across her legs and onto the floor, but she was unaware of them. She was deep in thought over Eugene Rose's death, laying out the few facts that were known to her. It had been an audacious plan:

Joan had informed her that one of her friends at the morgue said that the poison had been placed in the blowpipe, so someone had to know how much Eugene weighed in order to place enough of the Belladonna to do the trick. Plus, the murder took place in the middle of a class. So many things were precisely timed and prepared. Eugene's habits had to be well-known to the murderer—it was that fact that narrowed her personal list of suspects.

After she and Johnny left Jablonsky's office, Kate tried to reach Joan to talk about the funeral and the Rose family, but to no avail. Joan had back-to-back surgeries all day. Kate's reverie was interrupted by a knock at the door. "Come in," she called out, swiveling her chair back to face the opening door.

"Hey, gorgeous girl." Johnny flopped his briefcase and himself down onto her office couch. She took note of how professorial he looked today in his light cotton sweater vest, striped shirt, and stone-washed jeans. Johnny eschewed fashionable haircuts, choosing instead to keep his red-blond locks trimmed but not shaved. Kate's affection for him shone in her eyes.

"What brings you here, oh great professor?" It was rare that he visited her office. They usually met at his because he always wanted to use his elaborate, could-launch-a-rocket-to-the-moon coffee maker. Johnny and Antoine DeVille shared a passion for good coffee and expensive makers.

"I was thinking about your idea concerning Eugene's interest in glass objects and their provenance and just wanted to talk through your theories," answered Johnny.

"Did you locate any more of his papers? I've read what you gave me, but the police have his computer, so I can't look at other files." Kate paused, then she leaned forward in excitement. "Come to think of it, did he have a study carrel at the library? A doctoral candidate can get one and lock their books in it—you and I had one when we were writing our dissertations. The main library has some on each floor. Let's go ask Irene—the keeper of the carrels. Eugene might have left papers there." Kate jumped out of her chair and grabbed Johnny's hand. "Come on. It's a quick walk."

When the two friends arrived at the library, they showed their university IDs at the desk and asked to see Irene, an older lady in charge of assigning the coveted study carrels; she knew both Kate and Johnny from their student days and now as university employees. She also had known Eugene. "He was such a nice young man, don't you think, Professor McCarthy? He always had a joke to tell me."

"Professor McCarthy went to Eugene's funeral and met his parents. I don't think they know about his study carrel. Would it be okay with you if we clean it out and return his things to his parents?" Kate hoped that by dropping the fact that Johnny had met Mr. and Mrs. Rose, Irene would let them take any books or papers in Eugene's carrel. The librarian hesitated.

"I've never been in this position before. I guess it's okay if you sign for them…."

"I'd hate for his parents to have one more thing to do while they are grieving," Kate added in an intimate tone, implying that they were just trying to relieve the parents of an unhappy task. "There may be nothing in the carrel. He was almost finished with his dissertation." That last comment sealed the deal.

Irene showed them where to sign, then walked them to the third floor and unlocked the carrel. Kate assured Irene that she would return the key. Another key existed—it was the one DeVille had found in Sarah Braithwaite's house, but Kate and Johnny had no knowledge of that piece of evidence.

Eugene's carrel held a few library books that would need to be returned and a manilla envelope. Kate sat down in the carrel's chair, and Johnny leaned over her shoulder as she opened the envelope. They read through a few pages of notes on common images used in sixteenth-century Venetian glass. There also was a page with five surnames listed with a series of dates beside each name.

"Eureka!" Kate whispered. "I wonder what these are. Do you recognize any of these names?"

"Well, they probably are the names of wealthy people who had glass items made in Murano. That's just a guess." Johnny cocked his head to one side, obviously trying to remember something from Italian history that would be helpful.

"I'll take them and do some research. I'm going to copy this file and Google these surnames." Kate grinned at Johnny, enjoying having found what she suspected would be another important clue.

They decided to keep the library books. Kate officially checked them out in her name and paid the overdue fines on Eugene's library account. This afternoon would be spent in front of the computer, researching the names on the list.

Sarah Braithwaite was nervous. Not only was she emotionally undone by the break-in at the house, but she couldn't imagine what the intruder could possibly be looking for. Additionally, she was a young woman sitting in a police station, with no family to protect or advise her. Zane Davies had offered to accompany her as she made her formal statement, but she declined. She liked Chief Detective Jablonsky, but she had been settled in the interview room by Annie Lemon. Sarah decided she would ask if detective

Lemon was allowed to sit in during her statement; Jablonsky understood her request and agreed to it right away.

"Can we get you anything, Sarah? A coffee, a water, some crackers…?" Jablonsky sat down and opened his small paper notebook. Lemon sat beside him but positioned her chair to be a bit behind her boss'; Jablonsky began the interview.

"Sarah, did you know that there were security cameras on your house, and on several houses around you? No? Well, there are. Here are a few photographs taken from those cameras at the time the break-in occurred. Do you recognize this man?" Lemon carefully laid down several photographs of different views of the same man.

Sarah took her time looking at the photos; she would pick one up, scrutinize it, then move onto the next one. Slowly she began to move her head from side to side. "No. I don't think I've ever seen this man before. He's older, isn't he? He looks like he is at least in his forties." Jablonsky lowered his head, hiding his smile over her age comment.

"We hoped you could identify him; think about it—something may come to you later." As if she were an accomplished casino dealer, Lemon neatly slid all of the photos together and placed them next to the chief.

"Why did you call Zane Davies when you discovered the break-in?" Sarah looked surprised at his asking that same question once again.

"Like I said to you before, my parents are away, and my friends are out of state for various conferences. Zane is the only close friend I have right now in the city."

Jablonsky nodded. "I see. When we interviewed Zane after your friend Eugene died, he mentioned that Eugene was trying to dissuade him from visiting you when you return to Italy. Do you know why that would be?"

To the chief's eyes, a worried expression moved across Sarah's face that she quickly covered up. "Tell me about Eugene's concerns for you."

"Well, I'm not sure how this relates to the break-in, but Eugene felt that Zane manipulates me."

Jablonsky remarked, "Be more specific about his concerns."

"When Zane came to Italy, he stayed with me. I'm studying the origins of the four string violin, so I mostly stayed in Cremona, where the Violin Museum is, but my home base was Florence. Zane was insistent that we go to Murano to watch them blow glass. It was a really interesting trip but, um, I had limited time in Italy, it did take away from my research."

"Did you witness any arguments between Eugene and Zane?"

"Yes. A few in Italy, and again recently, when I began to make plans to go back. You see, Eugene was staying in Venice as an art history student, he was writing his dissertation. Zane came over as a visitor, not as a student—he said he was scouting objects to buy for his father's collection."

"And did he buy things?" Jablonsky was becoming really curious about this Davies family collection.

"Not that I saw. He would go off and meet people in the antique shops—I never paid any attention to it." Sarah furrowed her brow and was quiet for a few minutes. So far, Jablonsky's experience with graduate students like Sarah was that they were quick to assess situations. He watched as she began to put two and two together.

"Chief Jablonsky, you are speculating that there is a relationship between Zane Davies acquiring art objects for his family, the break-in at my house, and Eugene's death. Am I correct?"

"It's one of several lines of inquiry that we are pursuing. Sarah, is there any place other than the house that Eugene would have stored personal things?"

"Maybe at his parents' house. I'm not sure what things you mean? We're graduate students, we don't own anything except books and our writings—I mean, you have Eugene's computer, all of his work should be on it, or in the Cloud—perhaps he backed-up his work on an external storage device, like a flash drive."

Jablonsky turned his head slightly toward Lemon and softly repeated, "An external storage device," clearly communicating that either she or DeVille should have thought of that possibility. Flash drives are small and easy to hide. He looked back at Sarah.

"You gave us Eugene's notebook. Was there anything in that idea book that struck you as particularly interesting?

"Dr. Chambers, my academic advisor, asked me the same thing. Mostly it contains his private preoccupations with Italian designs, plus a few design ideas of his own. His doodles don't say anything special to me. Sorry."

"Sarah, have you seen the Davies' art collection?"

"No. Zane never showed it to me... I guess I never asked to see it. Like I mentioned, my interest is in antique musical instruments."

"Sarah, just for the record, where were you the day Eugene was murdered?"

"I was in a lecture at the Fine Arts building. Other students can confirm that." Jablonsky caught Sarah's smirk at having such a good alibi. But she didn't mention what time that lecture began or ended, so he asked. She was in the lecture during the same time as Eugene's glassblowing class. *But, the two buildings are close enough that she could have driven to the glass center, poisoned Eugene, and slipped back into her lecture,* thought Jablonsky.

"Thanks, so much for all your help. Please stay in the city, we may want to talk with you again."

Jablonsky ended the interview; Annie Lemon stayed to talk about the flash drive while Antoine walked Sarah to the elevator. She was a pretty young thing and the right age for Jablonsky's number one, but he knew DeVille rode on a different bus.

The chief assumed his position in front of the murder board. Under Eugene Rose's photo he wrote several new questions. Is there an external storage devise somewhere? Has forensics searched the Cloud? What is the importance of the notebook? Does Kate Chambers know more than she is saying due to her professional relationship with Sarah?

He then pinned two pictures from the security camera array on the board and scribbled, Who is this mystery man?

CHAPTER 7

IT WAS EARLY IN THE MORNING and Kate was curled up on her patio couch. Bourbon Ball was at her feet, madly chomping on a dental chew, while she researched the five names Eugene Rose had written on the sheet found in his study carrel. Contrary to the advice she had given Sarah Braithwaite, Kate was holding onto the potential evidence in order to do her own investigation before talking to the chief.

Jablonsky was such a stickler for drawing the line between amateur sleuthing and official police detecting that Kate felt it bordered on the absurd. But she was a law abiding person, mostly, and would eventually turn over what she found; it was all in the timing. Kate admired and respected Pittsburgh's Chief of Detectives, but there existed a tension between them over her role in the several murder investigations in which she had been involved. That same tension now permeated their dealings over Eugene Rose's case. He had never directly asked her why she would be involved in a case where she barely knew the victim. Perhaps she should say something to him about her motives for wanting to be involved; they were such personal reasons that she hesitated to reveal them. It was one thing to confide in Johnny, her adopted brother, but another to show one's sensitive underbelly to the Chief of Detectives.

She heard a woman's voice call her name. "Kate! It's me. Where are you? Where's that crack watch dog of yours?" Joan Weisner walked around to the side patio and plopped down on the couch beside Kate.

"What's going on?" BB finally let go of his doggy chew and ambled over to Joan, swinging his otter tail and hoping for pets, which he got.

"I'm so glad you are here! You know everything about everything—I can really use your knowledge." The two embracing women looked like sisters—both tall and dark haired—two different kinds of doctors committed to their professions. In that way, they were kindred spirits.

Joan Weisner had been in her general surgical residency when she first met Kate, who was in the midst of her post-doctoral training. The two became fast friends and had remained so. Joan was the surgeon who called Marco Rossetti to help with the extensive surgery performed on Eddie Fitzroy after his accident. She was Kate's closest woman friend, sometimes information advisor in sleuthing, a Scripps National Spelling Bee finalist, and a rabid Pittsburgh Pirates fan. Kate showed Joan the list of names and dates and asked if they rang any bells for her.

Joan responded with a drawn-out, "W-e-l-l. This one, Cantarella, everyone knows. The family was a wealthy Italian one, and like the Borgias, often associated with poisoning enemies. These three are also surnames, French or Italian in origin, and I'm pretty sure this one is an English surname. I suspect that the dates indicate when they lived. Are you looking for something in particular?" Apologizing for the pun, she often remarked that her profession could be cut and dry, so she liked the challenge Kate's sleuthing offered.

Joan continued. "You know, my family knows the Rose family. They go to the same synagogue as my parents. Eugene was younger than me, but I remember him from sleep-away camp where I was one of his counselors. Because of that history, we went to the funeral."

"I didn't know that you knew the Rose family until Johnny mentioned that he saw you at the funeral. Your relationship with the family might be a help with this investigation." Kate grinned at her. "And I really appreciated you calling me about the poison in the blow pipe. It made me consider the personality of the murderer."

Joan agreed that this murder was well-planned, so the culprit must be smart and detailed oriented. "What are your suppositions about the murder?"

"My working theory is that Eugene was unusually interested in following the provenance of glass items. What his dissertation teaches me is that in the sixteenth century, and beyond, owning something made of glass indicated status, both having pieces in your own household, and also giving them as gifts. The wealthy would gift them on the usual occasions, like a betrothal, marriage, birth and so forth."

Joan listened and then looked again at the names on the list. "You speculate then that he was following specific glass pieces as they moved through certain families of wealth and position, like these. But toward what end?"

Kate liked Joan's practical approach to motivation.

"That's what I don't know, yet. Did you know Eugene's grandmother? He mentioned to Johnny that she collected glass." Joan shrugged her shoulders, "I only saw her at Temple on the High Holidays. I can ask my parents or the Rabbi about her."

"Great! For now, I just started looking up these names. Want to help me?"

From her purse, Joan pulled out her own laptop, and as the sun moved higher in the sky, and a few blood red cardinals drank at Kate's birdbath, the two friends started their historical search of the names, working until Kate had to leave to meet Johnny for the glassblowing class.

Kate was attempting the second of her pair of *stangenglas*, tall glasses used to keep or serve wine. Typically, they had lids on them, but she didn't feel confident in trying to make those. She had a gather of glass at the end of the blow pipe, Johnny gently blew into the pipe, then Kate slowly elongated the hot glass until she had the height she wanted. Finally, she tapped it off the punty rod. Once again, Johnny took the glass piece to the annealing oven for it to cool.

Andy Ormsby had been standing by them, watching Kate work the glass. She was aware of his gaze, but it did not distract her from her work. He took the opportunity to point out the techniques of elongating the hot glass to the other students. Andy always created an upbeat atmosphere at the hot shop; Kate knew he was trying to keep everyone's attention focused on the work rather than on Eugene Rose's shocking death.

"How's the investigation going?" he quietly asked Kate and Johnny. When Kate was involved in a murder investigation, even tangentially, she played her cards close to the vest.

"I'm not really sure. I haven't talked with Chief Jablonsky much since he interviewed all of us. Johnny said he saw you at the funeral, did it spark anything?" Kate nicely sidestepped his question and turned it back on him.

"No, not really. I offered condolences to his parents and asked if they wanted his glass pieces. I told them I would drop them by their house."

"That was nice of you. Have you done that yet?" Kate and Johnny exchanged glances that were approving of Ormsby's gesture.

"Not yet. Since I don't know them, and didn't know Eugene all that well, I was hoping someone would go with me. I don't know what to say to parents who have lost a child," replied Ormsby, looking flummoxed.

Kate could hardly contain her excitement at having been offered this chance to talk to Eugene's parents. "Johnny has met them and was his dissertation director. I knew some of his friends, and you were his glass instructor. Sometimes grieving people just want to talk about the person who died with others who knew him or her. Why don't all three of us go together?"

"What a great idea! Thanks so much. Everyone is finishing up now, so we can pack his pieces. I'll give a quick call to let them know we are coming." While Johnny and Andy Ormsby went on their errands, Kate took the opportunity to examine Eugene's work more closely.

Ormsby returned with the kind of box that the center used to pack glass, and they wrapped Eugene's pieces. Johnny was the one who spoke about the items. "Well, these aren't very good, but he was just a beginner. His parents will love them anyway, just like all parents love the plaster handprints kids make for them at camp."

The Roses' Squirrel Hill home was only a short drive from the glass center. It was one of many traditional Tudor style homes that dotted that neighborhood, each surrounded by mature landscaping and yards large enough to accommodate swing sets or small swimming pools. The sound of children playing in the neighborhood mocked their somber errand.

Mrs. Ada Rose opened the rounded wooden front door and warmly invited them in. She escorted them to a covered flag-stone patio where her husband was already ensconced in one of the matching patio chairs; the generous porch was an inviting space on this warm fall day. Mrs. Rose excused herself for a minute, returning shortly with a tray of iced teas.

"Please let me help you with that, Mrs. Rose." Andy Ormsby gently took the tray from her and began to pass around the tall glasses of tea, decorated with fresh mint leaves and long glass stirrers. *His mom certainly raised him right,* thought Kate. Mr. Rose waved away the drink and spoke for the first time.

"You all knew my boy?" He slowly shook his head back and forth, saying, "The police don't have a clue as to what happened. They are stopping by to talk with Eugene's mother and me. I hope they have something to report!" Mr. Rose's voice gained strength through anger, and he slapped his hand on the arm of the chair. "Why would anyone do such a thing to my boy? He was a gentle academic."

"He was a light in our life," whispered Mrs. Rose, who suddenly covered her face with her napkin. Andy looked desperately at Kate for help as to how to respond to their anger and tears.

"One of the women at the library said he always had a joke for her, something inane and silly that would make her laugh. I wanted to tell you that Professor McCarthy and I went to the library to clear Eugene's study carrel. He had accrued some pretty hefty overdue book fines! We paid the fines, so everything is settled there—you don't have to be concerned." Kate spoke in an everyday tone of voice, looking directly at both parents as she spoke—she didn't shrink in the face of their grief.

"That would be Eugene. Big brain, but not much on the practical side," responded Mr. Rose, with a bit of a smile hovering at the corners of his mouth. Mrs. Rose chimed in,

"Those jokes! I'm so glad you mentioned that! When he would go to sleep-away camp in the summer, he always would send us any new jokes that he had heard. Even recently, when he was in Italy studying, he would include one in his letters or tell us one when we face-timed on the computer."

The atmosphere on the patio lightened, which was what Kate hoped would happen. She gestured to Andy to open the box of Eugene's glass pieces. "These were the items Eugene was working on. You may not think much of them, but what he was attempting to do with his glassblowing was really difficult. The pattern is very pretty." Andy took his cue from Kate and slowly handed the wine glasses to Mrs. Rose, who then handed them to her husband. "Thank you for these, Andy. They *are* a little lopsided, aren't they."

Everyone chuckled at the obvious truth. The change in mood emboldened Kate. "I've been reading Eugene's papers and find that his interest in that period of art is, well, unexpected in someone his age. Mr. Rose, do you and Mrs. Rose collect art, or have a special interest in glass?"

The chuckles over the wine glasses turned into outright laughter at Kate's question. Mr. Rose finally replied. "Art collecting? No. We are simple, hard-working people who put money away for education and the occasional nice vacation. I'm not sure where Eugene's interest came from—perhaps from my mother. She liked pretty glass things."

Mrs. Rose stretched out her hand to her husband. "I always thought it came from the family stories about the Italian arm of both of our families. You know, Kate, my father liked genealogy. He traced both my side and the Rose side back as far as the thirteenth century. It turns out several generations of our relatives were in the shipping business in Venice. They later emigrated to France, and finally to America." There was a hint of pride in her voice that Kate commented on and used as a springboard for her next question.

"You must be proud of that lineage. I suspect that the idea of Venetian merchants and sailors in the family would spark the imagination of a little boy like Eugene. Were there any special family possessions that survived from that time? I mean, family treasures like a ring, or maybe even a piece of glass?"

"Not that I know of." Mrs. Rose's expression softened, and she quietly said, "But your idea that our little boy was dreaming of adventures in Venice is a sweet one, and probably true. I appreciate that."

The intimacy of the moment was interrupted by a loud knock at the door. Mrs. Rose hurried off, and returned with Chief Jablonsky and Antoine DeVille, both clearly surprised to see Kate, Johnny, and Andy Ormsby sitting on the patio casually sipping sweet tea.

"Thank you for seeing us today, Mr. and Mrs. Rose. I happen to know these young people," he said, indicating the trio. "Dr. Chambers, Professor McCarthy, Mr. Ormsby, what brings you here?"

It was Ormsby who spoke first. "I wanted Mr. and Mrs. Rose to have Eugene's glass pieces. Because Kate and Johnny knew him better than me, I asked them to come along. We've been talking about Eugene and family history." Kate and Johnny remained silent, letting the discourse flow where it would and glad to be out of the range of Jablonsky's stare.

"Isn't that interesting," responded an annoyed Jablonsky. "Well, unfortunately I'm going to have to ask you to leave. I need to speak with Mr. and Mrs. Rose on police business." The chief gave Kate a stern look as if to reinforce that the professionals had arrived.

Goodbyes were exchanged with handshakes and a special hug between Kate and Mrs. Rose. "Please come back and see me again," she whispered in Kate's ear. "We can talk more about my boy and Italian relatives."

Kate was quiet as they drove away from the Rose's. She was thinking about how a death from murder wasn't like a death from disease. Disease is unfortunately a normal part of all living beings' existence, but in murder, someone consciously and purposely steals another's life.

When that drunk man got behind the wheel of his car and rammed head-on into her parents' car, he did just that to their life—he stole it from them, and from her. As she grew and matured, Kate increasingly longed for justice for the victims of crime: in grade school, she was known to be a fierce crossing guard; in junior high, she typically wore a police uniform at Halloween; later, at high school costume dances, she frequently donned a large mustache and wore spats, emulating her hero, Hercule Poirot. Her grandfather watched Kate's sensitivity to issues of justice grow, but did not encourage a career in policing, but rather one in helping others make good decisions.

In considering getting justice for Eugene, and after having met the Roses today, Kate was sure that there were things about the Rose family that would help solve Eugene's murder; perhaps she and Ada could suss out new clues.

CHAPTER 8

IT WAS DETECTIVE ANNIE LEMON who identified the man who had broken into Sarah Braithwaite's house. She excitedly marched into the chief's office and gave him the information.

"Here is our intruder. I'm not sure what his birth name was, but he goes by Sloppy Bogey Johnson. Yeah, that's his moniker. He has a misdemeanor sheet for being a golf hustler. Apparently Sloppy Bogey hustles at several country clubs. Here's his mug shot."

Jablonsky looked at the computer screen. It was an unusual mug shot in that the man was clean shaven and nicely dressed in an Izod polo shirt and a pair of plaid golf pants. Detective Lemon remarked, "My dad calls those 'jackass' pants."

Her comment brought a smile to Jablonsky's face, who responded with, "I never played the game myself. Good work, Lemon. Let's bring him in here for an interview."

"There is one more thing, chief. Coupe and I looked at the list of members of two country clubs where Sloppy Bogey frequently hustles, and we found this name." Lemon pointed again to the computer screen.

"Well, I'll be. Joseph Davies, Zane Davies' father. Zane called his dad when we were collecting evidence at the break-in. I'd like to talk to him, without Zane."

"Already taken care of," announced Antoine, who was standing at the door. "He's coming in this afternoon." After missing the external storage device, Jablonsky was glad that his number one and two were back in the game.

Mr. Joseph Davies was not what Jablonsky had expected. He arrived for the interview in jeans and a denim work shirt. His tan was the kind that one acquires from working outside rather than pleasure cruising on the river. Joe Davies' handshake was firm, and his eye contact direct.

"I was very sorry to hear about Eugene Rose's murder. I knew the boy—he was the same as Zane, if you get my drift. Nice kid, nice family. Any leads?" Joe Davies laid his smart phone on the table, face up. Periodically he glanced at it; he was a busy man.

"Yes. But nothing released to the public, yet. Do you know this man?" Jablonsky slid Sloppy Bogey Johnson's mug shot over to Mr. Davies.

"I can't believe it! Obviously, you already know that it's Sloppy Bogey. He's a golf hustler. You think he murdered Eugene Rose?" If Joe Davies could have gasped, he would have.

Jablonsky avoided the question. "Sarah Braithwaite called your son immediately after her house was broken into—I heard him call you from the scene."

"That's right. He was afraid you were going to arrest him. I can tell you that my son did not have anything to do with the break-in, or God forbid, the murder of his friend Eugene. You're barking up the wrong tree."

"Am I? What makes you so sure? We aren't talking about teenage boys here, Mr. Davies—Eugene was, and Zane is, a full-grown young man, and young men rarely tell their parents anything about their real lives." The intensity in Jablonsky's eyes spoke to his years of experience with prevaricating sons.

Joe Davies was silent for a few minutes, keeping his gaze down on his work-worn fingers. Finally, he spoke. "Look, my son has a problem with his temper. He acts out. He can be confrontational. And, he's a homosexual. I've always been there to protect him from himself and others—you understand? But just because he has a temper doesn't mean he is capable of murdering anyone. My wife and I encouraged his relationship with Eugene Rose, they were buddies. There are people who would physically hurt my son just because of what he is. Some probably work for me at my plants."

That's an intimate revelation for a man like Joe Davies, thought Jablonsky. He found the father's concern over protecting a gay son credible, but not convincing. "Tell me about Zane's art collecting."

"We knew that Zane wasn't going into the family business, so since he had an interest in art, and we have some disposable income, the wife and I decided that he could make a little career of collecting for us. The art would be an investment. Actually, he has become quite good at it. Who knew that in the long haul, fine art outpaces the stock market?" Joe Davies chuckled in disbelief.

"Did Eugene and Zane consult about which pieces to buy?"

"Probably not in the way you mean it. Zane talked about collecting, what he was looking at, and so forth, mostly because Eugene understood the drive to collect and to preserve culturally significant art pieces." It was clear to the chief that Zane's appreciation had affected his dad. Mr. Davies was not a man who would normally use language like "preserve culturally significant art pieces."

"Did your son tell you that he and Eugene had been arguing? Eugene felt that Zane was manipulating their mutual friend, Sarah."

"No, I didn't know that. Unfortunately, my son can be controlling." Mr. Davies shifted anxiously in his chair. "Is there anything else, Chief? I'm really busy—as you can see my phone is blowing up with texts and emails."

"Where do you keep your art collection?" Jablonsky wasn't going to mention that Sloppy Bogey had broken into Sarah Braithwaite's home looking for something. Was it an external storage devise, or perhaps an art object?

"We keep the collection in a couple of different places. We have a bank box for small items. Some of the paintings are hung in our home, a few pieces of sculpture are also placed around the house, and then, for several really valuable pieces, I have a safe in the downstairs of our home. Zane has made sure that everything is cataloged and properly insured. He is conscientious about it."

"Mr. Davies, do you know where Zane was the day that Eugene Davies was murdered?"

"Not really, where does he say he was?" Joe Davies sidestepped the accusing question. The chief didn't respond.

Joseph Davies offered his hand as the interview ended; Jablonsky shook it and said, "I'm going to say the same thing to you that I said to Zane. This is an ongoing murder investigation. Don't leave town."

"Message received. And I'll say to you, Chief Detective, that I will always protect my son."

Antoine, who had been observing the conversation, hurried into the room. "He came across as credible throughout most of the interview and then at the end, he threatens you! Unbelievable!"

Jablonsky snorted. "What else is new. Moving on, is Sloppy Bogey Johnson here?" Antoine nodded in the affirmative.

"Good, let's go."

Sloppy Bogey didn't appear to be the least bit nervous as he waited for the interview. He came dressed in golf clothes—another pair of 'jackass' pants with a matching polo shirt. He was an attractive man, tall and muscular, with skin ruddy from the sun. As Jablonsky observed him through the one-way mirror, he surmised that this grifter believed he could hustle his way out of any police problems. Thus, no anxiety.

The chief entered the room with a folder that contained Sloppy Bogey's misdemeanor sheet and the photos from the security cameras. Stefan sat down without any greeting, opened the folder, and placed the pictures in front of Johnson.

"These are photos of you as you entered Sarah Braithwaite's home on September thirteenth with the intent to commit burglary." Jablonsky leaned back in his chair and crossed his arms. He wanted to see if this man's tap-dance routine was muscular, like Gene Kelly's, or delicate, like Fred Astaire's.

"This is what you brought me in for? First, I don't believe this is me in the photos. Second, I have never committed burglary in my life. Third, I don't know any Sarah Braith... whatever. You've got the wrong man."

"Well, Mr. Sloppy, or Mr. Bogey, or Mr.... what should I call you? Okay, Bogey it is. We found DNA at Sarah Braithwaite's house and believe it will match yours. Officer Lemon is here to take a sample."

Before Bogey could protest, Annie Lemon entered the room, competently swabbed his cheek with a large Q-Tip, secured it in a sterile tube, and left with the sample.

Jablonsky placed more photos in front of Bogey. "Clearly you were looking for something specific, Bogey. Your prints were everywhere. No one slits couch pillows or searches ice cube trays without knowing exactly what he wants. What were you looking for?"

"I wasn't looking for anything because I wasn't there. You can put all the pictures on this table that you want, my story is still the same." Bogey looked directly at the chief as he lied through his teeth.

Jablonsky took out Bogey's police sheet and started to read the collection of offenses. Finally, he stopped and said, "You're a golf hustler. We've had many calls about you from members of local country clubs. If that is your main occupation, someone must have paid you a lot of money to commit a job like this—breaking and entering, destroying private property, theft—these aren't just misdemeanors. Who hired you, Bogey? If you cooperate now it will go better for you in front of the judge."

Bogey Johnson pursed his lips, taped his fingers on the table, then sighed. "What exactly are you talking about here, chief?" Bogey was a realist.

"You would do jail time, Bogey. That's what I'm talking about. This wasn't just filching rich country club guys out of their money. You would go into the system."

"Okay. What does filching mean?"

"It means hustling. Come on, Bogey, what's it going to be? The name or some jail time at the city's country club, where there are plenty of bars, but no drinks." The chief watched Johnson try to absorb the unpleasant reality of his situation—Bogey sucked air in between his teeth, rubbed his hands over his face, and finally decided to talk.

"The truth is, I don't know who paid me for this job. A typed note was left in my locker at the country club. It said that if I wanted to make a thousand dollars, just write yes on the note, and someone would leave the instructions and the money for me. I never saw anyone leave either the note or the envelop of money. I'm being really honest here, chief, you need to cut me a break."

"Do you have the sheet the instructions were written on?"

"No...well, I might. I'd have to check my car, or my pants pockets. It might have gone into the wash. Or, I might have stuffed it into my golf bag." Jablonsky couldn't believe this man kept a piece of incriminating evidence and he doesn't know where he put it. No wonder he was called Sloppy.

"Mr. Bogey. What were the instructions, exactly?"

"Um, exactly? I think it said that I was to get into the house and look for a small device, some computer thing, I don't remember what it was called."

Jablonsky thought, *He must be good at golf, because he surely has a single digit IQ. He doesn't even know enough to be worried about this situation.* "Was it called an external storage drive? Like a flash drive?" Jablonsky's tone of voice was even, masking the amusement he felt. If you're going to be a criminal, at least try to be a good one.

"Yeah! That's right. It had something to do with storage—you know, like a storage unit only tiny, to store video games and stuff like that. Now I'm thinking. Yeah." Bogey flashed an inane smile of bleached white teeth at the chief.

"Thank you, Mr. Johnson. This police officer will take you to booking and then you will accompany my detective and me to your apartment, where we will search for the external storage drive. Let's hope we find it."

CHAPTER 9

KATE HAD JUST ARRIVED HOME after work when she got a call from Joan. "I have information for you. Want to work out and then have dinner? My surgeries are finished for the day."

"Great! I also have been doing my research. Would it be all right with you if we meet at my condo? I need to feed Bourbon Ball. If you are up for a run, we could run through the neighborhood with the pup." Kate liked, no, loved, efficiency. If she could exercise herself and BB at the same time, and eat dinner and talk about research with Joan, the efficiency of it would satisfy her more than the food. By the time Joan arrived, Kate had changed into a turtleneck sweater and running shorts and worked her thick dark hair into one braid.

Since BB was with them, the two women set a relaxed pace. They passed many other runners along the length of the broad and tree-lined Ellsworth Avenue. Neither woman liked chit-chat, so they ran in silence until the evening sky turned yellowish pink and the streetlights came on. Once home, they ordered take-out from a local restaurant.

"I was thinking about the Rose family—I remember Eugene's Bar Mitzvah." Joan cut into a piece of rotisserie chicken. Kate knew she was operating the next day, so she placed a small bottle of Pellegrino next to Joan's water glass. "The Bar Mitzvah party was small but fun, not like the ginormous parties people plan today. Since I was his camp counselor, I stopped in at the service and party. I liked the Rose family."

"I particularly like Mrs. Rose. She asked me to come around again to talk about Eugene's work. She told us something really interesting." Kate reiterated the Roses' Italian heritage and how the family first emigrated to France and then to America. Kate, who loved to cook but ironically didn't have a large appetite, waited for her friend to finish her dinner, hoping she had some new information to add to the search.

Joan pushed her plate away, rinsed her hands, then opened her laptop. "Here are some of my notes on Eugene's list of names and dates. As I mentioned, the surname Canterella was in many historical documents because they lived at the same time, and were of the same social status, as the Borgias. I couldn't find any evidence that their family members ever left Italy."

Kate added, "I found records and pictures of art objects that the family collected. The provenance of the objects is clear. Many paintings are in museums, many remain in the family. The second name, La Rosa, clearly Italian for Rose, stood out to me because I had just had that conversation with Eugene's mother. La Rosa or Rose...it's the same thing."

"What are you thinking?" Joan stepped over the snoring and twitching Bourbon Ball to get a cup of coffee from the kitchen.

"Well, through genealogical studies, I speculate that Eugene discovered a glass object listed as belonging to the La Rosa family, that he subsequently suspected might have passed to the American Roses. If he did, I don't understand why he didn't note what the object was." Kate stopped and looked at Joan, waiting for her response.

"Okay. Maybe he mentions the type of object to a friend or has written it somewhere we don't know about. But how would that lead to someone wanting to kill him? It's not like we are talking about the Hope Diamond or a Vermeer. It seems a speculative and weak motive to me." Kate burst out laughing—this is exactly why she loved Joan. That scientific, unsentimental mind always kept Kate on her toes.

"Even if the object was valuable, why kill him? Why not just find out where the search was leading, wait until he had found something, and then take it? No real reason to murder him." Kate shrugged her shoulders to accent the Occam's Razor aspect of her theory.

"Agreed. The simplest solution is always the best. Let's follow your supposition. Perhaps he actually found an object that, by provenance, belongs to his family, and the killer knew it. That really narrows the list of suspects." Joan sipped her strong hot coffee while secretly handing BB a dog treat she had retrieved from the kitchen. Kate had a rule about feeding the dog at the table, but tonight, she let it pass, too immersed in her theory of the murder.

"I think we should focus our attention on the Rose family. I believe there might be clues in Eugene's grandmother's glass collection. Our research now narrows to glass objects that might have belonged to the family and that have been passed down to this generation. Potentially, the glass object might be very rare, therefore, very valuable."

"Whom do you know that is knowledgeable in this area?" asked Joan.

"Well, Andy Ormsby. I'll talk to him at the next class to see if the La Rosa name rings any bells." It was getting late, so Kate began to load the dishwasher. Joan stood in the kitchen doorway as she checked her cell phone to find out the score of the Pirates' game.

"By the way, I have my right behind home plate season tickets for this weekend. You would get to see Cheeks Malouskas, the new young pitcher. Why don't I invite Marco Rossetti to come? It will be fun!" Joan grinned at her friend and then began to wheedle. "Come on Kate, come on Katie girl, he really likes you and it's time you start to go out again."

Kate could feel her blood pressure begin to rise. The area of dating and men always seemed to be a hot spot between her and Joan. Joan had liked Eddie Fitzroy as a person, but never felt he was right for Kate. Obviously, she felt Marco Rossetti and Kate would be a better match and had been trying to advance his cause, even though Kate was still grieving Eddie.

"You can be so irritating! When I'm ready, I'll go out. Stop throwing Marco at me!" Unfortunately, Kate's anger didn't act as a stop sign for Joan.

"Come on, you can grieve and watch a baseball game at the same time." The comment was so insensitive, even for Joan, that she apologized, and occupied herself with saying goodbye to Bourbon Ball.

"Joan, go home. We can talk after I see Mrs. Rose and get more genealogical details." Joan blew Kate an air kiss and left, humming "Take Me Out to The Ball Game." *She always has to have the last word,* thought Kate.

Across town, Mr. Joseph Davies was in the kitchen of his home, drinking a beer with Zane. The atmosphere wasn't cordial. They were talking about the break-in at Sarah's house. "What the hell are you doing hanging around Sarah Braithwaite? She's a nice enough young lady but you know there is nothing in it for you. What is going on?"

Zane was always deferential to his father. In fact, when he was honest with himself, he was afraid of him. His father had never raised a hand to Zane, but he could, and at times had, made him feel like an inferior human being. Zane believed that his father really hated that he was gay but had held back from actually saying the words. What is never spoken is often heard the loudest.

"Was there something in particular that Eugene was doing that interested you?" Mr. Davies gave his son "The Look,"—all of his factory and administrative officers had experienced that unflinching and menacing hard stare.

"Yes and no. He was researching the provenance of certain glass objects that were privately held in the families of origin. I was interested because sometimes these families sell things for money, items I could buy, perhaps, for our collection." Zane took another bottle of beer from the refrigerator, flipped off the cap, and immediately chugged half of it.

"Is that why you want to go back to Italy—to follow up on his research?"

Zane finished the second bottle before answering, then moved toward the refrigerator to grab another.

"You've had enough, Zane!" barked his father. "What about Italy?"

"Since Sarah was going to be there, it seemed like an opportune situation for me. I'd know someone and have a home base as I looked around for things to purchase. That's all."

"That had better be all. Look, Eugene was murdered, and whether you like it or not, you are high on the list of suspects. You can't be gallivanting around Italy while they're searching for the murderer. Get real, Zane."

"Just ask me, Dad. Ask me the question!" Zane rarely was confrontational in his attitude toward his father, but with the help of the several beers, he managed it tonight. "Ask me the question!" he shouted.

"All right. Did you murder Eugene?"

Zane stood and slammed the kitchen chair under the table. "I can't believe you would even entertain the possibility that I murdered him. He was my friend, for God's sake." Zane blew out of the room, leaving his father at the kitchen table, thinking, *I hope he's telling me the truth.*

CHAPTER 10

CHIEF DETECTIVE JABLONSKY and Antoine DeVille arrived at Bogey Johnson's apartment in Aspinwall, a small residential community along the Allegheny River. It was a nice apartment, one of many which were situated in a complex sitting on the riverbank—it offered a workout center, a pool, and bicycle trails that ran along the Allegheny.

"Aside from hustling rich guys, how do you make a living?" asked the chief. Bogey was handcuffed to a kitchen chair.

"I'm one of the golf pros at the Greenwich Country Club."

"Is that what they call it? A pro? Do they know about your extracurricular activities?" Jablonsky chortled, then turning serious, asked Bogey to show them where his golf clubs were. Antoine zipped and unzipped the various compartments in the bag, and unbelievably, he found the note.

Coupe and the chief exchanged glances that confirmed their belief that Bogey was one of the most brainless perps they had ever meet. "Take him out to the porch with one of the detectives. I want to look around some more."

"Any chance of a beer while I wait?" asked a naively sincere Bogey.

"Where do you think you are, at the country club?" barked Jablonsky.

"You fellows are welcome to a cold one, there are plenty." The offers of beer were declined, and Sloppy Bogey was seated on the porch with a glass of water.

The chief continued to look around the attractively decorated apartment. He found many neatly ironed golf outfits hanging in the closet, the usual utility and insurance bills in the desk, and a refrigerator stocked with healthy foods right alongside plenty of cans of beer. On the kitchen counter, underneath a stack of Golf Digest magazines, he discovered a membership list of the Greenwich Country Club, with several names underlined. One of the names was Joseph Davies. They already knew that Davies was a member, but why were his, and other names, underlined?

"Look at this, Coupe." Jablonsky held out the list.

"Was Joseph Davies just a mark, or something else?" questioned Antoine.

"Bogey. Why are these names underlined?" Jablonsky asked, showing him the membership list.

"Well, these men are, shall I say, rather impaired golfers possessed of lots of money at the ready for a friendly wager." Bogey had the good grace to look sheepish.

"And that includes Joseph Davies?"

Bogey let out a whoop. "Especially Mr. Davies. Nice man, hardworking and all, but a terrible golfer. However, his son isn't bad."

Jablonsky replied, "His son? You mean Zane Davies? Young man, still at the university, private school snob. That son?"

"Yeah. That's a good description of him. He, however, doesn't gamble when he plays. I find him to be, well, an arrogant little you know what. He sometimes comes in the pro shop and buys this and that."

"Does he ever bring any friends?

"No. No pals his age. He does occasionally have lunch with two priests that play at the club. They are guests of various members."

"Priests?" Jablonsky replied, dumbfounded. "You mean, Catholic priests?"

"Yeah, regular type RC priests. I don't know how they know each other—the two priests are older. I don't know them. Like Zane, they don't gamble on their golf game either." Bogey chuckled and winked at the two detectives. "Maybe they believe they would have an edge with the man upstairs."

"I want you to give detective DeVille a description of them, their names and at what parish they are employed. By the way, is Zane Davies' locker close to yours in the men's locker room?" The chief kept his rising excitement out of his tone of voice.

"Hm. Now that you mention it, yeah. His locker is next to his dad's, a row back from mine. I rarely see the Dad in the locker room. Zane doesn't often play, which is too bad, because if he took some lessons and practiced, he could have been a good weekend golfer." Bogey casually sat back in the porch chair as if he were a golf analyst narrating a Sunday afternoon game.

Back at the police station, Coup and Jablonsky were adding more items to the murder board. Antoine wrote the new information while the chief enjoyed a chew on a fresh piece of cinnamon gum. There was the typed instruction note to Bogey Johnson from the break-in at Sarah Braithwaite's house—which he claims didn't turn up the external storage device. There was the membership list with Joseph Davies' name underlined. Finally, the information that Zane Davies sometimes had lunch with two priests at the club.

The priests were easy to find on the registry of local parishes. Antoine had downloaded a picture of each priest and pinned them up on the murder board—Fathers Carlotti and Lupinski. Both men were priests in east end parishes.

"Detective Lemon. Have you found anything on the biographies of these two men that can help us?" Annie Lemon left her computer and stood beside the chief. He offered a stick of gum, which she took, but as usual, she slid it into her back pocket.

"There is something interesting. Father Carlotti has family in Florence. In fact, he was there on some kind of retreat at the same time Sarah Braithwaite, Eugene Rose, and Zane Davies were in Italy. I wonder if Zane saw Carlotti in Florence. If so, what's the scope of their relationship?"

"Let's go visit the good father. Call him and tell him we are on our way."

Father Carlotti was one of several priests in a large, wealthy, east end city parish. Luckily, he wasn't possessed of a condescending manner, rather his body language simultaneously communicated irritation and fatigue. He welcomed the chief and DeVille into an office filled with books, papers, some religious pictures, and a fancy computer.

"Father, we are here to ask you about a young man named Zane Davies."

"Zane? Yes, I know him. Is he in some kind of trouble?"

Jablonsky took control of the meeting by asking the questions he wanted and at his pace; he slowly retrieved his small paper notebook and a pen. "How do you know him? Is the Davies family part of this parish?"

"Yes, they are. I can't say they come to Mass very often, but they are members in good standing. By that I mean they've all had their sacraments and pay their monthly allotment," Father Carlotti answered wryly while he held up a box of the ubiquitous envelopes mailed to every parishioner.

"Zane spent a semester abroad recently, in Italy. He was there at the same time you were. Did you two see each other?" Jablonsky looked up from scribbling in his notebook.

"I did see him in Florence—I was staying with family at the time. Zane and I had lunch." The priest was beginning to show his frustration at the personal questions being asked without the offer of any context.

"What did you talk about at the luncheon?" Jablonsky ignored the priest's attitude.

"Well, he and I talked about church artifacts. It's an obscure topic in which only art dealers and academics are interested. And me. Because Zane was headed to Murano, we talked about glass. Chief Jablonsky, I'm answering all your questions, now you tell me what this is about." Stefan took note of the increasing hostile edge to the priest's voice.

"Apparently you haven't heard. Eugene Rose, a fellow academic of Zane Davies, was murdered. We're inquiring into the circumstances of his death." The chief's tone gave no room for further comment, but the priest wasn't going to be denied.

"You think Zane Davies had something to do with a murder? I can't believe that is true. I know the name Eugene Rose. Zane referred to him as a close friend. He was in Italy with Zane at the time we are speaking about. In Pittsburgh, I think they had a house together. How is all of this related? How did you come to know that I knew Zane?"

"That information is part of our police inquiry. Back to your luncheon in Florence. Did Zane say that he was looking to acquire something in particular while he was in Italy?"

"Not that I remember. Well, wait, now that you say it, he did mention he was meeting a Rabbi to talk about items that are of value in Jewish ceremonies. Obviously, it would be something more than an everyday menorah. I just don't remember a specific item in which he was interested. Maybe he didn't say."

"If you remember anything else from that conversation, please let detective DeVille know." Antoine handed his card to the priest while Jablonsky stood up to leave.

Jablonsky and DeVille exited the church. Once outside, they both looked at each other and burst out laughing. Antoine spoke the obvious. "Two Priests and a Rabbi walk into a bar."

The interview with Carlotti did reveal a new angle. Why would the Catholic Zane Davies be looking for a Jewish antiquity and did Jewish Eugene Rose know something about it? It begged the question once again as to whether information about an art object was on the missing external storage device.

"Did you notice the religious pictures in Carlotti's office? The one was very large and prominent," mentioned the chief.

"I think that was a picture of St. Augustine. We had one in our high school."

Jablonsky chuckled. Talking about art objects certainly was rubbing off on DeVille.

CHAPTER 11

KATE KNOCKED AT MRS. ROSE'S FRONT DOOR. She had called Eugene's mother to follow up on the invitation extended to her the day they returned her son's wine glasses.

"Come in! I have us set up on the patio—tea and genealogy." It appeared that Mr. Rose wouldn't be joining them, which in Kate's mind was a good thing. Women always talked more freely without a man present.

"How are you doing, Mrs. Rose?" Kate asked in her normal speaking voice; she didn't believe in affecting the helium voice people use when asking about grief.

"One minute I'm okay and the next I'm prostrate on the bed crying, wondering how I will go on." She offered Kate a crooked smile.

"My grandfather always said that he called me his 'precious gift' because when my mother was killed, my very existence meant he could still see a future for his life. I guess he meant that parenting me gave his life purpose beyond his work."

"He was a wise man. I agree that we extend our life into the future through our children."

"I don't have any children yet, so I have to imagine the pain of the loss... I did lose my husband. Oh my, I'm so sorry to bring it up—it's a long story and inappropriate for me to mention it. They are two very different kinds of losses, aren't they?" Kate was surprised at her spontaneous revelation about Fitzroy.

Mrs. Rose put her hand on Kate's. "Call me Ada. I guess we are both down for the count." She poured two tall glasses of iced tea, then placed the family genealogy record in front of Kate, scooting her chair closer.

"This is the sheet that shows the Rose family in Italy in the sixteenth and seventeenth centuries." The neat boxes were labeled with the surname La Rosa with Rose next to it in parenthesis.

"They changed their name from La Rosa to Rose," Kate said, pointing out the obvious. "When did they do that?"

"When they came to this country, La Rosa became Rose. Historically speaking, that's relatively recent. They were still La Rosa in France in the seventeenth century, but by the time the family came to America, which was in the late eighteenth hundreds, it was listed as Rose. They came before the big wave of immigration that took place in the early twentieth century." Mrs. Rose pulled out the Ellis Island record. "Ellis Island opened in 1892. As you can see, the family arrived in 1895, and here is the name, Rose, and the list of family members—mother and father, two sons and a daughter."

"Did they stay in New York?" asked Kate, her finger tracing down the list of names on the Ellis Island record.

"No. They went to North Carolina. Yes, they went to a southern state! There was a factory that needed the father's expertise—there were furniture factories just starting to expand around the High Point area. That's what Sam's great grandfather Rose did, he organized and managed furniture factories." For some reason, Mrs. Rose found that to be humorous, and Kate was glad to see her laugh.

“I want to ask a delicate question,” remarked Kate. “Was there any problem with religion? I mean, it was, and is, predominately a Christian state, and the Roses were Jewish.”

“No problems that I ever heard about. There are family stories that indicate that they gave money to build a small synagogue. The Rose family did the same when they came to Pittsburgh. You know the synagogue that’s over on the other side of Squirrel Hill? They gave money for that building fund. Eugene had his Bar Mitzvah there.” Mrs. Rose’s flow of information halted as her voice choked with emotion.

“I’m sorry. Should we stop?” Kate waited until Mrs. Rose quieted her grief, then repeated a question she had asked when she, Andy, and Johnny came to return Eugene’s glasses. “Were there any special objects that the family brought on the journey from Venice to France to America? Things that would have ignited Eugene’s imagination?”

“Not that I know of.”

Kate sat back in her chair and waited. Mrs. Rose clearly had something she wanted to say, but hesitated. Finally, she spoke.

“You may already know this, but it was not uncommon for Jews to convert to Catholicism in order to evade horrible persecution. In family lore, it has been mentioned that the La Rosa family converted when they arrived in France.” Mrs. Rose looked directly at Kate. “It was a matter of survival of the family and the business. I don’t judge.”

“I don’t judge either, Ada—it all comes out of the same traditions. But what it does mean is that the family may have had art objects that were both Jewish and Catholic.”

“Could be. I’m just not sure that Eugene ever saw anything that the Rose family might have collected that wasn’t Judaica. When they arrived in America, they reverted to Judaism, and have practiced that religion ever since." Unconsciously, Mrs. Rose touched the discreet Star of David necklace she wore.

Kate had tucked the Xerox copy of Eugene's notebook in her purse and now brought it out, hoping it would interest Ada. It did. "Oh look! Eugene's book of doodles and ideas! How wonderful that you brought it." Mrs. Rose touched the pages as if they were made of gold.

"The police have the original. I made copies of it because I wanted to see how his mind worked. Do any of these images mean anything to you?" Kate slowly turned the sheets, allowing Mrs. Rose time to really examine the contents.

"The sketch of this object seems vaguely familiar to me, although I don't recognize it as belonging to Judaism. Eugene was widely educated in art, it must have meant something to him, though, because it looks like he tried to copy part of it onto his wine glasses. Let me get them and show you what I mean." Mrs. Rose hustled off and shortly returned with the rather misshapen glasses. Kate could not believe she hadn't noticed the similarities herself.

"Look at this round part. It's like a circle with some kind of image on it."

"You are brilliant, Mrs. Rose. It is the same—a circle, maybe like a pendant with a pattern or image in the center. I just don't have any idea what it is, do you?"

"No. I don't know what it is or what it represented to my boy. If you find out its significance, please tell me. I want to remember everything about Eugene and his beautiful mind. And Kate, thank you and Professor McCarthy, for taking such a personal interest in helping to find out why this happened to Eugene."

"In the glassblowing class, he always had a good word for everyone's efforts; he was a smart and lovely young man. It is easy to care about the horrible injustice that befell him." Ada reached out and took Kate's hand, gently squeezing it.

During the pause in their conversation, a hummingbird came to drink at the feeder that hung in the oak tree by the patio. Kate and Ada sat very still, watching the tiny, bejeweled bird defy gravity as it hovered to drink the honey water. The beauty and magic of the moment briefly soothed both women's broken hearts. When Kate left, their hug held a special intensity and warmth, an expression of their shared grief over the loss of a husband and a son.

Kate knew that she had to talk with the chief about the new clues and information, but she needed to devise a way to do it so that there was some kind of quid pro quo. She had an idea.

"Chief, this is Kate Chambers. Mrs. Rose had asked me to come for another visit to talk further about Eugene's art interests and his papers. She mentioned some things that I thought might be relevant to the case. When it is convenient, I could stop by the precinct. Yes, I can be there within the hour. I'll see you in a bit."

Kate immediately called Johnny, filled him in on her design discovery and the Rose family history, and asked if he would go with her to the precinct. "I wanted you to see the drawing in Eugene's notebook—it might mean something to you. I haven't told the chief that I made a copy of the notebook, so I'm going to ask to see the original, and work from that."

"No problem for me. It's our secret. I'm at the university, pick me up and we can head to the station from there." Kate smoothly maneuvered through the Fifth Avenue traffic, then swept around the circle in front of the Fine Art's building.

Johnny was standing outside looking quite dapper in his madras blazer and blue cotton pants. Kate gave him the short version of her information as she carefully drove down the steep roads in Polish Hill to the police station.

The detectives hadn't flipped the murder board to its blank side, so Kate took her time passing it on the way to the chief's office. She was surprised to see the names of two priests on it. *Who are these two priests?* she wondered. Detective Lemon caught her examining the board and quickly herded her and Johnny along to the chief's office.

Kate had made an effort over her outfit for the visit with Mrs. Rose. Her athletic figure was shown to advantage in a denim shirtwaist dress; her shiny black hair was pulled back in a simple ponytail. Kate rarely used feminine wiles with men, but if she looked pretty to the chief, and it helped to further collaboration, more's the better. The quid pro quo she had in mind, however, had nothing to do with looking good.

The chief was clearly curious as to what she was bringing to the table, so he got right down to business.

"What do you have?" he asked.

Kate reiterated the genealogy of the Rose family, speculating that Eugene was looking for a glass item that might have belonged to his Italian relatives. She described the design on Eugene's wine glasses and again in his notebook. Then she talked about the list of names that she and Johnny had found at the study carrel in the library.

"Give me the list," snapped Jablonsky. "Look you two, finding out about the study carrel was great detective work—work that a real detective should be doing. You blithely sailed into the library, ignorant of the fact that someone might have been watching the carrel, and therefore, watching you. And still might be watching you. This murderer was daring—he or she killed Eugene Rose in the middle of a class, do you believe this same murderer would think twice about taking a shot at you two in a large library? If there is an object that someone wants badly enough to murder for, and it is still out there—come on, use your brains. How long have you had this list of names and who has seen it?"

Kate had anticipated that the chief would be angry over the list, but she really didn't care.

"I just got the list. I've done a limited computer search on the names. It was only when Mrs. Rose talked about the surname, La Rosa, that I began to formulate my idea of a family antiquity. In my defense, I knew Eugene and so did Johnny. We were right there when he was murdered. I'm involved whether you want me to be or not." Kate's face flushed with adrenaline and her hands shook, but she didn't look away from the chief's gaze. She decided to continue.

"And, Mrs. Rose has asked me to come back for more visits. That means there will be more information that no one else could give us. I believe the answer to Eugene's murder might come from his family." Kate's tone held a "so there."

"Humph," was Jablonsky's only response. He began to twirl a pen like an airplane propeller.

"You and Johnny have a history of being stalked and shot at when you are involved in your, quote, 'research.' I'd like that not to happen again. Under no circumstances are you to have knowledge of a clue and pursue it on your own. Is that understood?" Jablonsky stood up, his large stature emphasizing the difference in their positions.

Kate stood as well. "Understood. But chief, I did bring you some important information. I think I deserve some consideration in terms of the leads you have."

"Oh, really? What do you have in mind?" Having gone through the teen years with his daughter Carly, he knew when a bargaining chip was about to be thrown down.

"I noticed that you have the names of two priests on the murder board. May I ask what involvement they have in the case?" Kate was going for The Full Monty.

"No. You may not. End of discussion. You two can go. Thanks for this information. But my main concern right now, Kate, is your and Johnny's safety. Am I clear?" Both mumbled yes and slouched out of the office.

Continuing to twirl his pen, Jablonsky looked at his number one. "Coupe. How do you think Kate's information helps us? Give me a theory that I can get behind."

"Well, I'm no art historian, but the fact that Eugene was looking at his Italian family history in terms of an antique glass object that might have belonged to them, that's a specific direction, and possibly, a motivation. Maybe he found an object and was trying to trace who was currently in possession of it. Coming from New Orleans, where old families have lots of European paintings and sculptures that are worth a bundle, I'd say we should see if an antiquity attaches to the La Rosa name, then to the Rose name. That's my takeaway." Antoine stood quietly, waiting to hear from his chief.

"Good. Speaking of European art, get me the skinny on the Saint Augustine reproduction that was in Carlotti's office. I want to know everything about it, so add that painting to your list of inquiries."

The chief smirked as he thought, *Wasn't St. Augustine the one who prayed, "Give me chastity...but not yet."*

CHAPTER 12

BACK IN THE CAR AFTER THE MEETING with Jablonsky, Kate turned to Johnny and said, "I want to talk to Andy Ormsby about the design. Are you in?"

Johnny nodded, and in admiration of her perseverance replied, "That's my girl! You and Bourbon Ball share Retriever genetics."

The small gift shop at the glass center was a magical place stocked with everyday items from glass pieces one could buy for a birthday to hand blown art objects. The windows in the shop were positioned in the building so the sun's rays illuminated other universes highlighted in the glass pieces. It was a tranquil space that frequently had rainbows cast onto the walls and floor as light refracted through the crystals suspended from the ceiling. Today, the staff was busy with soft dusters used to keep the glass looking pristine.

Andy was at his computer working on an article he was writing. Being the director of the glass studio in Pittsburgh had been a career coup; it was a community with a long history of large glass factories along the rivers that produced glass for everyday use like windows or drinking glasses, as well as a few shops where blown glass pieces were made. The position didn't pay as much as he would have liked, but that aside, it allowed him to teach and create. He suddenly noticed Kate Chambers' name pop up on his cell phone.

"Dr. Chambers! How nice to hear from you! What's up?"

"I need your expertise. There is a design that was in Eugene Rose's notebook which he also tried to create in his wine glasses. I wanted to show it to you to see if you recognize it. Is it okay to stop by, or do you want me to wait until our class?"

"No, no. No reason to wait. When were you thinking of stopping in?" Once again Kate could hear excitement in his voice. *Oh well,* she thought, *I can't control that.*

"Johnny McCarthy and I are in the neighborhood right now. Would this be a good time?"

"Johnny's with you as well? Okay, come along! I'll see if I can help." Andy met them at the entrance to the building and they walked back to a conference room. The walls were lined with tall bookcases filled with volumes on the history of glass. When Johnny went off to buy coffees at the tiny canteen, Andy remarked, "I remember Eugene's idea book. His designs required more than his beginner's skill in blowing glass. Which design were you interested in?"

"It is this one. It looks like a circle with something in the middle. Does it mean anything to you? Maybe a symbol used in Jewish religious rituals?"

Andy reached behind him, grabbing one of the art books from the shelves. He quickly thumbed through it, then pointed to the picture of an antique glass object. "It could be something like this," he said.

"This is really beautiful. It says it's a wine taster? The top is a circle, all right—it's in the Royal Ontario Museum in Toronto. I was wondering if the circle would be the frame for a small portrait of a wealthy patron. Anything like that?"

Johnny returned with the coffees, and everyone paused to sip their hot drink and think.

Andy nodded. "That's entirely possible. One that comes to mind is a portrait of Margaret of Austria. It's in the Corning Museum in New York. But that work was probably produced in the Netherlands, not Venice. Other common objects might have been a commemorative plate, or a plate used in religious services. There might be a roundel trapped in the middle of the plate with an image or design on it. A plate such as that might have been used to serve communion bread or matzo."

Kate stood to get a better view of the pictures and unobtrusively used her position to inch her chair a bit further away from Andy's; he had been creeping closer and closer to her as they talked. She looked up for an instant at Johnny, who gave her a secret smile that indicated he knew what she was doing.

They continued to look through the photos of historically significant glass art. Johnny said, "When you mentioned the idea of something used in religious ceremonies, for a minute I thought about a miniature picture of one of the popes."

Kate looked at him as if she were remembering something. "When I was looking at photos of old *stangenglas,* I noticed that some of them were beautifully decorated with pictures of saints, rich patrons or even the pope."

Using his teaching voice, Andy Ormsby pontificated. "Yes, items such as that were very lavishly gilded and often were cold painted with pictures of animals or the religious. It's possible that some chapels used them for communion wine." Ormsby paused and then added, "If Eugene's family was Jewish, they would have had these carafes for Friday Shabbat dinner—they would have been very expensive to make."

The three went on to talk about other possible glass objects that might have had a roundel or miniature picture encapsulated in it. Finally, they left, with Ormsby walking them out and holding the front door open for Kate. "See you in class!"

"Katie girl! You have two amorous suitors in the running. Who will move into first place?" Johnny assumed the voice of a television announcer. "Will it be the wealthy, bona fide genius but emotionally damaged, world renown surgeon, Marco Rossetti, or will it be the artist of modest funds but very decent and sincere, Andy Ormsby. Not that you need a man for funds—your grandfather made sure you are not dependent on anyone for money." Johnny giggled and poked Kate in the arm as they walked to the car. He had deteriorated into an adolescent boy.

"As did your mother, who left you a bundle, Mr. Annoying!" Kate retorted with equal levity. "You know I'm not romantically interested in anyone right now. I'm changing the subject! I want to talk to Joan about what glass objects a Jewish family might have owned in sixteenth-century Italy. Want to stay for dinner?"

"Of course. I need to see our big, adorable chocolate lab, Mr. Bourbon Ball. I'll walk him while you either call for take-out or make dinner. Deal?"

"Deal."

Andy Ormsby was busy finishing his article. The gift shop and canteen were closed, and glassblowing classes had ended. "See you tomorrow, Mr. Ormsby," called the maintenance workers, who were rolling their cleaning carts along the empty corridor.

Ormsby stood up to capture the sheets of paper as his printer extruded them. He tapped the sheets on the desk for good alignment and then deposited them in his briefcase—it was the last thing he remembered before he woke up on the ground with a security guard hovering over him.

"Mr. Ormsby, Mr. Ormsby, can you hear me? Wake up. Are you hurt? Oh, my goodness, you are hurt. I'll call the ambulance." The security guard immediately called for help, unnerved by the sight of blood on and around the director's head.

A short time later, Andy was shaken into consciousness again by a paramedic, urging him not to move. Right after that, detective Jablonsky arrived at the office and quietly spoke to the emergency technician.

"Is he all right? Will I be able to ask him some questions?" Jablonsky and DeVille watched as the medic cleaned a nasty cut on Andy's head. "That's going to hurt like hell," remarked the chief. The technician reported that Andy had sustained a blow to the back of the head with something heavy. He wanted to take him to the hospital in order to get some pictures of the skull and to assess him for a concussion. "Give me five minutes before you take him," requested the chief.

"Andy, did you see who hit you?" the chief asked in a low voice.

"No. I was leaving for the day. I was putting papers into my briefcase and everything suddenly went black. That's all I remember until the security guard found me." Andy winced as he tentatively moved his head.

"Has anyone threatened you recently?"

"Threatened me? No. I'm the director of a glass center, why would anyone threaten me?" Andy tried to get up, clearly became dizzy, so the paramedic muscled the chief out of the way. "That's it, Jablonsky. I'm taking him .... You can talk to him at the hospital." They wheeled a stunned and hurting Ormsby out to the ambulance.

"Chief. Take a look at this." DeVille held up a large, heavy book on the history of glass, its corner was dented, and the cover was speckled with blood. "Could be our weapon."

"Okay. Bag it. Let's have a look around and then head to the hospital."

Andy Ormsby was resting comfortably in a hospital bed when the chief poked his head into the room. "Feel like talking?" Stefan walked in and pulled one of the chairs close to the bed. "Was there anything unusual that happened at the center before you were hit?" The chief opened his tiny paper notebook.

"Nothing really. Well, Kate Chambers and Professor McCarthy stopped by to talk about one of the drawings in Eugene Rose's notebook. We looked at several history books to see if we could identify the object he drew and tried to replicate in his wine glasses. Kate had talked with Mrs. Rose and she was the one to notice the similarity."

Jablonsky was annoyed. *They must have left my office and gone directly to see Ormsby. Damn, it could have been her and Johnny lying on the floor along with Ormsby. When she's defiant, it's hard to keep her and her friends safe.*

"Andy, did anything interesting come out of that conversation?"

"Well, Johnny thought the design looked like some sort of roundel embedded in something with a picture on it. Maybe you would see it on a wine glass or a special serving plate. Perhaps even a pendant that a rich patron or his wife would wear."

"If Eugene had found such an item, would it be valuable?"

"Well, that's a really broad question. If it was hand blown in the Venetian style, and truly an antiquity, it could be very valuable. A wealthy patron of the early church might have commissioned one... I told Kate that I don't know of any private or public collection which houses such an object." Ormsby winced as he nodded his head.

"Was there any person that seemed out of place visiting the center yesterday?"

"It might be worth your while to talk to the gift shop people. They would know if someone unusual came in to look around or buy something. I'm typically not in the front of the house, as they say." Ormsby gingerly touched his sutured wound.

"If you think of anything else, call me day or night. In the meantime, we will talk to the gift store folks. By the way, you were hit with one of the books you must have been looking at with Kate and Johnny. It was a large compendium of the history of glass. We took it into evidence. Sorry."

The chief slowly walked around the gift shop at the glass center. The workers were grouped together like a bunch of bananas, their heads almost touching as they gossiped about what had happened to their director. Jablonsky flashed his badge and asked, "Who is in charge here?"

"That's me," said a youngish woman dressed in a Bohemian outfit, accompanied by the requisite long, curly, flyaway hair; clearly a Neo-hippy wannabe artist.

"Have you had a chance to look around to see if anything is missing? Mr. Ormsby said you would be the person who knows this shop best." Jablonsky flashed his best flattering smile.

"That's true, I would know best about this shop. We cannot find anything missing. Your detective DeVille asked me if there was anyone who came into the shop lately who didn't seem to belong. I've been thinking about it, and I would say yes—there was a man, probably in his forties, who didn't seem interested in buying anything, he just looked around. It was almost like he was taking mental pictures."

"If I showed you his photograph, would you recognize him?"

"Yes. I think I would." The perky shop girl flipped her hair and struck a confident pose. *She thinks she is in a reality television show,* mused Jablonsky.

"I'll have a few photos emailed over shortly. Thanks so much."

Jablonsky and DeVille revisited Ormsby's office and the conference room, not having any idea what might be missing. They commented on how organized everything was—all the books were alphabetically arranged on the shelves, the conference table and Ormsby's desk was dusted and clean, as were the cement floors. Either COVID 19 had had an impact on the glass center, or Andy was a compulsive cleaner.

Ormsby mentioned that he backed-up his work to the Cloud and not to a flash drive. All the drawers had been opened and the contents rifled through. They would have to wait until he left the hospital to know if something specific was missing. Forensics had already bagged his computer.

By the time Jablonsky and Coupe were ready to leave, detective Lemon had emailed photos of Father Carlotti, Bogey Johnson, Zane Davies and his father, Joe Davies, to the gift shop supervisor. She identified the priest as the man whose behavior seemed suspicious.

When the day wound down, Jablonsky was glad to head home to get to work on his latest model ship, the USS North Carolina. He poured himself some Jameson Black. *I wonder if Kate is right after all? Was the person looking for the external storage device the same one who is looking for Eugene's antique glass object?* He punched a telephone number into his cell.

"Coupe. Get that priest Carlotti in for another interview. And I want to see Bogey Johnson again. Nighty-night."

CHAPTER 13

"I DON'T HAVE MUCH TIME TODAY," said Father Carlotti. "I have a Baptism." The priest was clearly angry at having been summoned to the station.

"Father Carlotti, the supervisor of the gift shop at the glass center picked your photograph out of several that we showed her. Can you tell me why you were there?" Jablonsky's tone wasn't the least accusatory, yet.

"A niece is getting married. I was going to buy a hand-crafted piece of glass for her gift. Is this why I am here? I thought you had more questions about Eugene Rose." Carlotti's face flushed and he spoke through clenched teeth—he barely could control his anger. Father Carlotti's agitation stood in stark contrast to Jablonsky's calm demeanor.

"Do you know the director of the glass center, Mr. Andy Ormsby?"

"I do not."

"Did you walk around the center, perhaps looking at the hot shop?"

"I did not."

"Was that the first time you had been at the glass center?"

"Yes! It was the first and the only time. Why are you asking me these questions?" Carlotti yelled his answer at the chief.

"Mr. Ormsby was attacked yesterday. I'd like you to account for your time from the afternoon through the evening hours." Like a freight train slowly gaining speed, Jablonsky kept at the priest.

"After I celebrated morning Mass, I returned to my office and did some work. Look, I don't know this Ormsby fellow, and I didn't attack anyone. Did you just bring me in here to insult me? Do you or do you not have questions about Eugene Rose?"

"Can anyone verify that you were in your office?" Jablonsky looked directly at the priest.

"Yes!" Carlotti clenched his fists, he was seething.

"When you met with Zane Davies in Italy, are you sure he did not mention a particular antiquity he was looking to buy?"

"As I said before—not that I remember." The priest's foot started to jiggle and tap on the floor under the table.

"You stated that both you and Zane liked to talk about obscure religious antiquities. Does your family in Florence collect items of religious significance?" Jablonsky wasn't about to mention a particular glass item; he wanted to see how the priest reacted.

"First, I'm not sure if you are asking me a question, or if you are accusing my Italian relatives of stealing church antiquities. Second, you can ask Zane Davies directly what he was looking for." The foot stopped jiggling, the priest kicked back his chair and stood, his face flushed with color and his eyes flashing with anger.

"I have to leave. If you want to speak to me again, you should go through the parish attorney. Obviously, you are a lapsed Catholic who hates the church, and I will not bear the brunt of that." If Carlotti had been wearing a red bishop's cassock, he could have swept out of the room in a high theatrical manner. As it was, he just opened the door and left.

The two detectives stood in front of the murder board, both chewing some cinnamon gum; Annie Lemon's piece was nestled in her pocket.

"He's not wrong. We do need to talk with Zane Davies again, and his father. I want to take a look at their collection, including whatever is in their personal safe. He didn't mention a bank box, but he might have one. If Kate Chambers is right that the design in Eugene Rose's notebook is significant, we might find something like it in the collection." Underneath Eugene Rose's photo Jablonsky wrote "a glass roundel."

"Chief. I will do a more thorough search on Father Carlotti's family in Florence, with a special focus on their finances, their genealogy, any collections of note, and so forth." Annie Lemon moved over to her computer and immediately began to work. DeVille added that he would track down the second priest of interest, Father Lupinski.

"Good. He might know something about Carlotti and Bogey Johnson that we don't. For instance, he might know where Carlotti's defensiveness and hair-trigger temper come from. Plus, Andy Ormsby was discharged from the hospital; they only kept him overnight for observation. Before I meet him at the glass center to see if he knows what might have been taken from his office, I'm going to try and get a warrant to view the Davies' art collection."

Jablonsky's drive back to the glass center took longer than anticipated; the traffic in the Strip District was once again bumper to bumper. He finally arrived and found Ormsby standing in the middle of his office looking overwhelmed.

"Hi, Andy. Take it one step at a time—we can start with your desk. How's the head?" Jablonsky pulled out the office chair and Andy sat down, clearly grateful to have someone tell him what to do. The chief had brought Ormsby's computer back—he took it out of the evidence bag and laid it on the desk while Andy was systematically checking his desk drawers.

"I don't really keep anything important in my desk, even so, there doesn't seem to be anything missing. I keep everything on my computer—thanks for bringing it back. Give me a minute to look through my files." Some time passed before Andy shook his head, then said, "I don't see anything out of the ordinary—it looks like all my files are here, and in order. If someone copied them, I'm not sure I would know." He looked at Jablonsky, obviously at a loss as to where to go from here.

"Let's talk about Eugene Rose again. You first met him at the glassblowing class?"

"No. He came in first to talk about his dissertation, and his interest in Murrine technique. Then he decided to take the class. He was a nice kid." Suddenly, and unexpectedly, Andy's eyes filled with tears. "I'm not someone who is used to murder."

Jablonsky handed him the Kleenex box. "And I hope you never get used to it." The chief paused, thinking. *Either his tears are real, or he is a very good actor.* Stefan continued with his questions. "Tell me again about Zane Davies."

"He came along with Eugene a couple of times; they had been roommates. Like I said, there was clearly tension between them. It seemed like it was over a girl—although as I mentioned before, both men were gay. That's really all I know."

"Pittsburgh has always been a prosperous town. Everyone in the one percent pretty much knows everyone else in that same strata, some of them are probably on your board. That said, have you heard anything about the Zane's family art collection?"

"No. If it was a really significant collection, the Carnegie might have had an exhibition of it, but I don't think they have. I can make some calls to my friends at the art museum and find out what they know. Shall I?" Like most men, Andy Ormsby wanted a task to perform.

"That would be helpful. We will be taking a look at the collection." Jablonsky let that sentiment hang in the air. Would Ormsby offer to go with him? Getting a warrant to view the collection had been a difficult sell, even to a sympathetic judge, but Ormsby didn't need to know that. Jablonsky had promised that he would only use it if needed. When Ormsby spoke again, he didn't offer to go with the chief, rather he jumped back to Eugene Rose.

"You think there is a relationship between what happened to me and the murder of Eugene? I can't even imagine what that would be. I think the break-in here was just that, a break-in. Someone was probably looking for things to sell for drugs."

"Does the center have expensive glass on the premises?" Jablonsky didn't realize that the center had its own glass collection.

"Yes. Right now, nothing is on display. Our collection is kept in the basement. It is clean and climate controlled and we have special packing boxes that protect the art pieces. Do you want to see the space?"

"I would." Ormsby wasn't yet completely steady on his feet so he, the chief, and Antoine took the elevator down a floor to the storage stacks. The whole side of the basement was filled with sturdy shelving upon which white boxes had been placed.

Stefan looked around, walking up and down through the organized shelving, noticing that each white box was clearly labeled and had a photograph of the contents. If someone wanted to steal an object, where it was stored was clearly visible. Ormsby had needed to rest at one of the tables scattered around the room, so Jablonsky joined him.

"If there was anything missing in these stacks, would you know?"

"Oh yes. That's the first thing I had the intern do this morning—match the boxes to our inventory sheet. And we looked through the security footage. Those are the cameras." Andy pointed to numerous small cameras discreetly positioned where the ceiling met the walls. Once they had arrived back at Andy's office, he promptly brought up the security footage on his computer screen.

Jablonsky asked for a copy of that file and the inventory list, then he asked if Ormsby thought he could add anything to the investigation by looking at the Davies' collection.

"I'm only well-versed in glass. The person you would want with you would be Professor McCarthy. No one knows more about the different genres of fine art than he does. I called Kate Chambers early this morning to let her know what happened. She said she might stop by today."

Figures, thought Jablonsky. *And I'm sure her side-kick Johnny will be with her.*

"Hey, speak of the devil!" Andy's grin said it all—gone was the strained look from the pain of the head injury. In its place was the exuberant look of a man who has eyes for a young lady. Jablonsky turned toward the door and there was Kate, with Johnny.

"How are you feeling?" asked Kate, wincing as she looked at the neat row of sutures in Andy's head. Ormsby bypassed her questions by saying the chief was going to look at the Davies' art collection.

"I suggested that Johnny go with him because he can offer such an educated perspective—particularly if the collection is broad in scope. You should go too, Kate."

At that last comment, Kate turned to Jablonsky. "We both have the time. Johnny would be really helpful—I'm the civilian assistance." She blushed at her own self-promotion.

The Davies' home was in a wealthy suburb of the city where the nouveau riche had built what was commonly referred to as McMansions. Joseph Davies' home was no exception—the stone house sat on a five-acre plot replete with a large circular drive, a fountain, and a four car garage, with the requisite Porsche Panamera and Range Rover parked in front. Joseph Davies answered their knock at the door himself, dressed again in casual jeans and button-down shirt.

Davies only greeting was a terse, "I want you to know that I have willingly agreed to this viewing, but that it is only for our collection, nothing else." Jablonsky introduced Dr. Kate Chambers and Professor Johnny McCarthy as experts and advisors. Like all self-made men, Joseph Davies scoffed at titles, but he did know that Professor McCarthy was one of Zane's teachers, so he offered his hand. They moved into the center hall, then an oversized living room, replete with a vaulted beamed ceiling and stacks of windows. Slowly, they were led around the room by Mr. Davies, who stopped at the various art items.

Johnny eased the tension by giving the historical perspective on each piece of art—there were several table-sized bronze sculptures and a few very fine oil paintings representing some minor American Expressionists of the twentieth century. There was even a small Andrew Wyeth. Johnny complimented Zane's choices of oil paintings.

"These are important and beautiful works. They constitute a coherent point of view within your collection; they should substantially increase in value."

"Mr. Davies, you mentioned that you keep items in a safe in the house. May we see those things please," Jablonsky asked, trying to move things along. So far, there had been nothing of interest in terms of Eugene Rose's murder. There were no pieces of glass.

In response to Jablonsky's request, Joseph silently led them into a finished basement where a large personal safe stood behind a wet bar. Blocking the chief's view, Davies tapped in the electronic combination to open the door. On the four deep shelves stood two solid gold communion chalices studded with semi-precious jewels, several sets of sterling silver repoussé candle sticks for use on an altar, and layers of hand embroidered altar cloths and priest's robes, sheathed in tissue paper.

"These chalices are stunning, and very old. Italian, right?" asked the entranced Johnny.

"That's what my son tells me. I really don't know," snapped Davies.

Johnny held up an open collar chasuble with stunning gold embroidery, vibrantly colored flowers, and Christ the King religious symbols around the shoulders and running down the sleeves. "I've rarely seen such beautiful hand work on a priest's chasuble. Now patterns like this are machine made; these, however, were done by hand. Local ladies spent hours embroidering the various designs. This is quite a find."

Johnny kept touching the fine silk and cotton work on the priest's garment.

"Does Zane regularly collect religious articles?" Jablonsky asked. He and Kate locked eyes, both thinking about the break-in at the glass center.

"Some. He brought these altar cloths and priest's robes back from Italy when he was there with Sarah Braithwaite, and the unfortunate Eugene Rose."

Jablonsky continued. "I understand that your parish priest, Father Carlotti, had lunch with him there. Does he advise Zane on purchases of religious artifacts?"

"I wouldn't know. I hardly know Father Carlotti. I see him now and again at the club, golfing. Chief Jablonsky, it is clear you are looking for a stolen object. It is also clear that you think my son had something to do with it, and that Eugene Rose's death is also mysteriously related. I can assure you that neither is true. Now, I think I've been very accommodating. Let's finish up." As Joseph Davies shut the door to the safe, they heard Zane call from the top of the stairs.

"Hey Dad! What's going on?" Zane walked down the stairs, halting in mid-step when he saw Jablonsky and Dr. Chambers, his academic advisor. Kate hadn't realized Zane would be at the house; if she had known, she wouldn't have tagged along.

"Have a seat, Zane," said the chief, motioning to one of the large leather couches. Joseph Davies briefly explained to his son why the police were there.

"How long have you been collecting religious artifacts?" Jablonsky asked, flipping open his tiny paper notebook.

"For a couple of years. I was looking for more when I was in Italy but didn't see anything I thought was worth the money. I take it you saw that I brought back some beautifully embroidered altar cloths and priest's chasubles."

Zane was now in possession of himself—he sat comfortably, straightened his Ralph Lauren cotton sweater and flicked his thick hair off of his face. He primarily addressed himself to Professor McCarthy.

"Is Father Carlotti advising you?" Jablonsky didn't raise his head from his notebook to ask the same question he had asked of Zane in an earlier interview; repeated questions sometimes catch lies.

"Well, yes and no. He has the interest, but no funds. For him, it is about the history of the church. As you already know, I spoke with Father Carlotti while I was in Florence. I also talked with a Rabbi, just to cover all bases, so to speak." Zane chuckled, clearly finding himself to be quite amusing.

"Did Eugene Rose discover a piece of glass that had a religious function?" asked the chief, hoping to get some direction on what a possible glass object might be.

"No. I don't think there are many religious artifacts made from glass, except stained glass for windows, or perhaps serving plates. Glass is too easily broken. Eugene wasn't interested in those things. Besides, he was Jewish. Isn't that right, Professor?" Zane skillfully put the focus on Johnny, who barely nodded his agreement. Kate finally spoke.

"Zane. What do you make of Eugene's interest in a design that was a circle, like a roundel. He had sketched it in his idea book and also tried to fire it in his wine glasses." Jablonsky sat back, letting her take the lead.

"Let me show you." The chief handed Kate a piece of paper and his pen. She quickly drew the design and gave it to Zane.

"It does look like a roundel. You know, it kind of reminds me of a famous glass wine taster that's in the Royal Ontario Museum in Toronto. Maybe he had seen it and liked it. It was done in the Venetian style, his favorite."

"Yes, Andy Ormsby showed us a picture of that wine taster," responded Kate, who knew that Zane was once again deflecting from himself to someone else.

"So, this design doesn't look like anything else to you? Had you ever seen Eugene save his designs on anything other than his computer? I mean, you lived with him—all three of you would have been writing papers at the same time—mid-terms or finals." Kate became insistent about the intimacy of their living situation, forcing Zane to produce an answer.

"Eugene was scrupulous about backing up his work. I only ever saw him use the Cloud, or paper, like his notebook. Sorry. Perhaps Sarah would know more." Another deflection—first Professor Johnny, then Andy Ormsby, now Sarah Braithwaite.

"Mr. Davies. I was curious as to how you ship your art finds. Do you use a particular carrier or just the regular mail?" Kate oozed innocence.

Mr. Davies recognized an end run when he saw one. "We use many different carriers and we have the requisite paperwork on each item. I think that is all for today. You have seen the collection, there are no stolen art pieces and no glass objects. You will contact my attorneys if you need anything else." Davies stood and pulled Zane up beside him.

"Mr. Davies, I am going to want to see all, and I mean all, the paperwork on each item in your collection. Have those attorneys send them. We will be in touch when we receive your paperwork," Jablonsky said. Neither Zane nor his father moved to escort the group out of the house.

As they walked to their cars, Jablonsky stopped Kate. "What exactly were you getting at in there?"

"I wonder how Zane ships his art finds. For instance, the lightweight altar cloths and priest's robes. I know that Customs rarely checks a collection of student luggage for contraband in the same way that a regular traveler's are checked. If Zane was smuggling, did Eugene know about it, and was that one of reasons they argued? And further, did he sneak light weight things into Sarah's luggage so he wouldn't have to pay duty on them?"

Jablonsky didn't admit it, but he had never thought about the duty that would be assessed on art and antiquities. "Smuggling. I like the way you think; I can see why you have that PhD. I'm anxious to see the list Davies gives us in regard to his collection. We will check who delivered each piece. Why did you raise this question with Mr. Davies and not directly with Zane?"

"I didn't think it was my place, and Zane was an advisee. He isn't any longer. I didn't think he would be here today, or I wouldn't have come along." Jablonsky flashed her a grin—it was unusual hearing the words "not my place" from Kate.

Back at the station, the chief added new information to the murder board. Under Zane's picture he wrote, 'smuggling?' under Joseph Davies' photograph he wrote, "What does he know, when did he know it, how far would he go to protect his son?" Under Eugene Rose's picture he posed the question, "Is there an actual glass piece and if so, where is it?"

DeVille and the chief made plans to interview Father Lupinski about his friend and fellow priest, Father Carlotti.

CHAPTER 14

KATE AND JOAN MET IN THE LOUNGE of the university club. Kate had just finished seeing Sarah Braithwaite for her final academic advising session.

"I was able to give Sarah good news," she told Joan. "The head of Johnny's department, and hers, came to an agreement that she could spend another semester in Italy, looking at violins and finishing her master's thesis. She was thrilled." Kate sipped her dry vodka martini, which she liked with one olive and a little dirty. As she imbibed the ice-cold drink, its salubrious effects helped her relax.

Kate shared her belief that Zane Davies had snuck some antique Italian altar cloths and priest's robes into Sarah's suitcases in order to avoid payment of duty.

"You think Eugene knew about it and confronted him? The Roses are clean and straight in their business dealings—Eugene would have had a moral problem with any criminal behavior, particularly since it might get Sarah into trouble." Joan, as usual, had ordered Pellegrino water with plenty of lemons and limes on the side.

"I did a little more research to help you in your investigation. I went to talk with the Rabbi at the synagogue to which my parents, and the Roses, belong. After he scolded me for never attending, he did offer some interesting information: There are records of the original building plans, and contributions to the building fund, that date to the early twentieth century. Guess who is listed?" Joan squeezed more lime into her bubbly water in obvious glee.

"Mrs. Rose did mention that the Rose family had made a sizable contribution to the building fund. Where are you headed with this?" Kate was typically savvy about following a line of reasoning, but she didn't quite grasp why this was so interesting to Joan.

"How does an immigrant family, only in this country for a couple of generations, come up with the amount of the contribution? I'm thinking something like family jewels brought from the old country—only in this case it was Italy, to France, to America." Joan grinned.

"You are right! There might be more to the story than just a religious object made of glass. Jewels were easy to carry, easy to fence. Would the Rabbi know anything about an exchange like that—money to go into a synagogue building fund in exchange for jewelry?" Suzie handed them the menu, and without being asked, brought Kate some bottled water instead of a second martini. Kate was controlled in her appetites.

"Let's order, then we will talk." In honor of Pennsylvania's garden bounty, the menu offered homemade tomato pie with a corn relish, accompanied by warm dinner rolls that melted the pads of butter smeared on them. Both women ate with enjoyment, then asked Suzie for coffee.

"Okay. Back to the subject," said Kate. "Would a Rabbi know a person who could exchange jewelry for cash? There's nothing illegal in it."

"Pittsburgh's Jewish community is well known all along the East coast. I'm sure the diamond merchants in New York City would have been only too happy to buy good quality stones. In fact, I believe it was probably just the stones that the Roses brought with them, rather than jewelry pieces." Joan paused, then added, "I'll go back to our Rabbi and find out."

"I can also talk again with Mrs. Rose and her husband. They might know more than they are saying about the early history of their family. Immigrant families have many secrets," remarked a wise Kate.

Jablonsky and Antoine were seated in Father Lupinski's parish office. They explained why they were there, which the priest took in stride because Father Carlotti had already called him concerning Eugene Rose's death. Lupinski cleared his paper stacked desk and chairs, offered coffee, which the chief accepted, but Coupe declined.

"As you know, I'm investigating the murder of Eugene Rose. We have spoken to Father Carlotti, who confirmed that the Davies family are members of his parish. We are under the impression that you know Zane Davies but didn't know Eugene Rose. Correct?"

"That's correct. I sometimes golf with Father Carlotti at the Greenwich Country Club. He and Zane are interested in church antiquities. That's about all I know in regard to Zane." The priest looked puzzled.

"What can you tell me about Father Carlotti? Have you known him long?" Lupinski appeared to study Jablonsky, then apparently having made up his mind about something, decided to answer the chief's questions.

"I have known him for a long time. We were in Catholic high school together, then seminary. We also traveled to Italy where I met his Florentine relatives."

"To your knowledge, has he always had an interest in religious art?"

"Religious art? I'm not sure about that. He likes church history. In fact, he and his uncle talked about church history a fair amount. He spent his senior year in seminary as an exchange student in Florence. Chief Jablonsky, I'm not sure what Carlotti's personal history has to do with the murder of Eugene Rose."

"This is an active murder investigation. We are exploring anything related to that act. Please just answer my questions." Jablonsky allowed for a silent interlude, then continued. "I'm not accusing anyone, I'm collecting information. So, is Father Carlotti's family one of means?"

"No, his parents are definitely working class. I think the branch of the family that lives in Florence, however, is wealthy. They have a beautiful house in Tuscany and a town home in the city. They were generous to us when we stayed with them." Lupinski had settled back in his chair, giving himself over to what seemed to him as prying and irrelevant questions. Since the decades of sexual criminal activity had been revealed, priests had to become used to that attitude.

"Do you remember if they had art collections—paintings, sculpture, or Venetian glass objects?" Jablonsky was glad to see the priest finally relax.

"They had many beautiful things in their home, but I don't know about an actual collection. I took a vow of poverty—it all looks like an embarrassment of riches to me." Lupinski threw up his hands and laughed at the difference between his life and the life of wealthy people.

"Have you noticed a change in Father Carlotti's mood recently?"

Lupinski stared at the stained-glass window that graced his office, then coughed, then sat more upright in his chair. "I'm not sure what you mean?"

"I found him to be hostile when I questioned him about his relationship with Zane Davies. He threatened to sic the diocese lawyers on me. That's what I mean." Lupinski slapped his leg in amusement.

"He has a short fuse, I admit. As far as any changes in his temperament, well, honestly...." Once again, the priest hesitated before continuing. "When he came back from Italy, he seemed different to me. More, well, irritable. Whatever is bothering him would be between him and his mentor, or his confessor."

"Do you suspect that something happened to him when he was in Italy?" *This is a new direction in the case,* thought the chief.

"Yes. I'm no psychologist, but a change in mood is usually brought about by an event or an interaction, correct? In seminary, he gained the reputation as a prickly personality. In fact, we still call him PP. He did love talking about church history with Zane, though, it seemed to relax him."

"Would he be involved with a woman?" Jablonsky knew how common it was for priests to have a liaison with a female parishioner.

"Not that I know of, but that doesn't mean there isn't one. Carlotti likes the ladies. On and off, he sees a psychologist about his mood and for ways to keep his vow of chastity," offered Lupinski, clearly uncomfortable with this admission about his friend's personal life.

"Since you are such good friends, have you asked him directly if anything happened to him in Italy?" Jablonsky looked closely for any struggle over lying that might be taking place with the priest.

Lupinski leaned forward in his chair, sincerity wreathing his face. "I have asked, and so far, he hasn't told me. Look, Father Carlotti is a good priest, just a difficult man. Those are two different things—neither adds up to being involved in a murder."

"I'll be the judge of that," replied the chief.

Jablonsky and Antoine left Father Lupinski with more questions than answers. They arrived back at the office with take-out lunch. As they unwrapped two warm Pittsburgh-style Muffuletta sandwiches loaded with deli meats, good quality cheeses and olive salad, Antoine commented, "I'd say Carlotti has something to hide. He admits to being a womanizer, maybe we should *cherchez la femme.*

"Maybe. It's hard to tie together a woman and his obsession with historic church objects, unless there is a rich female patron we don't know about. Here's what I surmise from all the interviews so far. Eugene Rose was looking for a family antiquity and perhaps found it. I believe that Zane Davies knew this. To Eugene, a family antiquity was personally valuable, but, to Zane Davies, it was monetarily valuable. Did he want the glass antiquity for his own collection, and what would he do to get it?"

Antoine put down half of his round sandwich and wiped his mouth with one of the paper napkins. "Kate Chambers did a good job bringing out the issue of smuggling. Has Zane Davies been smuggling more than altar cloths and priest robes out of Europe? Like her, I believe Eugene knew about the altar cloths, but I can't imagine that would have been enough of a motive for Zane to murder him. I think you are right; it has to be a valuable glass antiquity."

"Two cases are developing that are related. We have the murder of Eugene Rose. Then we have a second case that is about Zane Davies, the family art collection and possible smuggling. For example, on the murder side, who hired Bogey

Johnson to break into Sarah Braithwaite's house? Would Father Carlotti go that far in his search for an important piece of church history? On the smuggling side, I wonder if Mr. Davies showed us his entire collection."

Jablonsky and his number one continued to savor their Muffulettas while considering the intersection of desires related to finding and possessing fine art objects.

CHAPTER 15

"WHAT DID THE DETECTIVES ASK YOU?" Fathers Carlotti and Lupinski sat together on the patio of the Greenwich Country Club having lunch and tall glasses of cold beer. Their choice of sandwich was not the New Orleans' staple, but rather New England fried cod, with lettuce, tomato, and a healthy dollop of tartar sauce made with pickles. The beauty of the rolling manicured lawns was lost on both men as they dove into their sandwiches.

"They asked me about your temper and your relationship to Zane Davies. Carlotti, what is going on? You are like a cat pacing in front of a mouse hole. I didn't think you knew Eugene Rose—your connection is to Zane. Has he done something wrong, or worse, illegal?" Lupinski's expression was filled with concern for his long-time friend and colleague.

"I'm not sure. Zane doesn't always play by the rules. The police asked him if he knew whether Eugene stored his work on a flash drive. If there is a flash drive, I don't think the police know what's on it." Carlotti ate his sandwich with quick snapping bites.

"I told him that you seemed changed when you came back from Italy. I've never asked you about it, but I am asking now—did something happen to you there?"

"What could have happened? I was in one of the most beautiful cities in the world, living with my loving relatives.

Weekends at their country house in Tuscany, school days in the city...." Carlotti picked up the lone Dill pickle on his lunch plate and broke it in half.

"I preferred Florence," he commented under his breath.

"We can talk about Italy some other time," Carlotti replied, putting off his friend.

"You can count on me if you need anything. I don't share your interest in or passion for church history or breaking my vows to date women for that matter, but I do care about you. I know you have been struggling for a long time. Is there a woman in your life right now?" Lupinski put his hand on Carlotti's shoulder, which he quickly shrugged off.

"Come on, Lupinski, priests are in enough trouble as it is. We are two heterosexual males—we don't hug or touch each other."

Bogey Johnson stood at the window in the golf pro shop watching the two priests lunching on the patio. He suspected they were talking about Eugene Rose or the break-in at his house. Bogey went into the back room of the shop and wound a rubber band around a wad of hundred-dollar bills, then zipped it into a side compartment in his golf bag.

Kate went with Joan to the synagogue. She immediately liked the Rabbi, who didn't adopt a cleric's accusing tone, but rather made a few jokes about educated people who were too smart to talk to God. He took them to the synagogue library and pulled out the building plans that dated to the decade of the nineteen thirties. Kate slowly turned the pages of the architect's drawings, commenting on this or that. Joan and the Rabbi gossiped about the Rose family.

"Rabbi," asked Kate, "in the early decades of the last century, when so many people left Europe to emigrate, you mentioned that it was not uncommon for a family to have brought precious stones with them. Portable cash—a bulwark against hunger."

The Rabbi immediately replied, "Yes! Many immigrants sewed small valuable items into their clothes. Who could blame them, the pogroms were devastating, especially in old Russia and Lithuania. Sadly, Jews were persecuted in Europe as well, long before Hitler's Germany."

"When they were building this synagogue, would the Rabbi at the time have had connections to merchants who could give cash for, say, gemstones?" Kate and Joan looked expectantly at him.

"I don't know for sure, but if I had to guess, I would say yes. Here is the earliest ledger we have for the synagogue." The Rabbi slowly slid an old-fashioned ruler down a long list of names and stopped at Rose. "Here is David Rose. Here is the family contribution."

Kate let out a low whistle. "Wow. That's a substantial gift, even by today's standards." Then, as if they shared one brain, both women asked, "Where did the money come from?"

"I don't know, and there is no living Rabbi who would know the answer to that question. Why not talk to Sam Rose yourself? Perhaps he knows family stories about the old days."

"It is a sorrowful time for them. I have a nice relationship with Mrs. Rose, but I don't know her husband at all. I don't want to intrude on their grief, you can understand." Kate spoke directly to the emotional issue hoping that the Rabbi could offer a solution, which he did.

"Joan and I could go with you; we both know the family. I officiated at Eugene's Bar Mitzvah and sadly, at his funeral. This could just be a condolence visit. Besides, Rabbis are inherently nebby! I'll make the call."

"I'd feel much more comfortable getting around to family history with you there." One wouldn't exactly say that Kate was manipulative, but she wasn't above maneuvering people to go in the direction she wanted; in that way she was more of a Border Collie than a Retriever.

It was a warm, breezy Sunday afternoon, the sound of thunder was audible, but distant. Kate had stopped at Rosalie's Bakery and procured a selection of baked goods to take as a hostess gift for the Roses. Because of their grief, she doubted they had much of an appetite—maybe a little something sweet might tempt them.

The Rabbi and Joan were already there. Joan had been thoughtful enough to bring along a few pictures from the summer camp in which she had been a counselor and Eugene a preteen boy. The photos provoked laughter and tears. Joan's reminiscing about Eugene provided a smooth transition for the Rabbi to talk about the founding years of the synagogue.

Going along with the flow of the conversation, Kate asked, "Mr. Rose, did you know your great grandfather, the one that helped fund construction on the synagogue?"

"I was a very young boy. The truth is I only knew him from our family albums."

Mrs. Rose added, "You did know, however, that your mother adored Eugene in the same way your grandmother did you. Your mother couldn't shower him with enough special treats—food, clothing, toys. It was hard to keep him from becoming spoiled."

The Rabbi, like Kate, who was also used to maneuvering people, circled back around to the grandparents. "Sam, how did they make their money? I know they had worked in North Carolina running furniture plants, but they were so generous to the community—that couldn't have come from someone on a salary. His contribution required capital." No one seemed to think his question was blunt or prying, money wasn't a taboo subject in this culture.

"You know, the last time we were all together for one of the holidays, Eugene asked my father the same question. But then, Eugene was always asking about family history. We got out the genealogy papers that very day, and it was the first time that any of us knew that our name, Rose, started out as the Italian La Rosa. We sat in the dining room, drank coffee, and talked and talked. Eugene was interested in everything... how did we come to America, why didn't the family stay in France, the Italian shipping merchants...." His voice trailed off.

"Did your grandfather ever answer the question as to how he made his capital?" Kate admired the way the Rabbi stayed on topic.

"Well, my father said that his father told him that they brought gemstones from France, just the stones, and sold them. Untaxed cash. That seemed to spark Eugene's search into the French and Italian parts of the family. That's why he traveled to Italy."

"Isn't that interesting," Kate said. "But how did he go from family gemstones to being fixated on glass?"

Mrs. Rose paused in pouring iced tea for her guests. "He loved glass. He had a tiny glass animal collection when he was very young—his Bubbe, Sam's mother, bought it for him. She said that 'her side of the family' always loved beautiful things, particularly objects made of glass. When she died, we inherited many special pieces—come, I'll show you a few. I put them in the breakfront in the dining room."

Kate couldn't believe her good luck. Here was the origin of Eugene's interest, and perhaps the key to the object for which he was hunting. Mrs. Rose pointed to the various pieces. "As I recall, this is a Royal Flemish vase, and this is a mercury glass bowl, here is a ginger jar—apparently there is actual gold fused into the network of threads. This was Eugene's favorite."

Kate recognized the Venetian technique of 'vetro a reticello'; very beautiful, very hard to execute. *These pieces definitely ignited Eugene's search for a glass family heirloom. I wonder what he found.*

"Where did your mother-in-law keep her glass pieces when she was alive? Were they on display in the house?" Kate remembered how the Davies family had their art pieces arranged in their living space.

"Well, she believed that art should be enjoyed, so she did place the pieces around her home. She wasn't my mother, so I'm not sure if I know where every piece went. My husband has a brother and a sister. I know that they inherited a few objects." Mrs. Rose suddenly stopped talking, then said, "You think someone murdered my son over a piece of glass?" Horror can't adequately describe the look on Mrs. Rose's face.

Joan, who had come into the room, took over. "No, no. We were just wondering if Eugene's interest in glass was learned from his Bubbe. That's all. I don't remember Mr. Rose's mother, but I do remember your mother from synagogue. She was such a nice lady, always dressed in the latest fashion. My mother and she were members of the National Council of Jewish Women—both interested in social justice. Did you belong to that organization?"

Joan's diversion worked; she and Mrs. Rose began to talk about their mothers. After her parents were killed, like Scout with Atticus Finch, little girl Kate was always able to curl up in her grandfather's lap whenever she felt overwhelmed with her hyphenated identity of "the little girl who had no

Mommy and Daddy." Later, from years of hearing friends talk about their mothers, Kate was happy to be free from the restrictive knots that bind mothers and daughters; of course, it also meant that she didn't have any of the joys of that relationship either.

Mrs. Rose urged the Rabbi to take some of the pastries along to his family, to which he readily agreed. As they walked to the cars, Kate thanked both him and Joan profusely—both had been instrumental in getting the Roses to talk about family history, and their son, in a way that allowed more clues to emerge.

Most importantly to Kate was the fact that Mr. Rose's mother had such an extensive glass collection. How could she find out where all the pieces were? Had Eugene made a list of his grandmother's glass and was that list what the intruder wanted from the break-in at the glass center or Sarah Braithwaite's house?

CHAPTER 16

MRS. ROSE COULDN'T SLEEP. The pictures of summer camp that Joan had brought to the house prompted Ada to retrieve Eugene's childhood photo albums from the bookcase in the den. She settled into one of the comfortable armchairs, slowly turning the pages and remembering the carefree times of watching her son grow. She had kept a box of special cards that Eugene received over the years—most of them were from her and her husband, an equal number were from his grandparents.

One card in particular caught her attention. It was from Eugene's grandmother on the occasion of his Bar Mitzvah. Grandmother Rose had penned a note saying that a "special gift" that only he would appreciate was on the way. What had it been? Not money, that wouldn't have been interesting to Eugene. Ada couldn't remember Eugene receiving any special gift; she would have to ask her husband, Sam.

Perhaps some might have thought looking through the photographs and cards a masochistic activity, but in those moments, Ada felt filled to the brim with love for the young boy who had been such a cheerful and sweet gift to her; if only she could have kept him longer. As the grandfather clock softly chimed the passing of the late night hours, a deep fatigue engulfed Ada—a fatigue that came from knowing she never really would recover from the loss of her only son.

She dozed in the chair, waking at what she thought was her husband coming down the stairs, looking for her. But it was not him. Mrs. Rose slowly stood up and walked to the open den door, peered into the entry hall, then tip-toed into the kitchen. The cellar door was open, and she could see the beam of a flashlight moving on the walls.

Oh, my God! Someone is in the cellar. She crept back into the den and had the presence of mind to quietly call the police on her cell phone. The sound of her voice must have disturbed the intruder—the cellar steps squeaked under foot, then the kitchen door slammed, and a figure bolted into the dark night. Ada screamed for Sam.

Jablonsky was used to being called out in the middle of the night. As he drove into Squirrel Hill, he felt nothing but compassion for Mr. and Mrs. Rose, who were enduring an attempted burglary so close to the death of their son. The chief was sure the three events—the break-in at Sarah Braithwaite's house, the attempted robbery at the glass center, and now another attempt at the Roses' home—were related to Eugene's murder. Unfortunately, there was a limit to what he could reveal to Mr. and Mrs. Rose about these connections

Everyone was in the basement. Mr. and Mrs. Rose had changed out of their night clothes and were scanning the neat storage boxes that were arranged on shelving to see if anything was missing. The forensics team was dusting for prints and securing the samples of dirt that the intruder had tracked in and taking impressions of his footprints outside the kitchen door. Ada and Sam began arguing.

"What were you doing downstairs? Why didn't you call me first, then the police? This person could have hurt you!

Damn it, Ada." Mr. Rose sputtered with frustration over not being able to control anything.

"Let's go upstairs," Jablonsky softly suggested. "We can talk there while the team does its work." Antoine followed, then stood unobtrusively behind a living room chair; the chief always talked about how one should both observe and listen in an interview, and this was exactly what Coupe intended to do.

"In your own words, tell me what happened," prompted Jablonsky. Mrs. Rose reiterated that she couldn't sleep, so she had gone to the den and was looking at family photo albums and some cards that had been given to Eugene. "I must have dozed, then heard a sound, I went into the kitchen and saw that the cellar door was open and realized that someone was in the basement with a flashlight. I went back to the den and called the police. The man, and I do think it was a man, must have heard me and ran out through the kitchen door." As she spoke, Mr. Rose repetitively put his hands to his face. "Oi, Oi, Oi," he repeated under his breath.

"Do you remember anything about the intruder? What he was wearing, his height—things like that." The chief held the pen over his paper notebook.

"He was dressed in a black shirt and black pants. His arms and neck showed so I could see that he was a white man. He wore a black knit cap. I'd say he was around six foot tall, normal build...that's all I can remember." Deep lines of fatigue creased Mrs. Rose's face.

"Mr. Rose. Does it look to you like anything is missing from the cellar?" The chief turned to engage Sam, who was about to blow a gasket.

"Not that I immediately notice. I keep some tools, cleaning products, outside items like rakes and leaf bags down there. An old bike of Eugene's." Sam's voice was hoarse, his jaw clenched.

Mrs. Rose interrupted. "There are boxes from Eugene's house and the box that Kate and Johnny brought from the library."

"Would you show us where those are?" The chief rose, ready to go back to the cellar.

"Don't you think she has been through enough? Can't that wait until tomorrow? This was just a break-in, not a murder! What are you doing about our son?" Mr. Rose stood and yelled at Jablonsky, the veins on his neck standing out in protest against his emotional strain.

"I want to show them, Sam. I'm fine. Just this one more thing, and then I'll go upstairs and rest. Come along, Chief Jablonsky, I'll take you to the boxes." Everyone trooped back down the steps and the forensic team took every box that Mrs. Rose pointed to.

"Are there any missing?"

"Not that I'm aware of. The only unsealed box was the one from the study carrel at the library. Here it is." Mrs. Rose stared at the box for a few minutes, clearly trying to remember something. "Kate and Johnny brought this to us. Kate was here today, well, it was yesterday now, with the Rabbi and Dr. Joan Weisner. Joan had been Eugene's camp counselor—We know her and her family. She brought some pictures along, which is what spurred me to get out our family album and cards. I know there is something I wanted to tell you, but I can't remember what it was. I just can't remember what it was." Ada Rose suddenly seemed unable to focus.

Jablonsky put his hand on her arm. "Whatever it is, it will come to you once you are rested. You can call me when you remember." Jablonsky knew from experience when enough was enough. These poor parents needed to rest. He directed the forensic team to take all of the boxes that belonged to Eugene.

The chief and Coupe left the scene at the Roses and since the dawn had already broken, decided to stop for some breakfast at Sophia's Café. Once Jeanne had seated them, Jablonsky called Kate, not caring how early it was.

"Dr. Chambers. Did I wake you? What a shame. There was an intruder at the Rose house in the middle of the night. Mrs. Rose mentioned that you, the Rabbi and Dr. Weisner paid them a visit yesterday. I want to hear about it. Make yourself available for a report this afternoon. The chief hung up before Kate could respond, which is what he wanted.

"Kate was sleuthing, against your direct order, if I remember correctly." Before answering, two steaming plates of food arrived, and the men, who had ordered the same thing, addressed their plates of an egg and cheese frittata, a side of homemade pork sausage patties, and home fries. The only difference in the attack was that Antoine used hot sauce on his frittata and the chief stuck to the traditional stream of Heinz Tomato Ketchup.

With her usual impeccable timing, Jeanne arrived with two hot cups of strong coffee just as the men were wiping up the eggy remains with the last of the toast; she refilled their water glasses and cleared the table. The chief eventually leaned back against the red-orange vinyl that covered the bench seats, wiping his mouth with his napkin, happily sated.

"Okay. A third break-in. We are not looking hard enough for the flash drive or some other kind of external storage device. If we don't find it, I'm afraid someone is going to get hurt. What is your strategy, Coupe?" It wasn't just Kate who was on the hot seat this morning.

"I spoke again with Sarah Braithwaite. She is sure that she never saw Eugene use a flash drive but says that doesn't mean he didn't have one. Sarah was unaware of the study carrel but thought there might be a chance it would be there, which as far as we know, it wasn't. By the way, Sarah mentioned that our Dr. Kate was able to negotiate another semester abroad for her in Italy. Zane wants to visit her while she is there." Coupe tilted his head to the side, looking dubious about the student's plans and waiting for the chief to weigh in on the traveling.

"No way that is happening unless we have solved the case. We received an email from Davies' attorneys detailing the dates of purchase of the art objects. Annie Lemon checked the provenance, and everything appears in order." Once again, Jablonsky built a steeple with his fingers, then added, "Something is really fishy about that father and son and their collecting."

When the two detectives left for the precinct, Jeanne handed the chief his 'to go' cup, with the requisite two shots of espresso in twelve ounces of regular grind. "This ought to help me stay fresh during the interview with the elegant Kate Chambers."

Kate was indeed dressed like an elegant professional woman when she arrived at Jablonsky's office. She wore a lightweight black suit with a patterned silk blouse and gold jewelry. Once again, the murder board was right side forward, so this time she was able to catch the names of the two priests written on it. Seated in the chief's office, she was the first to speak.

"Are Mr. and Mrs. Rose okay? As I count, this is the third break-in—it has got to be related to Eugene's murder." Kate pulled out a sheet of notes from her briefcase and placed it in front of her on the desk.

"Hold on there, young lady. What were you doing at the Roses' yesterday, after I expressly forbid you to collect information without me or one of my detectives present?" After his rudeness on the crack of dawn telephone call that morning, Kate expected ire from Jablonsky; she chose to ignore it and proceeded to weave a believable story from equal parts prevarication and truth, ending with the fact of Grandmother Rose's glass collection.

Jablonsky turned to his number one. "Coupe. I want you to find out if there is a complete list of the family glass pieces. For valuation of an estate, such a list must have existed and would be with their attorneys. Also ask Mr. Rose if his siblings inherited any glass pieces."

Annie Lemon appeared in the doorway holding the box from Eugene's study carrel. "Kate, since you and Johnny emptied the carrel, I want you to look through this box again, to see if something is there that you missed before. Take your time."

Kate looked at every paper and book once again. There simply was nothing new. "Perhaps he left something in the books that Johnny and I returned to the librarian? I could go and have another look."

"Give the name of this librarian to DeVille and we will meet you there."

The librarian had the most recent books which Eugene Rose had checked-out ready for Jablonsky, Antoine, and Kate. They sat at a table and carefully turned each page, delicately running fingers over the entirety of the pages. Out of the corner of her eye, Kate watched Jablonsky slowly become captured by the pictures of hot worked glass. He would pause, read the identifying information, and then look again. She saw him pay particular attention to the pictures of glass produced in Eastern Europe, his ethnic roots. *Fine art has the power to completely engage us and change our consciousness,* she mused.

When they found nothing relevant to their inquires in the books, Kate showed them the way to the study carrel; the search of every inch of the desk yielded nothing. Kate turned over the swivel chair and ran her fingers along the piping of the leather seat.

"Wait! I think there is something here!" Jablonsky and Antoine held the chair upside down while Kate fished something out of a small slit in the pipping. "Gotcha!" she cried in excitement, as she held up a small flash drive.

"Let's try it in my computer." They trooped back to the librarian's office and Kate opened her purse, pulled out her laptop and plugged in the flash drive. Up popped a picture of a large necklace and pendant—Kate and the librarian unconsciously drew in a quick breath—it was exquisite.

This was the kind of necklace that titled men and women wore for stately events in the sixteenth and seventeenth centuries. There were large ruby-colored glass beads that had been flattened on one side in order to lay comfortably on the neck and chest. The ruby beads were decorated with gold leaf and spaced with small gold beads, one placed on either side of each glass bead, stabilizing it. The ruby glass appeared to be strung together with many thin gold wires. But it was the pendant that held everyone in its grasp. It was a large hand-blown roundel, heavily gilded and as big as a man's hand. There was a cold-painted vibrantly colored miniature picture of someone obviously important. It was stunning and very old.

Someone had taken the time to photograph both the front and the back of the necklace and its pendant—Kate found herself flicking the screen, moving back and forth between the two images.

"Where did Eugene find this?" Kate looked at Jablonsky.

He replied with the obvious, "I don't know. Are these two photos the only thing on the drive?"

"No. There is a third page with dates next to the La Rosa name. See, 1680, then 1700, then 1720. The dates are every twenty years. The surname La Rosa would indicate that this necklace and pendant was owned by Eugene's family. So, he was able to trace it after all." Kate leaned back in her chair, both exhausted and exhilarated by the find.

"The question still remains, where is it and was he murdered by someone trying to get ahold of it?" Jablonsky stood. "Antoine, call Andy Ormsby, tell him we have something we'd like him to look at."

"Chief, you have to let me come along. I have to hear what Andy says. Please." Again, Jablonsky was reminded of how his daughter always used that wheedling tone when she wanted to do something outside of the family rules.

"All right, Dr. Chambers. Let's all go to the glass center."

CHAPTER 17

"MR. ORMSBY. THANKS FOR SEEING US." Jablonsky looked at the shaved patch on Andy's skull. The wound still had an angry red look to it, but the chief was focused on the pictures of the necklace and pendant.

Kate was practically toe-walking with excitement. She couldn't wait for the niceties. She blurted out, "We found a flash drive that Eugene had hidden. Look what's on it!" She booted up the photo of the glass necklace, its exuberant colors practically leaped from the screen.

"Holy *merde*!" exclaimed Ormsby. "I'm gob-smacked. I've never seen anything like this except in museums, but even then, not of this quality. It takes my breath away." He leaned closer to the screen, almost as if he wanted to reach in and grab the necklace. When he straightened up, he offered a few educational statements about the object.

"Without seeing the physical necklace, I'd say with ninety percent certainty that these ruby beads were made in the sixteenth or seventeenth century in Murano. The necklace was probably commissioned by a patron for himself or by a bishop or cardinal of the church. If you walk through the Uffizi Gallery in Florence you will see many paintings of important men and women wearing something like this, but most of those necklaces either have not survived or were made from gemstones. A glass one is exceptionally unique."

Ormsby mimicked Kate's behavior of flicking the screen back and forth between the two photographs.

"You know, the back of the pendant looks like it has two tiny gold hinges. It's thick, I wonder if it opens?" Ormsby grabbed a magnifying glass and leaned into the screen again. "Yes, there's a chance it opens—one could store a tiny memento, like a lock of hair." Ormsby straightened up. "Where is the necklace and pendant?"

"We don't know where they are. Look at these dates. What do you make of them?" Kate turned the screen so he could more easily see the numbers.

"I'd say they represent generations. You know, twenty years more or less equals a generation. The fact that the La Rosa surname is beside each date means to me that this object was handed from one generation to the next. A private family antiquity. If it still actually exists, an auction price would be substantial, but it is even more valuable historically. It might be one of a kind. Anyone who brings this object to light would go down in history. Do Eugene's parents know about this?"

Jablonsky answered. "I don't think so. Just like your center, their house was broken into in the middle of the night. We now think the intruder was looking for this flash drive, evidence that the necklace did exist and evidence of the provenance."

"I wonder if this necklace is in Grandmother Rose's collection?" Kate looked expectantly at Jablonsky, who took the cue.

"Ormsby, would you be willing to look at their glass pieces, and perhaps those of the Aunt and Uncle? You are the expert. I can set it up at a time that is convenient for all parties," Andy whole heartedly agreed, saying he would wait to hear from the chief.

"I want to remind all of you that these pictures are evidence in a murder investigation. Don't talk about them with anyone. Understood?"

While Jablonsky secured everyone's confidentiality, Kate downloaded the photos and date sheet from the flash drive onto a file on her laptop. She knew that the chief would have to take the drive as evidence, so she wanted her own copy of the material. Jablonsky was aware of what she was doing, and when she put her laptop back into her purse, he held out an evidence bag for the drive. "Now that you are finished downloading the pictures, Kate, I'll take the flash drive."

The detectives left the center and Andy once again walked Kate to her car. "Would you want to get a coffee and talk about the necklace? Plenty of nice places here in the Strip."

Kate was unsure of how to handle this direct of a romantic advance. Since the chief was now using Ormsby as an expert, she needed to know when he would be viewing the Roses' collection, so she could get Mrs. Rose's permission to also be present. If she said no to this invitation, would he later resist giving her information?

"Well, I really can't right now, but I'm meeting Johnny and my friend Joan for dinner at the university club. Why not join us?" Kate was pleased with herself—she found a way to keep his interest, and to avoid being alone with him. It was a shame, Ormsby and she had shared interests, but she just wasn't interested in him.

"That's sounds great! What time?" answered Ormsby.

"Around six is good. We usually meet right after work. Joan is a surgeon who has to operate early in the mornings, so, dinner with her is never on continental time. See you later."

Joan and Kate arrived at the club around the same time and found Johnny looking at the kiosk in the lobby. "It's nice to know someone is being recognized for his work," he remarked. On the kiosk was a picture of Marco Rossetti with an announcement of an honor he was receiving for his invention of a surgical technique routinely used in war zone operating theaters.

"Did you know about this?" accused Kate. Both Johnny and Joan looked at her as if she was speaking in a foreign language.

Johnny defended Joan. "What's your problem? Does Marco's presence cast a spell so strong that you can't resist him being in the same building?" The absurdity of his statement, and the amusement on Joan's face, caused Kate to laugh. "Okay, okay, you're right, and I am duly chastised."

At that exact moment, Andy Ormsby walked up to the group, interrupting what would have been an evening of endless teasing. Suzie showed them to the usual table, only taking Andy's drink order because she knew everyone else's.

After dinner, Kate pulled out her laptop and showed Joan and Johnny the photo of the necklace and pendant. She enjoyed the fact that Johnny couldn't stop looking at it. "There is something so familiar about the person in this miniature portrait. I just can't place it. It will come to me."

"He's like you," she commented to Andy, who preened at the compliment.

"If you formally appraise and take photos of all of Grandmother Rose's glass pieces, I could add a small text about provenance and historical significance. I'd like to use some of those pictures for teaching purposes. Would that be proper?" Kate watched Johnny try to get access to the collection for himself, as well as for her. She tapped him on the leg under the table as a thank you.

Ormsby responded. "Sure. But the Roses would have to agree. It would be a nice remembrance of Eugene—that is, to present the glass pieces as an official collection. Glass was his thing."

While the two men were deep in conversation about whether the necklace and pendant would be found, Kate decided to venture to the ladies' room to wash her hands and freshen her makeup; it had been a long day. Her head was down as she zipped her purse—she walked straight into Marco.

"I'm so sorry! Oh, it's you! Hello. I see you are getting a much deserved accolade tonight." Kate tried not to babble. In spite of his having been dressed in an attractive tuxedo for several hours, he still exuded that fresh soap smell. *What brand is that?* she wondered for the umpteenth time.

"The evening is winding down. Thank goodness." Perhaps it was Marco's height, or how close he stood to her, or the pleasure in his eyes at seeing her, but it was as if a curtain had been pulled around them, creating the feeling that they were alone in the busy lobby.

"I'm glad to run into you. I wanted to let you know that I'm leaving for Poland tomorrow evening. My surgical team and I are headed to a Polish medical center to teach the Ukrainian surgeons my techniques for saving soldiers who have battlefield wounds."

"That is such important work. I can't say I'm glad you're going, at least it's in Poland, adjacent but not close to the fighting in Ukraine." Marco's was the kind of career that Kate understood; careers that her young university advisees were training for, careers that made a concrete difference for good in the world.

"I'll be staying on in Europe. First I'll be in Germany and then I'll take a brief trip to Italy." Marco paused. "I could drop you a postcard, if that's okay?"

"A paper postcard, with an interesting picture on the front. I'd love that! There's something so timeless about them, much better than getting an email." *How nice it would be to get mail that isn't a condolence note,* she thought.

"Hey, you two!" Joan's greeting acted as a hand that pulled back the invisible curtain that had been guarding their privacy. "Oh," said Marco, who cleared his throat in order to recover his public self. "Dr. Weisner. Hello."

Kate, also yanked back into lobby reality, jump-started her brain by fiddling with her purse. Joan leaned close to her and whispered, "What was going on there?" Kate pinched Joan on the arm in retaliation of her inference.

"Congratulations on your award, Marco. It's well-deserved. Hear! Hear! Let us stand you a drink. Come on. We are in the other dining room." Kate chuckled as she watched Marco try to resist Joan's cajoling invitation; she had tried it many times and always failed.

Kate decided to go with the flow—when she passed Suzie, she ordered a bottle of champagne for the table. Marco was introduced to Andy Ormsby; no one mentioned anything about the flash drive or the necklace and pendant, or Marco's impending travels. They talked instead about Eugene Rose. At one point it occurred to Kate that Marco might know the names of the two priests listed on the murder board. When he left to return to his own post-award festivities, she walked half-way with him.

"Marco, I'm not sure where your mother goes to church, but I was wondering if the names Father Lupinski or Father Carlotti are ones you know?"

"Yes. I've heard her mention both, but the priest at her church is Carlotti. That's the big parish in Shadyside. Why?" Kate watched his expression change as it dawned on him that her request was related to Eugene Rose's murder case.

"I guess we will both be in a war zone. Thanks for the champagne, Kate, it was thoughtful. Keep an eye on your mailbox." He walked away, then turned back to watch Kate returning to her friends, just as she turned back to watch him. They laughed and waved, both caught in the act of taking one last look.

"I've heard through the grapevine that the police found a flash drive with an actual photo of the necklace on it."

"Who told you that? Do the police have it in evidence?" Carlotti leaned against his golf club for support, feeling so much physical tension upon hearing the news, that he thought he might either cry or have a stroke.

"I have my sources, and yes, the flash drive is locked up in evidence." Zane hit a long drive down the emerald green fairway. It was a warm fall day, sunny with blue skies and a perfect sixty degree temperature; migrating ducks swam together in the large ponds that dotted the course, quacking out their flight plans. Father Carlotti was deaf and blind to the relaxing sounds and countryside beauty all around him.

"And can these sources get to the flash drive?" The priest was unable to concentrate on taking his shot. Grumbling began from the group playing behind them.

"Drive the ball, let's move on!" Zane pointed to the group waiting to play through.

Carlotti hit the ball, put his club back in the bag, and they both drove off in the cart. "I want to see the pictures. It might not be the same necklace that I'm looking for."

"There aren't any other glass necklaces or pendants like this one. When you approached me in Italy to find it, I never really believed that there was one. I thought you had mistaken a regular gemstone necklace for a glass one. Let me think about it, there may be a way to get you photos."

Zane worried that Carlotti was becoming more and more unstable; he seemed okay in Italy, but since they came back, the priest's obsession with the object was growing, and not in a good direction.

Davies understood obsession—after all, he was a collector. But the collecting didn't rule him. To that extent, the therapy his father had paid for had been effective, except when it came to controlling his temper. Zane decided to visit Professor McCarthy to see what he could find out about the flash drive.

Late in the afternoon, Father Carlotti knelt in the confessional. "Bless me Father for I have sinned. It has been two weeks since my last confession."

"Go on, Father," encouraged his confessor.

"The urge has come upon me again. I try to resist it, but I haven't been successful."

"You mean the urge for sex or the urge for the glass object?" Carlotti replied that it was both, but mostly he was obsessing about the object. "Is it worse than the last time?" asked the confessor, his voice infused with worry.

"Yes. I broke into the glass center not realizing that the director was still there. I struck him across the back of his skull with a heavy book. A few days ago, I broke into a private home. In both cases I came up empty. I'm so sorry, I can't control this need, it is like an ocean wave that overtakes me and tosses me under the water."

"Father Carlotti. You must see the psychologist again, and I want you to go back on medication. The fact that you hurt another human being is of grave concern to me. Have the police realized that you are guilty of these break-ins?"

"They have interviewed me. I think the chief of detectives believes I am lying about something, which of course I am. And, I did pay that grifter at the golf club." Through the screen in the confessional box, the confessor could see that Father Carlotti was tearful and that his clasped hands shook.

"You are confessing to several crimes—hiring someone to break into a home, illegally searching the glass center and the Roses' private house, and most egregiously, injuring a person. I fear this obsession could escalate into you killing someone. For your penance, you must see your psychologist every day, go back on medication, and you must agree to his reporting to me about your emotional stability. I cannot absolve you of your sins until you have confessed to the police."

"I know. I am in the state of sin. I will do everything you suggested." Carlotti left the church and walked back to his office, knowing he had just lied to his confessor. He would not, and could not, stop until the necklace and pendant were in his possession.

CHAPTER 18

JOHNNY CALLED KATE AT HER OFFICE. “Zane Davies was just here fishing for information.”

“What did he want?” asked Kate.

“He was asking about new evidence. Do you think Ormsby might have mentioned that he saw a picture of the necklace on Eugene’s flash drive?”

Kate thought for a minute. “No. The chief warned him not to. And I was under the impression that Andy had only met Zane once or twice at the glass center. They move in completely different circles. The people who know about the flash drive are Jablonsky, Antoine and the other detectives, you, me, Ormsby ... oh, and Irene, the librarian. It’s got to be her. I wonder if she knows Zane, I mean, he’s a master’s student, he doesn’t have a study carrel but he frequents the library. I’m going to call her. Talk to you later.”

Kate made a few notes to herself before she called Irene. The conversation had to have a certain tone to it so that Irene wouldn’t feel like a suspect.

“Hi, Irene, Dr. Chambers here. I wanted to call and thank you for all your help with locating the flash drive. That was surprising, wasn’t it? I hope it helps find Eugene Rose’s killer. He was such a fixture at the library—do many people ask after him?” Kate was hoping she struck the right balance between a thank you and sympathizing over the loss of a student.

"A few. The most recent was Zane Davies, whom I know. I think Zane said that he and Eugene were roommates at one time. Must be hard to experience murder at such a tender age. It's hard on me and I've seen my share of sunrises!"

"I know what you mean. I think about Eugene's family. I paid a condolence call and it turns out that Eugene's grandmother was a glass collector. His interest in glass must be genetic. What did Zane think, I mean when you mentioned we had a picture of the necklace and pendant?"

"Oh, Zane was tremendously interested—of course he and Eugene shared a love for art objects and art history." *There it is, there is the leak—an innocent leak, but one nevertheless,* thought Kate.

"Thanks again, Irene. You've helped the police find a significant clue. I hope to see you soon." Kate ended the conversation, swiveled her desk chair and began to doodle on her notepad. All in all, the chief had been generous lately with her requests to be included in things. This time she would just give him the facts and not ask for anything in return—paying it forward was always a good idea.

Zane and Sarah Braithwaite were having a heart-to-heart conversation at her house. They sat on the couch in front of a coffee table littered with a few beer bottles and an empty pizza box, talking about going back to Italy; they both agreed that it would be different without Eugene.

Someone pounded on the front door. Sarah jumped up, shaking; after the recent break-in, any unexpected noise brought terror with it. Zane looked through the side window panels around the front door and recognized the uninvited guest. "Stay here, I'll take care of this."

"Father Carlotti? What are you doing here?" demanded Zane as he stepped out onto the front porch, closing the door behind him.

"Bogey Johnson mentioned that you were going to see this girl, so I Googled her address. I need to talk to you." Carlotti's white shirt was stained with sweat. On the golf course, Zane had noticed that the priest had lost weight. He looked gaunt.

Sarah heard the conversation and opened the door. "We haven't met, I'm Sarah Braithwaite. What's going on, is there some kind of spiritual emergency?" she remarked sarcastically.

"Actually, there is. I'm sorry to intrude, but I need to talk privately with Zane for just a few minutes. We can stay on the porch—we won't come into the house."

Sarah replied, "Good. Stay out there," and closed the front door without slamming it.

"Are you crazy? What do you want from me?" Zane started to feel scared. Carlotti looked almost hysterical—the priest reached into his pants pocket and brought out a small handgun. He kept it down by his leg.

"I want you to get me the photographs of the glass necklace and especially that pendant. You've been jerking me around since Italy. Your daddy's rich and has influence, use it. Get the photos—I'm warning you Zane."

"Or what? You'll shoot me? You're a priest! You've lost your mind. They are just objects—I'm a person!"

"They are not just objects to me. It's ... it's ... I can't explain it to you. Just find them or I'll find you." Carlotti turned on his heel with the gun still in his hand. He got in his car and sped down the street.

Zane almost fell down on the front steps from nervous exhaustion. He couldn't stop shaking and his throat was parched. "Crap," he said to himself. "What am I going to do? This guy is nuts."

Zane didn't realize that Sarah had been watching and listening to the interaction. She opened her front door and sat down on the porch steps beside him. "Look. I don't know what is really going on between you and that priest, but he had a gun. I saw it. First the break-in and now this priest shows up with a handgun? This can't be a coincidence. Call the police and tell them what happened, or I will. Do it for Eugene."

Little did Zane know that Sarah had already reported the incident to detective Lemon and the police were on their way to Carlotti's parish to bring him to the station.

Jablonsky sat down in the interview room, and without any niceties, placed an unloaded revolver on the table. "What can you tell me about this weapon—we found it in your office at the parish."

Father Carlotti looked haggard. The veins in his arms and neck resembled rope and his black eyes were filled with anguish. He kept his hands at his sides, unconsciously opening and closing his fingers; he evidenced no surprise that the police had his gun.

Father Lupinski had been at the parish office when the police arrived and had decided to accompany his friend. He turned to Carlotti. "Go ahead, tell them everything."

"The gun was my sister's. My father gave it to her when she moved to an apartment after college. She thought she had lost it years ago, but when I returned from Italy, I took it and kept it."

"You took it after you returned from Italy," Jablonsky repeated in a neutral tone.

Lupinski addressed Carlotti again. "You must talk about what happened to you. This is the time and the place. Come on. You won't be describing anything these men haven't heard before." *What the heck had happened to Carlotti?* wondered the chief, anxious to hear the story. Carlotti clasped his hands in front of him on the table and began his story.

"I, um, I stayed with my uncle's family in Florence. Along with their city house, they also had a house in the country, in Tuscany. Very rural, very isolated." Carlotti's intake of breath became audibly staccato.

"So, you went to your uncle's home in the country. What happened there?" The chief was on the alert, knowing already that this story was going to end badly, he casually slid the revolver to his side of the table and put it in his lap. Even unloaded, it still could be used as a weapon.

"It was summer, the evenings were long and warm, so after dinner I used to go for walks. Some of the local girls also did the same. Over time, I came to know these young women, and well, one thing led to another, especially with one young woman." Carlotti paused for what seemed like a long time.

"Tell them everything, Carlotti," urged a frustrated Lupinski.

"You see, I have a problem with chastity. I've always had a problem with chastity. In high school, at seminary, vacations in the summer. That's why I was sent to Florence. My mentor felt I should spend some time counseling with one of the priests from the Order of St. Augustine."

"Why that religious order in particular?" asked Jablonsky.

It was Father Lupinski who responded to the question. "St. Augustine is the patron saint for those who struggle with their faith."

The chief nodded. "I remember a paraphrase of the famous St. Augustine prayer about chastity." Lupinski and the chief smiled at each other.

Carlotti watched them, then suddenly barked at Jablonsky. "Easy for you to smile about it but struggling with one's faith and vows is a serious endeavor."

"Duly noted. Go ahead with your story, Father Carlotti," Jablonsky prompted.

"I've always been drawn to women; I find them beautiful and interesting—I'm weak in the face of sexual pleasure with them. The one young woman whom I saw in Italy lived around my uncle's estate. There was a private chapel on the property, so this young woman and I often met in the chapel to talk, and, well... to have sex. One evening, right after she had left, I was praying over my duplicity with my counselor, the Augustinian priest. I distinctly remember the buzzing of the evening insects. Suddenly the heavy chapel doors swung open and several men came in. The sound of their boots on the slate floor was deafening—it sounded like a battalion of men coming to kill me. One of the men grabbed me around the throat—it was the girl's father." Carlotti began to hyperventilate in earnest so Father Lupinski made him bend over at the waist.

"Slow your breathing, slow down, you aren't there, you are here in the police station in Pittsburgh. You are safe." Minutes passed, Carlotti slowly sat back up.

"What did they do to you, these men?" Jablonsky's voice was even and quiet.

The atmosphere in the interview room became supercharged, almost as if a spark could ignite a flame; Carlotti stood and gasped out his story. "The girl's father called me horrible names in Italian, he said that I had defiled his daughter who had trusted me because I was a priest, that I had betrayed God ... they started to beat me. They shoved me down to the ground and kicked me all over with their heavy boots. It went on forever. I remember the smell of their sweat and the manure on their boots."

Carlotti stopped, exhausted, and collapsed down into his chair. He didn't look at anyone, he kept his gaze on the table. Jablonsky believed the priest was in the midst of a flash-back, that he was psychologically in that chapel. The chief was correct.

"I was dying. My nose was broken, several of my fingers were dislocated, my hips and legs burned. I tried to call out, but my ribs were broken, and I couldn't get air. The floor was hard and cold. I made a bargain with St. Augustine—if he would spare my life, I would be true to my vows. No more women."

Carlotti finally raised his head, looked at the two men, then slumped in his chair, spent, his hair soaked in perspiration from the effort of reliving his trauma. Jablonsky snapped his fingers in the air and an officer quietly opened the door and handed in a bottle of water.

"Drink some of this," said Jablonsky, who along with Lupinski, remained silent.

"Tell the chief the rest of the story," prompted Father Lupinski.

"A groundskeeper found me, and I was taken to a hospital. When I returned to Florence and my uncle's house, everything was hushed-up. My uncle told me that if I wanted women, I should just leave the priesthood and marry. He also told me that the girl I was with is a distant cousin of the family. He didn't speak to me for a month. Then, one day he came home with a gift for me that he said a grandfather, many generations back, had bought from the family who owned the Tuscan estate before his family did. It was a very old necklace made with Murano glass beads and a pendant with a beautiful painted image of St. Augustine on it. I kept it with me—I would touch the image of St. Augustine when I prayed. It helped me be strong spiritually. When I left for the States, my uncle said he would mail it to me, but he never did. Zane Davies told me he saw pictures of it, so I know it still exists, I just don't know who has it." Father Carlotti wept as if he were a young child, asking for help from the adults in his world.

Jablonsky turned to Father Lupinski. "I take it you knew about this beating in Italy," to which Lupinski replied that he only recently heard the story. The chief went further. "Has your friend been treated for post-traumatic stress— PTSD? Even I can see that he has most of the symptoms."

As if Carlotti weren't in the room, Lupinski and the chief talked about the therapy that the church was providing their priest. "What was the most recent trigger?" asked Jablonsky, who had seen his share of Afghanistan war survivors go off the rails.

"I think there were two triggers. First, when he went to Italy recently, thinking he was strong enough to be there again. Second, it was what Carlotti just said—Zane mentioned that Eugene Rose was tracking the provenance of a glass necklace that he believed belonged to his family." Jablonsky thought, *So Zane lied to me. Eugene did talk to him about the necklace and pendant. I wonder what else he is lying about.*

"How did Father Carlotti even know these young men, much less talk about an antique necklace?" Of course, Jablonsky already knew the answer to that question.

"It was through casual conversation at the golf club. At least that's what I think." Lupinski turned to his friend and asked directly. "How did Zane Davies come to know about your desire to find the necklace?"

"It was as you thought. The Davies family are members of my parish and somehow, we both knew that other was going to Italy. When we were there, I asked him to find it for me. I'd like to go home now. I'm afraid I can't answer any more questions. Please." *So, Zane also lied about being asked to find it. What else?*

"I have a few more questions. Did you hire Bogey Johnson to break into Sarah Braithwaite's house?

"Yes, I did."

"Did you break into the Roses' home looking for the flash drive?"

"Yes, I did."

"Did you break into the glass center and assault Mr. Ormsby, looking for the flash drive?"

"Yes, I did."

"One last thing, Father. Did you take the gun with you to Sarah Braithwaite's house intending to shoot Zane Davies?"

"I don't know what I was thinking. I felt Zane was leading me on. I just feel crazy. Can't you see that I am standing outside of God's mercy?"

"Zane isn't pressing charges, but even so, I will have to book you for the break-ins and for the assault on Mr. Ormsby. Get yourself a good attorney. I will have to have a talk with your superior about your behavior because, as you are now, I feel you are a danger to the community, and yourself." When Lupinski went with his friend to booking, Antoine appeared.

"Whew. That was really intense. I agree with you that this priest has symptoms of post-traumatic stress. And, well... do you think he is telling the truth?"

"I think he's telling the truth as far as it goes. This is a man who routinely lies to himself—like an addict, he tells himself that he can pray away his womanizing. That type of addiction needs a special kind of intervention and I'm not sure he's getting it. Then there are the post-traumatic symptoms from the beating. Let's get the Italian police report on the incident. The Catholic Church keeps excellent records and since it was fairly recent, it should be easy to get all three reports—the physician's, the police's, and the priest's. We already have the information on his Italian relatives that detective Lemon gathered. For the first time, we have motive—if he gets out on bail, I just don't trust that Carlotti is going to stop his search."

CHAPTER 19

A FEW DAYS AFTER THE CARLOTTI INTERVIEW, Ada and Sam Rose drove to the precinct to see Jablonsky. The chief arranged to talk with them in his office rather than in an interview room—it was more comfortable and less formal. Annie Lemon's manner was respectful and warm as she guided them into the chief's office.

Mrs. Rose began. "I mentioned to you the night of the break-in that there was something I wanted to tell you. Remember? Okay. When I was looking through the box of special cards, I found a note written to Eugene from his grandmother. I had never seen it before. Here it is." Ada handed over the hand-written note.

"A special gift?" commented Jablonsky. "What was the special gift?"

"We don't know. I asked the aunts and uncles and they had never heard of such a gift either. When I was talking with Kate Chambers, she asked me what Sam's parents were doing around the time of Eugene's Bar Mitzvah, and I remembered that they had traveled to Italy, to Tuscany to be precise. Kate and I wondered if Grandma Rose had bought something special for Eugene while she was there and died before she had a chance to give it to him."

"And no one in the family ever saw this gift? It's not in Grandma's glass collection? Would she have stored it someplace else—like a safe deposit box or in a home safe?" *Curiouser and curiouser,* thought the chief.

Sam answered him. "They didn't have a home safe, but we do have a bank box. When I settled my parents' estate, there was nothing in the box that I hadn't already known about. By the way, and this is just an aside, my mother made a substantial monetary gift to the glass center around this time period."

Sam, a businessman who was always prepared, continued. "I brought the key to the safe deposit box. We can go there now, if you like."

Jablonsky walked into the bullpen and asked Lemon to take Mrs. Rose home while he and Mr. Rose drove to the bank. Luckily, Ada didn't fight the chief—she often found herself suddenly exhausted from her grief; at those times, and now, she felt like a parched piece of land longing for rain—a rain that will never come.

The chief and DeVille followed Mr. Rose the few short miles to the local bank. After all the security measures were met, they opened the long rectangular box and laid out the contents. There were several pieces of family jewelry and some documents. Mr. Rose shrugged his shoulders and remarked, "That's all there is."

"What's in that pouch?" The chief pointed to a small silk pouch that had been under one of the antique jewelry pieces. Mr. Rose opened it and turned it inside out— "It's empty."

Jablonsky stared at the objects. He then picked up each marriage, death, and passport document, taking them out of their individual envelopes and riffling through the pages. "Wait a minute. There is something else here." From Grandmother Rose's passport, the chief fished out a yellowed piece of paper—a bill of sale mostly in Italian.

Mr. Rose touched it gingerly. "I never saw this before. It looks like she bought a piece of glass when they were in Italy. My mother was always up to something—I didn't know about this purchase, nor did Ada."

"Is this date close to the time Eugene had his Bar Mitzvah?" Jablonsky circled the date on the bill of sale with his fingertip.

"Why, yes. According to this receipt, it was about six months before. So, whatever this item is, it must be her 'special gift' for Eugene."

"There is a description of the object in English," said the chief, who began to read it. *One sixteenth-century ruby glass bead necklace lavishly gilded with gold leaf strung with gold wire and gold bead spacers. The image on the glass roundel is Saint Augustine of Hippo. Solid gold hinges on the back.* Mr. Rose looked at the chief with disbelief. "We are Jewish. Why would my mother buy Eugene something with a saint's face on it?"

"It is possible that she had proof it had originally belonged to the La Rosa relatives. She knew Eugene would like the idea that it came down to him through the generations." Jablonsky didn't mention that the necklace probably had ended up in the Carlotti family. Instead, he put his hand on Mr. Rose's shoulder and quietly said, "No antiquity is ever worth taking a human life over." In an effort to control his tears, Mr. Rose distracted himself by continuing to ask rhetorical questions.

"I wonder why she hid this bill of sale in her passport. This is all very odd. Do you read Italian? I was wondering what it says at the top of the paper?" The three men studied the sales slip as if staring at it would make them fluent in Italian.

Antoine, who knew some New Orleans-style French, a close relative to Italian, offered his translation. "I recognize the word for estate and for Tuscany. You mentioned that you thought your parents traveled to Tuscany."

"They visited Florence, so, it would make sense that they would drive into the Tuscan region. I have to ask my siblings what they knew about that trip. I was always working and didn't pay much attention to their travels." Antoine continued with Mr. Rose's train of thought.

"Did Eugene travel to Tuscany when he was in Italy? I mean, it was before the country was locked down over COVID-19, so he would have been free to roam."

"Maybe. Ada would have known his itinerary. They face-timed—you know, on the computer." Mr. Rose slowly closed the safe deposit box and returned it to its niche in the wall. Jablonsky handed the evidence bags with the silk pouch and the bill of sale to Antoine.

Back at the station, they stood in front of the murder board, writing down the new clues. Finding the bill of sale confirmed the connection between Carlotti's story, the necklace, and pendant, and that Zane had been lying. The chief handed out the assignments. "Let's get ahold of Carlotti's family in Florence and specifically ask about their estate. According to him, if the necklace and pendant belonged to his Florentine relatives—how did Grandmother Rose get them? And, until the necklace and pendant are found, everyone is still in danger—Kate, Johnny, Andy Ormsby, Ada and Sam, Sarah Braithwaite, and even Zane."

Johnny and Kate jogged around the Highland Park Reservoir before heading to work. Even though it was very early in the morning, the humidity hung in the air like guests who have overstayed their welcome. Kate was describing the glass pieces she saw at the Roses' with so much enthusiasm that Johnny hoped he could finagle a visit to see them in person. "And those aren't the only pieces that Ada and Sam have; there are more," added Kate, like she had just topped a sundae with a bright red maraschino cherry.

"You heard me mention to Ormsby that I'm interested in using the collection as a teaching tool for my graduate students. He hasn't called me yet, but I'm hoping he will let me be there when he appraises it. What do you think?" Johnny picked up the pace. He knew they both liked a good sweat in their workouts. They agreed to meet at Kate's house for dinner to review what they knew about Eugene's murder; then both left to get ready for work.

The house was alive with the chat of these two good friends, the smell of food, jazz standards on the radio, and the doggy kisses of Mr. Bourbon Ball. Kate had decided to make a light dinner of broccoli salad. She steamed the broccoli until fork tender and added it to a mixture of mascarpone cheese, some citrus vinegar, dried cranberries, chopped walnuts, fresh bacon bits, and some grated carrot. Johnny placed spoonfuls of the salad on a bed of Butterhead lettuce and served it with slices of a freshly baked baguette. Since rosé wine was the fad, Johnny had brought along two bottles from France.

"Let me see the photos of the necklace and roundel again," Johnny requested when they finished eating. Kate retrieved her laptop, and the two friends scrutinized the photos. "You know, the image on the pendant has the look of a very famous portrait of St. Augustine of Hippo painted by Sandro Botticelli. Let me show you." Johnny Googled the picture, and when Kate saw it, she instantly agreed.

"Remind me again what St. Augustine is known for?"

"As I remember my saints, he is special to those having trouble with their vows." Kate grinned at this information.

"Some of my colleagues at work attend services at Father Carlotti's parish, and they reported that it is well-known that he has a history of being a womanizer. He was in Italy at the same time Sarah, Zane, and Eugene were in Italy. And the parish gossip is that Carlotti had an affair with a young relative while he was there, and there might have been a baby. Lots of motive packed into him as a suspect."

"Lots of reasons to want a talisman of St. Augustine. The original fresco of *Saint Augustine in His Study* is in Florence in the church of Ognissanti. All things lead to Florence," Johnny remarked.

"Why would a thoroughly Jewish boy like Eugene want such a Catholic item?" asked Kate.

"Eugene, as an art historian, would see the necklace and pendant both as representing the best of hot glass work at the time and as something that his family kept throughout the Diaspora. He would have researched the iconography of Saint Augustine, but the importance of that saint in the church wouldn't mean anything to him personally. It would be a family treasure, but not for religious reasons."

They continued to talk about the necklace as they cleared the table. "Ada mentioned that the family owns a condo in, wait for it, St. Augustine, Florida, so that Grandmother Rose might have stored the pieces there. And here's another new thing, Ada also told me that Grandma contributed to the glass center around the time of Eugene's Bar Mitzvah, which means to me that she might have talked about the necklace and pendant with someone there. I think someone else could have known about the glass pieces!"

Bourbon Ball stood by the kitchen door, ready for his nightly visit to the side yard, so the two friends went out onto the patio, sat down, and watched BB sniff for raccoons. Johnny and Kate were comfortable in silence—they gazed at the night sky, which was dark and thick like a length of velvet; a few frogs had found their way into the small pond she had installed for her collection of water lilies and were croaking out their contentment.

"Marco Rossetti and his team have left for Poland to teach his surgical techniques to the Ukrainian surgeons." Kate spoke into the darkness, making no effort to turn and look at Johnny.

"You know, some people do more with their lives than the rest of us. I admire that he has put that genius brain to good use. My mother and the ladies at Rosalie's Bakery used to talk about him. They all liked him as a youngster but, even at that age, found him a little odd—they chalked it up to what had happened to his siblings. It's impressive he has come through all that loss able to carve out such a meaningful life." Kate was aware that Johnny was watching her from the corner of his eye as he spoke.

"Agreed," responded Kate. "He emailed me before he left just to report on what his mother and her friends think about Father Carlotti." Kate changed the subject.

"Their views confirmed the gossip my colleagues gave: he's been known for years to be a womanizer, he has lost a lot of weight, and his eyes look like charcoal briquettes, and his mental health has deteriorated to the point that he sometimes will cry during his sermons or when handing out communion. Half of the time, no one can find him. Interesting, isn't it?" Kate finally turned to look at her Johnny.

"I'll say. Carlotti has got to be on your suspect list. Say, he is the right height and age for the man who broke into Mr. and Mrs. Rose's house, correct?"

"You bet he is. It was one of the first things I asked my friends at work—you know, how tall is he, what does look like, how old—the basics. He's definitely on my list."

They fell silent again. When Bourbon Ball was finished touring his yard, they went inside. As Johnny was helping her clean their few dinner dishes, he remarked in passing that he thought it was darn nice of Marco to take time to email her as he was heading to Europe. Kate didn't comment, so he left it at that.

Before falling asleep, Kate thought about the parallels in her and Marco's lives. One thing she knew for sure was that no one who had a happy, adjusted upbringing ever gave the world anything really important. It is the person who had transformed pain and rage into healthy avenues who is driven to help enrich the world.

Kate had transformed fate's cruelty of losing both of her parents into helping her university advisees make good choices; Marco transformed the hideous loss of two siblings into directly saving lives. Kate wondered if her and Marco's paths would continue to cross.

Another kind of human drama was being played out elsewhere in Pittsburgh that night. At the same time, Kate and Johnny were discussing Eugene Rose over dinner, suspects in his murder were pointing guns at each other.

"Call the police," yelled Joe Davies at his wife. He grabbed the loaded shotgun he always kept by the front door. He flew out, cocked the shotgun, and screamed at Father Carlotti. "Get off my property! The police are on their way."

His son Zane was caught in the crosshairs of the priest's revolver. "Where is it? Where is my pendant?" Carlotti's gun hand shook so badly that he had to steady it with the other.

Jablonsky arrived on site. He sprinted up the Davies' long driveway, his Glock held down at his side, out of sight; he also had a spare closely holstered around his left ankle. DeVille crept around the side of the house and hid in the bushes with the chief's command in his ears. "Take the shot if you have to, but don't kill him. We want everyone alive."

Several police cars were present, their flashing lights creating a strange aurora borealis effect. Officers were positioned behind their vehicles, weapons loaded and aimed. "Don't fire unless I say so," whispered Stefan as he moved past them.

"Father Carlotti, this is Chief Detective Jablonsky. You know me, you and I just talked. I understand that you need to see the pendant—I can make that happen. Just drop your gun and we will leave together." In the midst of the chief trying to lower the temperature of the confrontation, Zane Davies smashed his efforts by screaming hysterically.

"I don't have either the necklace or the pendant. Carlotti, please, I don't know where they are. Don't shoot me!" So scared was Zane that as he looked down the barrel of the priest's gun, he struggled to take air into his lungs. Unlike the day at Sarah's house, this time, it looked like the priest was going to shoot him.

The group collectively held their breath, time felt suspended, and there was complete silence. The actors in the drama were outlined in the full moon's silver light. It was eerie. Jablonsky held up his left hand and lowered the gun in his right, placing it on the ground.

"Father Carlotti, I'm unarmed. I'm going to walk toward you, and together we will leave. No one has to get hurt." DeVille remained crouched in position on the side of the house; he had a straight sight line to Carlotti. Joe Davies remained frozen, his shotgun still trained on the priest—he simply wasn't going to follow anyone's command to get out of the way.

When Father Carlotti moved to lower his gun, Zane shot him. The loud sound of the report blasted into the night and bounced around inside everyone's eardrums. Not even his father knew that he had a gun. Like the flick of a snake's tongue grabbing its dinner, Zane had pulled it out from his back waistband and fired at the priest.

DeVille stood up, ready to fire his weapon, just as Jablonsky yelled out to everyone, "Don't fire!" He bellowed at Zane to drop his pistol—as if the handgun were on fire, Zane opened his fingers, lifted his hand, and let the gun drop. At the sound of the clatter of his weapon hitting the concrete driveway, Joe Davies sprinted toward his son, grabbing him and shoving him down to the ground, almost sitting on him.

"No one move," commanded the chief. "DeVille, you and the officers get everyone's weapon. Someone call an ambulance. The priest is bleeding badly."

CHAPTER 20

JOAN WALKED OUT OF THE OPERATING ROOM, taking off her cap and mask and wiping her face. She had been informed that Jablonsky was in the waiting area and wanted her report, so she went right to him. "He will live. I must say that this man has a great many scars on him from other injuries. Do you know anything about that?"

"Yes. When he was younger, he was attacked in Italy. We just received a fax of the police and hospital reports on the incident—he was almost beaten to death. I'll send a copy of the physician's records to you. Were you able to get at the bullet?"

"Yes, I retrieved it. I have another surgery. May we speak later? My assistant will hand the bullet to you." The chief appreciated Joan's directness. "No problem," he replied.

Jablonsky ordered an officer placed outside of Carlotti's room. He didn't expect anyone else to try and kill the priest, but he wasn't going to take any chances. The situation this evening highlighted the strangeness of this case. *I knew he shouldn't be out on bail, but the church's attorneys said he would be supervised. Some supervision,* thought the chief.

Eugene Rose's murder had turned out to be much more complex than Jablonsky initially thought, with its tentacles reaching into the international smuggling of antiquities and the human desire to possess those antiquities. The situation certainly didn't fall into his usual wheelhouse.

DeVille called. "I have Mr. Davies and Zane at the station—both are being processed. Zane and his father are claiming self-defense, and a high-priced attorney is present. When do you want to interview them?"

"First, I want you and Lemon to find out where Carlotti got a second gun—did he obtain it legally? Later this morning, we are due to head to Mr. and Mrs. Rose's home to look at their family glass pieces. The Davies can cool their heels in holding. You and Ormsby meet me at the Rose's, and we will see if we can discover something about the elusive glass necklace and pendant." After a night of only a few hours of sleep, the chief arrived at the Rose house, tired but determined to find something that would point to Eugene's killer.

Jablonsky wasn't surprised to see Kate at the house. Mrs. Rose had also given permission for Johnny to accompany Andy Ormsby; as the two men cataloged the items in Grandma Rose's collection, Kate pulled the chief aside and informed him about the condo in Florida and reiterated her belief that someone else knew about the special gift.

Kate offered to talk to Andy again about Grandmother Rose's monetary contribution. "You know, I can find out who would have taken the contribution, who would have been around the office, that kind of thing." The chief okayed the conversation, and Kate left.

On the one hand, Jablonsky was glad that she and Mrs. Rose had become close, but on the other hand, the relationship was worrisome for the chief. Father Carlotti might not be the only person in hot pursuit of the necklace and pendant.

An expensively dressed attorney sat beside Zane Davies. He snapped at Jablonsky, "It's about time. My client has been waiting for a long time."

Jablonsky slowly lowered himself into his chair, then slowly arranged his coffee cup and his small paper notebook. The absurdity that someone took Eugene Rose's life over a glass object shaped his mood and response to the attorney's whining.

"Has he been waiting long? That's such a shame. Well then, we'd better get started," his tone dripping with sarcasm. "Zane, I want to talk about the shooting of Father Carlotti, who, even though you didn't bother to inquire after him, is still alive."

"That's a cheap shot, Jablonsky. Question my client without the moral indignation." The chief ignored the attorney's admonition.

"Let us not forget that this inquiry is fundamentally about the murder of your close friend, Eugene Rose. If you cared for him at all, I would hope you would be as truthful as possible about your relationship with him, Father Carlotti, and the missing necklace and pendant."

Zane looked exhausted. Gone was his normal arrogant posture, now replaced with fear over the distinct possibility that he could go to jail: Accordingly, and amusingly, he had dressed himself in all black. "Go ahead, tell the chief what happened at your parents' home," encouraged the attorney. "Remember, you defended yourself."

Jablonsky interrupted. "We will start with your conversations with Father Carlotti when you both were in Italy."

Zane looked surprised, but he recovered and gave a well-rehearsed answer. "He approached me about finding a glass necklace and pendant which, years before, his uncle had given him as a gift and had promised to send to him, but never did. At the golf club, he overheard me say that I frequently went to Europe to buy for my parents' art collection. He wanted me to ask my connections there if they knew of this piece.

"Was that the first time you had heard about the necklace? And Zane, I want the truth this time, not your usual cadre of lies." The chief contained his anger, but it was evident to everyone that his very last nerve was rapidly shredding.

"Well, to tell the absolute truth, it was not the first time I had heard about the two pieces. Eugene had shown me a picture of the necklace and pendant before we went to Italy. He said that his grandmother had bought it for him as part of a Bar Mitzvah gift but that she had died before she could give it to him or tell anyone where it was. He said that she said that a long time ago, it had belonged to the La Rosas, his Italian ancestors.. May I have some water, please?"

Jablonsky snapped his fingers to alert the detectives watching in the media booth—a bottle of water was immediately handed into the interview room. "Tell me about the estate in Tuscany. What did you know about it?"

"I knew that Father Carlotti's family in Italy currently owned it and had owned it for a century or so. Through the Italian records, I could verify that in the seventeenth century, the La Rosa family were the owners of the house and the surrounding farmlands." Zane drank deeply of the water, then continued.

"I also was able to find the distribution of the uncle's estate when he died—both real estate and art objects. Cui bono, I asked myself. All the adult children, Carlotti's first cousins, got everything. But there was no mention of the necklace and pendant."

Jablonsky still didn't understand something. "Why didn't the priest just talk to his cousins about the necklace?"

"I asked him the same thing; after all, it was family. He said he didn't want the cousins to know anything more about his private life than they already did. I'm not sure what that meant. When we came back to the States, he kept calling me. He was... persistent." *So, Zane never knew about the beating Carlotti sustained in Tuscany,* thought Jablonsky.

Zane gave his recitation in rapid-fire, declarative sentences. Jablonsky could see that he just wanted out of the situation and figured these details, spoken in that style, offered the best way to get home.

"You originally lied to me that Eugene told you about the necklace and pendant. Now, I want the truth. Did Eugene confide in anyone else that he was looking for this special gift from his grandmother?" Jablonsky was trying to whittle down his list of suspects even further.

"Honestly, initially, it was just me, then I told my father, and then I told Carlotti I could get the photographs from the flash drive. Eugene might have told Sarah Braithwaite or even Mr. Ormsby at the glass center. Sarah denies she knows anything about the necklace, and I haven't spoken to Ormsby. Then there's Carlotti's friend, Father Lupinski. He knows about the necklace and pendant through our luncheons at the golf club. That's all I know." Zane ran his hands over his hair; the young man's agitation was building.

Zane's attorney placed his hand on his client's arm. "Just answer the questions to the best of your memory."

"When Carlotti showed up at your parents' home, did you know he had a gun with him?"

"I figured he might because he had come to Sarah's with one. Chief, I'm no shrink, but it is clear to everyone that Carlotti is having a breakdown. He was outside my dad's house, screaming for me to get him the necklace and pendant. In his mind, if I knew where the photos were, then I knew where the two items were. But that isn't true!"

"When did you get a handgun?

"I purchased it after Carlotti showed up at Sarah's. It's legal. I registered it and everything. I had a creepy feeling that I needed protection from this wacko priest." DeVille had already checked on the status of Zane's gun; it was legal, all right.

"When Father Carlotti arrived at your dad's house, did you actually see his gun?"

"No, I didn't see a gun until he pulled it out. It was night, and the floodlights were on, but everything was still half in the shadows. I was afraid, damn it! He had already threatened me, so I wanted to protect myself. I'm telling the truth when I say I had no intention of killing him! When my dad heard the arguing, he came out with his shotgun. At that point, you showed up, and... you saw the rest."

"I saw Father Carlotti start to put down his gun."

Zane jumped out of his chair and pumped his fists into the air, yelling, "I didn't know what he was going to do. I feared for my life, so I protected myself! Damn it!"

The Davies' attorney had shown remarkable restraint during the questioning, but now he intervened. "I think that is enough for this interview: You were at the scene; you assessed the level of confrontation; the priest had already threatened Zane with a gun. This is textbook self-defense. I want my client released."

"One more question Zane. Did you murder Eugene Rose?"

"I did not! And I didn't intend to kill Father Carlotti!"

Jablonsky stood and spoke to the attorney. "I will let you know what the District Attorney says about bail. But there is still the issue of this young man's smuggling and the unknown extent of it. For right now, Zane goes back to holding." The chief walked out of the room in the midst of the attorney's protestations and Zane's weeping.

CHAPTER 21

JABLONSKY AND ANTOINE WERE REARRANGING items on the murder board. "Eugene Rose's murder was well thought out. A calculating and cool head was needed to set up all the details necessary for the murder to be successful. Do we think Father Carlotti has such a state of mind? In the short time we have known him, his behavior has begun to look like an ice skater in one of those spin turns going faster and faster. I spoke with the bishop about my concerns; he assured me that Carlotti will be taken care of."

"Is Carlotti your man for the murder of Eugene?" Antoine asked the chief.

"He was. He had the strongest motive; he is driven by a personal spiritual crisis. He is educated enough to read and understand about poisons and would know how to order a poison online. He was seen at the glass center, probably casing it. His obsession with the pendant makes him unstable to the point of being out of control—and that makes him dangerous." Jablonsky unwrapped a piece of cinnamon gum, folded it flat, and put it on his tongue. "Coupe, anything new about the Italian side of the family and the beating Carlotti took there."

"Everything that Zane said about the history and transfer of the estate from the La Rosa family to the Carlotti's was fairly easily researched, if you knew what you were looking for and could decipher a bit of Italian."

"Did you or Lemon ever actually talk to Carlotti's cousins?" The chief kept tapping his marker against the murder board. *Something doesn't quite jive here,* he thought.

He turned and eyeballed his number one and number two. Coupe answered first.

"I spoke to one of the older detectives who was working in the Tuscan area when the priest was attacked. Between his English and my limited Italian, what he conveyed was that no one was ever arrested for the crime. He intimated that the Patron, Carlotti's uncle, wanted it kept quiet." Annie Lemon chimed in with the result of her research.

"The medical records describe that the young Carlotti almost died from the beating. I did speak with Carlotti's cousins, trying not to reveal much about the details of our investigation." Jablonsky could always count on Lemon for her discretion.

"Did they know about the sale of the necklace and pendant?"

"Yes. It was the oldest cousin, Antonio, who said that Father Carlotti's behavior had caused his father great humiliation. After their father's death, when they were dividing the estate and its contents, they placed the necklace and pendant with an antique dealer. It was that antique dealer that met Grandmother Rose, presented her with the estate background of the La Rosa/Carlotti family, and sold the pieces to her. Antonio said the sale of the necklace and pendant was their way of getting back at Father Carlotti for having caused their father so much shame."

"Did he say how much this necklace and pendant sold for?"

"I asked, and he said the dealer sold it for five thousand dollars."

The chief was surprised at the small amount. "Did Antonia have any idea what it would be worth today?"

"Yes. He said that if the Vatican knew about the piece, they would potentially pay upwards of a million for it. I don't know if that is an exaggeration or not—this side of Carlotti's family is quite wealthy, so they know what art objects cost. Grandma Rose did pay the requisite Italian county and state tax—if that is what it is termed there." Lemon made a face that communicated how little the family wanted to keep the necklace and pendant.

"What Grandmother Rose paid and what the Carlotti family could have auctioned it for is an unbelievable difference. By the way, which mail carrier shipped it?" Shipping was a detail that niggled at the chief.

"None. Grandmother Rose took it with her. There is no shipping trail. When she came into the country, I assume she declared it and paid the duty."

"I guess she thought it was safer with her. See if you can dig around for the declaration of purchase—I know it has been a decade, but our government might have a receipt for the duty." The chief turned his attention to the murder board.

"There are other people who are in the frame. Eugene Rose was murdered because of this glass piece, which hardly anyone knew about. I think it is reasonable to add Father Lupinski to the list of suspects because he was privy to conversations between Zane and Carlotti at the golf club. He also knew about Carlotti having been attacked in Italy and the meaning of the necklace and the pendant to him. He knew that Carlotti hired Bogey Johnson to search for the flash drive and that his fellow priest had broken into two places looking for it. He knew that Carlotti had a gun and had taken it to Sarah Braithwaite's house looking for Zane. Does he also know where the necklace and pendant are?" In his shorthand, Jablonsky listed the statements under Lupinski's picture on the murder board.

"I'll do a deeper dive into his past," remarked Antoine, "but I can't ascribe a reasonable motive to Lupinski."

"I have the same problem—lots of knowledge of events, but other than greed, no motive that immediately makes sense. Then there is Joseph Davies and Zane. Here are my questions. Did we see everything Zane has collected for his father? Are there some art pieces for which there is no provenance? Were most of the foreign items in their collection smuggled into this country?" The chief had already written the word smuggling; now he added "antiquity theft" under Zane's picture.

Lemon spoke up. "We could talk to Professor McCarthy about that. Since he is considered an expert in fine art, he might know the best person to help us find out what antiquities have recently been stolen, both here and in Europe. I'll contact him." Lemon took the initiative since she had been involved with Mrs. McCarthy's case last year and communicated easily with Johnny and Kate.

"Good. You both have some research to do. We haven't heard from the two amateur sleuths for a day or two. I wonder what's going on?" They chuckled over their ongoing problems with the likable civilians.

"Detective Lemon called me today," remarked Johnny.

"What for?" Kate was surprised.

Johnny was loading high-quality photographs onto his computer of American portrait artists to present in one of his class lectures. Johnny was an organized professor.

It was a rainy, moody afternoon, so he had steamed some cappuccino for himself and Kate, who lounged in one of the comfortable chairs he had long ago brought into his university office. Aside from the desk and floor-to-ceiling bulging bookshelves, he had arranged the space to resemble a cozy den rather than a sterile office. Kate loved the warm atmosphere; today, she had slung her legs over the arm of her chair while delicately sipping the milky coffee out of some hand-decorated cups Johnny had bought when he had last traveled to Rome.

"Why did Detective Lemon call me? It had to do with the smuggling of antiquities. She wondered who the best people were to contact about what special objects across Europe have gone missing in the last couple of decades. I gave her Julian's name." Johnny's ex-partner, Julian Castillo, was an attorney who specialized in antiquities theft and, in fact, was the person who had traveled with him on the Roman vacation.

He nonchalantly stirred his cup of coffee with a small spoon, and as an aside to the theft issue, mentioned the shoot-out at the Davies' home, unaware of the bomb he had just dropped.

Kate's feet hit the floor as she sat up. "What shoot-out?"

"You don't know? Detective Lemon told me about it, but I thought it was on the news or that Joan would have told you. Carlotti showed up at the Davies' home, wielding a gun and demanding the glass necklace and pendant. Zane had a pistol, with which he shot Carlotti. Joan was the surgeon on call, so she operated on him."

"Is he alive?" Kate was furious! How could Joan not have telephoned her immediately with this news? If it were possible for steam to come out of her ears, like the espresso machine, it would have.

"He survived the surgery. Jablonsky was at the hospital and talked with Joan after the operation. He put a guard on Carlotti's room. So, the ladies of the parish were right in their assessment—Carlotti has gone off the rails." Kate knew that Johnny's lame joke was an attempt to lighten her mood, but it fell flat. Johnny tried to calm her down.

"Why don't you call Joan? Since the rain is now just a drizzle, they probably restarted the double-header the Pirates are playing late this afternoon. Maybe they are in the seventh inning stretch."

Kate agreed and walked into the hallway outside of Johnny's office. She paced up and down the empty corridor, unable to relax. She called Joan, her voice tight with anger.

"Joan? Are you at the game? Why didn't you tell me that Father Carlotti was shot? You know I'm involved with this."

Joan, used to demands from all sorts of hospital administrators, other surgeons, patients' families, and insurance companies, responded in an aggravated tone. "I caught the case. And you knew that I had tickets to today's double-header; it's almost the end of the season. You also know that I should not talk to you about a patient. The game is starting again; we can catch up later." Joan abruptly ended the telephone call, leaving Kate to stew. She remained standing in the hallway for a few minutes to calm her anger.

Johnny opened the door to his office. "Come back in; I have the news on my computer. They're talking about the shooting."

"In a follow-up to a previous news story, it has been reported to us that the person who was shot in an altercation at a

Pittsburgh suburban home has died at the university hospital. The victim's family has been notified, so the hospital has released the man's name. The victim is a local priest named Father Timothy Carlotti. The police are investigating his death as a possible murder."

~

If Kate was furious with Joan in the afternoon, Jablonsky was seething that evening. "Where were you?" he snarled at the officer who had been posted at Carlotti's door. "I told you in no uncertain terms that only medical personnel and fellow priests were allowed in his room. Man, you are hanging over the edge here. What happened?"

The young officer mopped his brow with a paper napkin and tried not to stammer. "Only the nurses and his physician went in the room. Oh, and two priests came." The officer looked at his paper register, "A Father Lupinski and a Father Nolan."

"Did they come together?" Jablonsky snapped out his question.

"Ah. No. Lupinski came at 7:35 and Nolan at 9:30."

Jablonsky turned to Antoine. "Who the hell is Nolan? Call the Pittsburgh diocese and find out if there is such a person. I want some answers." Antoine turned away and walked a short distance down the hallway to make his call.

Jablonsky eyed the officer. "What did Nolan look like?"

"Well, he was around six foot, probably in his forties, had black glasses and an old-fashioned black fedora—he had an everyman look to him. He was dressed in a black suit and wore the collar."

"Did he say anything to you?"

"I asked him his name. He gave it and said that he wouldn't stay long. He said he was here to give Carlotti communion. He held up a little bag, which I assumed was the communion stuff. I—I didn't check the bag. Then he went in, stayed less than five minutes, and left."

The chief just grunted and thought to himself, *Lupinski would have been the one to bring communion to his friend. Nolan is our perp. I wonder what was in the black bag.*

"I want you to give a description of this Nolan person to our sketch artist. Do it now!" The chief shouted at the officer like he was a frustrated Dad faced with a recalcitrant little boy.

DeVille walked back to the chief. Jablonsky quietly raised the obvious question. "Why would someone want to kill this man? Had he found the necklace and pendant, and we didn't know about it? The pieces don't fit."

"Chief. The person I spoke with at the diocese checked his records and no Father Nolan is listed anywhere in the city. This perp knew enough about our investigation and Carlotti's role in it that he came disguised as a priest to a public space and, we suspect, killed him. It has the same cool-headed stamp as Eugene Rose's murder. The fact we know it was a man is at least something."

"I'll be at the morgue with Doctor Patel. Between us, this is definitely murder. See you back at the precinct."

CHAPTER 22

IT HAD BEEN FIREWORKS NIGHT for the second Pirates game, which meant that Jablonsky hit all of the post-game traffic. He relaxed into the rhythm of tapping the breaks, then inching forward—tap, inch, tap, inch. The delay would give Patel more time with the body.

No matter what time of day or night Doctor Patel was called to examine a body, she always looked beautiful to the chief. When he arrived, Aashi was bent over, peering into her microscope, a pencil stuck through the bun at the back of her neck.

"What do you have for me?" he asked.

As was her habit, she twirled her chair around, then continued to rotate it slowly back and forth while she gave her report. "It was an air embolism. The oldest trick in the book! A syringe filled with nothing but air was injected into the priest's IV. When air goes into a vessel, it forms an air embolism, which may or may not cause death. In this case, the embolism traveled to a blood vessel in the heart and was large enough that it cut off the blood supply. Death was probably painful and not necessarily immediate. I also wanted to show you Carlotti's body."

They moved to the autopsy table, and Patel pulled back the sheet. "Look at all these old injuries and scars. At some point in his life, this man took quite a beating. Frankly, you usually see these kinds of injuries in someone who had been a soldier, imprisoned, or tortured."

Jablonsky nodded and recounted Carlotti's history. "Carlotti said that he had trouble with chastity—in everyday parlance, he was a womanizer. True to his nature, when he was in Italy, he carried on with a girl there—her father and his buddies beat him up. It was his uncle who bought him the elusive glass necklace and pendant. He believed that meditating on the image of St. Augustine, which was painted on the pendant, would help him with his desire for the ladies." Jablonsky rolled his eyes, waiting for Patel to weigh in on the topic.

"All old cultures have talisman objects, but a pendant with a picture of St. Augustine is a new one for me. Were the men who beat him prosecuted?" Patel asked.

"No. Interestingly, the Uncle never brought charges against any of the local men. Sad. He said he didn't want the notoriety."

"Or, there was something else to it. Perhaps a pregnancy resulted, and the families wanted it hushed up." Patel covered the priest's body. "He survived all of that only to be murdered in Pittsburgh by a tiny air bubble."

"Your official findings are?"

"The cause of death was an air embolism created by injection into his IV, and the manner of death is murder. This is the second murder related to the glass neckless and pendant. To me, it is very strange indeed. What could be the motive?" While Patel busied herself with maneuvering the body into the cooler, Jablonsky left for the precinct.

The chief and his best detectives were gathered in the bullpen considering just that—motives. Carlotti's picture was moved next to those of Eugene Rose and Zane Davies. Jablonsky added the photo of Father Lupinski, and DeVille tacked up the sketch of the man described by the officer guarding Carlotti's hospital room.

Jablonsky remarked, "He does look like an everyman. But there is something familiar about his posture. It will come to me."

Annie Lemon pointed to the picture. "Both murders could have been committed by this man. We know they were both bold and well-planned. If the priest's motive for wanting to possess the neckless and pendant was spiritual, I think the perp's motive is monetary."

Jablonsky passed around some sticks of his cinnamon gum. Once its innervating flavor burst onto his taste buds, he added, "Our friend Andy Ormsby has remarked on several occasions that, if it could be authenticated that the necklace was crafted by Murano artists in the sixteenth or seventeenth century, it would be worth a bundle. It follows that whoever found it would become famous in glass circles."

"That certainly wasn't why Eugene wanted it—it was a piece of their family history," interjected Antoine.

Lemon, DeVille, and Jablonsky were surprised to see Kate and Johnny stroll into the bullpen. Lemon flipped the murder board.

"I just heard about Father Carlotti. I'm so sorry. In light of his murder, I thought I'd stop by to mention that Ada Rose called me and reported that a search of the Florida condominium didn't turn up anything," Kate, casually dressed in cut-off jeans and a pale blue cotton sweater, stood like an awkward student waiting to see the principal. Jablonsky motioned them toward his office. "With me, Coupe. You too, Lemon," he commanded. Jablonsky sat at his desk while his number one and two slouched at the back of the office, arms crossed.

"So, they didn't find the necklace and pendant in Florida. Too bad. What about you, Johnny? What have you got?"

"I've been in regular touch with Julian about any missing antiquities being tracked in Europe. So far, there is nothing related to the necklace or pendant, but Julian says there are underground rumblings about some canvases of American Expressionists that were recently sold off-market."

"Off-market?" repeated Jablonsky.

"Well, off-market means they were sold out of a private collection to a private buyer. Cash exchanged hands, but no taxes or duties would have been paid."

"Any idea where these transactions took place?" asked the chief.

"Rumors say the buyer was American and the seller was French, from somewhere around the Cote D'Azur. Right now, Julian said that no one knows where these canvases are. I didn't see them in the Davies' collection and frankly, would have been surprised if they were there." Johnny paused. "How much wealth does the Davies family have because even the smallest canvases would be a fortune to buy."

Jablonsky turned to Annie Lemon, who had the facts at her fingertips. "The wealth search engine I looked at estimated the company's worth to be around thirty million. That includes their manufacturing plants in Brazil."

"That's a lot of money, but if the canvases are important American Impressionists, it may not be enough." Johnny's officious facial expression told the story of the bank account necessary for high-end collecting. Everyone paused to take in the operating rules of a world they would never experience. Jablonsky turned to Kate and changed the topic.

"You are educated in the behavioral sciences—what motive do you think is strong enough that the murderer would strike twice, and I might add, strike in two public places?"

"I think it is about money and reputation. Because Eddie had been an archeologist, I came to understand how finding a rare antiquity in one's field could launch a person to academic and public fame. The value of the find is a secured reputation and perhaps offers of a position that would include funding for further explorations and a much better salary. To find this antique necklace, and especially the pendant, would be a really big deal for a specific, but small, group of people."

"You mean like collectors—like the Davies," responded the chief.

"Or, in her own way, even Grandmother Rose, who wanted the glass piece primarily for her grandson, whom she believed would make a career at a university. He would stand out among his peers if the family owned such a piece." Jablonsky had to admit to himself that he hadn't considered that aspect of the grandmother's special gift. Kate continued.

"And then there is the church. Valuable antiquities from the Catholic Church have been stolen or have 'mysteriously disappeared' for centuries—they always want the return of such items, like this roundel pendant—especially since it has a beautiful portrait of Saint Augustine of Hippo on it."

"Would you add Andy Ormsby to the list of people who would be tempted by such an object?" Jablonsky built his finger steeple as he scrutinized Kate's face.

"Yes, I guess you would have to add him to the list. Unless, as an artist, he produces several critically acclaimed pieces of studio glass that sell with big price tags and is ensured a steady clientele—like Dale Chihuly has fashioned for himself. I can't see him as having personal aspirations to collect because he simply doesn't have the means. But as the director of an important glass center, he would want to add to its collection. You remember all those special boxes in the basement of the center? They hold the current collection." Kate furrowed her brow thinking about the possibility that Ormsby would murder over the necklace and pendant.

"To summarize, you postulate that for a specific someone, the discovery and possession of the rare glass necklace and pendant would be enough motive to commit two murders." Jablonsky pushed Kate, wanting to hear this kind of motive worked through.

Kate was confident. "Absolutely, I do. From all my years with my grandfather and Eddie, I'd say some anthropologists, archeologists, and art collectors would definitely commit crimes in order to possess something rare. Remember the premise of the movie, *Raiders of the Lost Ark?* If the person felt that Eugene and Father Carlotti could make some sort of claim on the antique necklace and pendant, then they would have to be silenced."

The chief stood on the front steps of the precinct and addressed the media. "We are circulating this artist's drawing of our prime suspect in the murder of Father Timothy Carlotti. We ask the public to contact us if anyone has seen this man. Do not approach him; we believe he will be armed and dangerous."

The city buzzed with the sensational murder of the priest. The phone lines at the police's call center rang day and night; no one slept much, so busy were they sorting through the legitimate versus the imaginary leads.

Kate sat on her patio, sipping some sweet tea and making telephone calls. After talking with Jablonsky, she was convinced that someone other than the obvious suspects had known about the glass piece, so she made calls to the museums, art dealers, and estate evaluation groups. Her first call was to the Carnegie.

Kate was accomplished at the skill of being chatty and getting information all at the same time. Applying that ability, she learned from the acquisition department that no one had seen or ever heard of these two objects. She moved on to the glass center, speaking with someone in the "development" department, who first gave her the standard rules of privacy on monetary gifts. After a bit of conversation, they confided that it was entirely possible that several people could have overheard a supporter talk about an acquisition, especially one as unusual as the glass bead necklace and pendant.

"Well, people are only human." Kate empathized with her contact. "Something that rare, you'd want to tell a colleague about it."

She was writing her notes when her cell phone rang; it was Joan. "Are we still friends?" This directness was just another reason Kate loved her.

"Of course. I know the rules about patient privacy; sometimes, I just want you to break them. Where are you?"

"I'm standing on the other side of your patio wall." Joan's head popped up, Bourbon Ball barked, and Kate laughed. "Come on in, have some tea." The two good friends hugged, then remained seated outside. Kate had ringed her patio with pots of fall mums, which still attracted butterflies, some tall dracaenas, and a couple of mature scheffleras. The plants made for a private green space to eat, sip a drink, and think about clues in a murder.

"I love your patio, Kate. You've made it like a small bistro. Speaking of ubiquitous tiny restaurants, did you know that our famous Marco is still in Europe, maybe having a coffee at a bistro right now," mused Joan.

"He mentioned he would be traveling after his work was finished, and that he would send me postcards." Kate gave Joan a quizzical look that asked for her to comment; Kate usually didn't know when a man was flirting with her unless it was unmistakable, like Andy Ormsby's behavior.

"He'll probably send pictures of opera houses! He's on the board of the Pittsburgh Opera and has a box at Heinz Hall. Everyone who goes comments on the tall, well-dressed surgeon who always slips into his box right as the performance starts and slips out when it ends. He always attends solo. Did you know his nickname is The Leopard?" Joan laughed at the improbable tag.

"The Leopard? How did he come by that?"

"Because he is always alone. No one ever sees him with anyone other than colleagues. Interesting, isn't it?" Joan paused to see if she could interest Kate in talking more about Marco, but when her friend remained silent on the topic, she changed the subject. "I see you are doing some research. What knot are you trying to untie?"

Kate reiterated her conversations with the people at the Carnegie and the glass center. "Everyone is interested, but no one has seen the two pieces." She repeated her mantra, "Someone else knew."

Joan agreed with Kate but went in a different direction. "Since we talked to the Rabbi and Mr. and Mrs. Rose, I've begun to wonder if there wasn't more to Grandmother Rose's gift. A Bar Mitzvah gift is usually money that is put away for the child's education. Everyone I know who had a Bar Mitzvah or a Bat Mitzvah, me included, primarily received gifts of money."

Kate asked, "Are you speculating that there is cash stored in the neckless or the pendant?" She immediately brought up the photos she had downloaded from the flash drive. "Let's take a look." She swiped the screen back and forth in order to see the front and rear. Both women peered at the photos, trying to assess if there was a place one could put paper money.

"It's so hard to tell from the photo. But, on the back of the roundel are two tiny gold hinges, which means the back opens up—something very small could be stored there. It's an interesting idea, though. Joan, you always have an unusual take on things."

They fell silent, thinking about the possibility that there might be more to the story than just a family heirloom. Kate had unconsciously been circling the top of her glass with her finger when suddenly the sunlight struck her emerald ring, deepening its rich green color. She stared at it, then was caught off-guard by a deep wave of nausea.

"Are you okay?" Joan asked. But Kate wasn't okay. She bolted into the house, into her bathroom, and vomited into the toilet. Joan ran right behind her to pull Kate's hair away from her face.

"It's Eddie, isn't it?" Joan's observation was right on target. Kate knew that her friend had seen many patients and family members fall apart upon hearing bad news—she didn't have to hide any emotional reaction from Joan.

"Yeah. When the light hit the emerald he gave me, it ignited my grief. That's all." Kate brushed her teeth, swished a capful of mouthwash, splashed water on her face, and they both went back outside. Bourbon Ball, who had been standing sentry at the bathroom door, now laid across Kate's sandals, periodically licking her bare toes in doggy affection and concern.

"You know, when Eddie died, a part of my early life died with him. He was at all the important occasions, knew my friends, and got all my jokes… no one else shared the memories that he and I shared; he was there as I grew into a woman. During one of the summer sojourns in Nantucket Island, I remember the two of us floating in the Atlantic Ocean, spread eagle, just one hand touching—the saltwater held us, the sun warmed us, and we talked about everything and nothing. I can still smell the suntan lotion." Kate exhaled deeply, then added, "No one else knows these things. Plus, it was important to me that my grandfather loved him so."

Joan spoke with her usual directness, "I'm so sorry, Kate. He was a part of you, and he loved you—I knew that to be true."

Once she had recovered, Kate returned to formulating a new theory about Bar Mitzvah gifts.

"Does the monetary gift have to be actual paper money? Where I'm going with this is that I remember the Rabbi telling us that the earlier generation of the Rose family might have given gemstones as a gift gave to help build the synagogue. Maybe Grandmother Rose was gifting Eugene a few gemstones and hid them in the roundel?" Kate looked for confirmation of her new theory.

"You know, there is a kind of symmetry to your idea. Eugene's grandmother might have bought a few gems and stored them in the medallion—thereby linking the family past to the present—the portable money of the Diaspora and a family heirloom. Eugene would have appreciated that." Joan paused, then added, "I don't know if Ada mentioned that Grandmother Rose worked downtown at a respected jewelry store. I believe she was a certified gemologist. My father bought a few pieces of jewelry for my mom from her.

Pretty interesting in terms of your theory." Joan offered Kate her widest smile.

"I didn't know about her jewelry connection. That's very pertinent. The people who knew about the necklace might also have known about the gemstones. It would be an added inducement to possess it." Kate's excitement caused her eyes to shine with the anticipation of sharing this information with Jablonsky.

When Joan left, Kate Googled the jewelry store where Grandmother Rose had worked; the distraction helped her calm down from her grief reaction. This was not the first time that grief had highjacked her mood—one minute, she was seeing an advisee at the office, and the next she was weeping at her desk. She wanted to think about gemstones that had nothing to do with her emerald ring and Eddie's death.

Back at work the next day, Kate called the glass center. "Andy, it's Kate. I wanted to thank you for the information on Grandmother Rose's contribution to the glass center. It was kind of you to take the time to look into it for detective Jablonsky and me. I do have a follow-up question."

"Anything, Kate, ask away." Once again, Kate felt a tinge of guilt when she heard the affection in Ormsby's voice, but it didn't stop her from asking her question.

"Is there a record of the staffer in the development department who took Mrs. Rose's contribution?"

"Yes. Let me look. Here it is—it was a woman named Elise Ballard. She is now at the Corning Museum in New York if you want to contact her—although I'm not sure why you would. It was a simple transaction, a supporter giving a monetary gift. And thank goodness for that! It's how we stay afloat." The glass center relied on contributions from the community and the city to exist.

Kate didn't want to show her hand, so she lied. "I visit Ada Rose periodically, you know, just to check on her. We talked about her mother-in-law's support of the Center, and she was curious to know more about it. I'm really acting on her behalf. It helps her to know every detail about Eugene's relationship with his grandmother. A sensitive person like yourself would understand." She knew she was laying it on a little thick, but it worked.

"Of course. No problem. Here is Ms. Ballard's telephone number at Corning. I'll see you in class, right?"

"That you will. Thanks so much, Andy."

Using Andy Ormsby's name, Kate was able to get through to Elise Ballard, who actually remembered Mrs. Rose. "She was a really nice person. She and her husband were quite generous to that organization. I heard about the murder of her grandson—murder at the glass center was big news. Is there something specific you want to know from me that the Pittsburgh center wasn't able to answer?"

"Well, I was one of the students in the glassblowing class where Eugene Rose was killed, and I know his mother. She didn't realize that her mother-in-law had made the contribution, so she wanted me to find out the details—how Grandmother Rose seemed that day, if she bought a glass piece while she was there—that kind of thing. Her son and this particular grandmother were very close." All of Kate's statements were true; she just strung them together to elicit maximum sympathy.

"Poor woman, to lose a son like that. I imagine every little detail is important. The one thing that I do remember about our interaction was that she had an appointment with Dr. Isabelle Aubert, who was our blown glass appraiser. I didn't know about the meeting until she arrived that day. She seemed very excited to meet Dr. Aubert." Kate's excitement fizzed inside of her like an Alka-Seltzer tablet.

"If she had a meeting with your appraiser, then she must have had a glass piece with her. Did she show it to you?"

"Now that you mention it, she was carrying a very large purse, almost a leather carry-on you use for traveling. She might have had it in that purse. I remember thinking that women's purses had gotten ridiculously large!" Kate chuckled in recognition.

"That's really helpful, Elise. Where is Dr. Aubert now?"

"She has retired. Actually, she lives in Nice, on the Cote d'Azur. Her daughter followed in her mother's footsteps and is an appraiser for one of the museums in that beautiful French city. I have her email—would you like it?"

"Yes! I'm sure Eugene's mother would want to know if she appraised a glass piece that day. You've been so generous with your time. I can't thank you enough! I'll mention your generosity to Andy Ormsby."

The two women finished their conversation, and Kate jumped out of her office chair and skipped around the room. "I was right! I was right! Someone else knew about the necklace and pendant, and there is an official appraisal from Dr. Isabelle Aubert. I'm going to email her right now."

CHAPTER 23

THE JEWISH COMMUNITY WAS FURIOUS over the lack of an arrest in Eugene Rose's murder, and the Catholic diocese demanded justice for their priest; crooks, however, were happy to have the spotlight shine on someone else. Jablonsky remained positive that Zane and Joseph Davies were lying about the legitimacy and extent of their art collection. He put a plan into action.

DeVille and Lemon were dispatched, along with several search warrants, to the Davies Tool and Dye Company. A large contingency of uniformed police and plain-clothed detectives arrived en mass at the company, their vehicles kicking up clouds of dust as they drove onto the property, three cars across in Formula One style. Lemon led the charge into the office areas, and DeVille went onto the factory floor—everyone's side-arms were visible, making all the employees nervous—which was precisely the idea.

The warrants covered everything: computer files, paper files, invoices, employee information, outbuildings, the whole shebang. Someone had called Davies' attorney, the one who was with him at the last interview, and he arrived on the grounds in record time. "You can't take these," he shouted at Lemon as her officers confiscated the computers.

"Oh, yes, I can," she said, holding up the warrant. Lemon turned to one of the middle-aged secretaries, "Open this safe, now." The attorney sputtered and took the chief operating officer aside to confer about a strategy to stop the search and seizure. Then he tried to call in favors from several young district attorneys. "Which judge issued these search warrants?" he demanded. "This is a private business!"

Outside, it was as if the factory had been a sleeping beehive, and now DeVille interrupted that peace. His group of detectives arranged the workers in an orderly queue and then took their statements. Several were immigrants who usually worked at the Davies fabricating plant in Brazil; they were rightfully anxious over the police presence.

Each worker was asked the same two questions. "Do you know anyone who works here that does off-the-books, illegal jobs for Joseph Davies?" And, "Are there any buildings on the property that are locked and off-limits to everyone except the boss?"

DeVille struck pay dirt with the latter question. He and several other detectives were directed to an outwardly dilapidated building behind the factory. It had old-fashioned security in the form of large padlocks. Antoine didn't wait to find a key—he just shot off the lock. When they stepped inside, they found a large climate-controlled pristine room with two large tables, some chairs, and no windows. There were three black safes of substantial size that lined one wall. He called Lemon on her cell.

"Annie, get the top office staff down here. We found three safes. I want the combinations. We have legal warrants to open anything; they must comply." Once the three key senior staff were marched into the room and were read the warrants once again, Joseph Davies' personal secretary announced that she wasn't going to break the law and so handed over the combinations. The staff were led back to their offices, and Antoine began to empty the safes.

They found a tube that contained six rolled-up canvases, three monstrances made of gold and heavily adorned with gemstones, several gilded antique tall wine decanters, similar to the kind Kate was trying to make. Among many other items, inside a soft cloth bag, they found an antique violin.

"We are going to need to speak with Sarah Braithwaite about this," Lemon remarked as she held it up for everyone to see. All of the items were tagged and bagged so forensics could work their magic. Unfortunately, Antoine had to tell the chief that they found no glass bead necklace or pendant.

After the work was done, Lemon and DeVille leaned against their car, swigging bottles of water. "The chief sure was right on this one. I don't remember seeing any listing of these pieces of art in Davies' official report on his collection. And Johnny's friend Julian was also right about the underground collector's network. By the way, did you get a name from the workers?" Lemon asked, referring to their inquiry about a personal thug for hire.

"Yeah. Finally. Several employees whispered the name of a crook that sometimes works here but who mostly is Davies' fixer. Deuce Lewis. Ever heard of him?"

"Maybe. I have someone in mind. I'll check when we get back to the precinct." Lemon crushed her water bottle and threw it in the backseat of her otherwise neat car. She and Antoine drove back to the precinct, content with the raid.

~

Jablonsky stood next to Johnny in the conference room, where the contents of the safes had been laid out. The chief had called in Johnny as an authority on fine art; he, of course, called Kate, who had no invitation to see the evidence, but showed up at Jablonsky's office anyway, saying she had some new information for him. She mentioned Grandmother

Rose's work as a gemologist and her theory that a gift of money for Eugene might have been loose gemstones, which she would have had access to at her jewelry store. She did not yet mention Dr. Isabelle Aubert.

"These paintings are worth a fortune," she spontaneously uttered as she walked alongside the table where the canvases had been unrolled. Johnny and one of the technicians were looking at the canvases with a black light to ascertain if any of them were overpaints. He remarked, "We have taken a few discreet scrapings of the paint to see which century and decade each one belongs in. These certainly look legit—all of them appear to be painted by American masters, and, most importantly, all are signed and dated. Three Homer Winslow paintings, two Frederick Childe Hassams, and one very rare John Henry Twachtman. These are really important artists that fall into the genre that Zane already has been featuring in their collection."

Jablonsky asked, "Anything else that is important?"

"To my knowledge, none of the canvases have been in a major museum show nor are owned by a museum either here in the States or in Europe. I'm searching each *Catalogue Raisonné* on the three artists—the catalogs will detail all of the known works by the artist, the medium, like oil paint or watercolor, and who owned it. This is going to take some time. I sent Julian pictures of the glass and the violin and asked the Carnegie to send over their specialist on American Expressionism. Sorry for the delays, but if you want to build a solid criminal case for tax evasion, this is the only way to do it."

Before the chief could answer, Joseph Davies stomped into the detective's area, swearing like a sailor; his attorney was right on his heels. Jablonsky walked out of the conference room and stopped Davies, positioning himself menacingly close to him. The other detectives opened the locked desk drawers where they stored their guns—no one knew where this confrontation would lead.

"Who the hell do you think you are? You cannot just take belongings from my safe! Damn you, Jablonsky ... You crossed the line with the wrong person." Davies' lawyer stepped close to his client, physically trying to ameliorate his client's aggressive body posture. The attorney knew every detective there was armed and capable of shooting him and Joseph Davies if they threatened the chief.

"Are they your belongings? Prove it! I have probable cause to obtain a warrant to search any premise for any item, personal or public, that I want." The attorney entered the conversation, twisting the narrative.

"That is just the point, Chief Detective. You will have to prove that these objects belong to my client. Just because they were at his place of business doesn't mean he owned them." He turned toward Mr. Davies, who continued to sputter with indignation and said, "Shut up, Davies. Let me do my job. Is Mr. Davies under arrest? No? Then we are leaving." Like a puppy being led away by its owner, Joseph Davies kept turning his head back to look at Jablonsky and shout expletives.

Kate had poked her head out of the conference room to watch the heated interaction. Once things calmed down, and Jablonsky stepped back into the room, she pointed to the tagged violin. "Chief. Sarah Braithwaite's specialty is the origins of the four string violin. That's what she was studying in Italy. The fact that this antique instrument was in Davies' safe could have implications for your case."

"You are absolutely right, Kate." The chief went into the bullpen and pulled aside both detective Lemon and DeVille, giving them directions that Kate couldn't hear.

Kate also mentioned her idea about the gemstones and that Joan had told her Grandmother Rose had been a certified gemologist who had worked at a ritzy downtown jewelry store. Had Grandmother Rose hidden gemstones in the pendant?

“Thanks, Kate. We are busy here right now; you can go back to your office.”

Johnny McCarthy remained, assiduously working to identify the provenance of each of the found canvasses.

CHAPTER 24

THE PUBLIC PRESSURE TO FIND THE MURDERERS of the "decent young man, Eugene Rose," and "a respected cleric, Father Timothy Carlotti," as the press dubbed them, was building in intensity. Newspaper articles and television reporters hounded the police for answers, not knowing that the two murders might be linked. Jablonsky was slowly building his case but wasn't forthcoming with the details, which the media hated. The police tip line hadn't produced any significant leads—Kate was the only civilian who had brought useable information to the manhunt.

Standing at the murder board, the chief pointed to Sarah Braithwaite's and Zane Davies' photos.

Antoine speculated. "Did Sarah and Zane conspire to smuggle items as a team—for example, that violin and the glass bead necklace and pendant?" Coupe had made coffee from his personal super-duper coffee maker and was sipping the rich, frothy drink as he examined the board.

"I don't know. She seems like such a straight arrow girl from a straight arrow background. What makes more sense to me is that Zane Davies took advantage of her knowledge to either purchase the violin and smuggle it in, or he outright stole it, and had it shipped to his father." Coupe knew that Jablonsky had little use for entitled boys of any color or ethnicity, who were the progeny of rich daddies. Just like

Kate believed that everyone is lying about something all the time, the chief knew that rich boys were guilty of some kind of indiscretion during every stage of their development.

"I wouldn't rule her out," remarked detective Lemon. "I know she doesn't fit the typical profile of a crook, but this case doesn't either. I mean, two human beings were murdered over a pendant with a picture of a saint on it. To me, that's bizarre."

"Humans have been killing each other over religion since Jesus was a baby and over other Gods centuries before that," answered the chief, who wrote a few sentences under Eugene's picture. Then he wrote the words "gemstones and violin."

"Did Grandmother Rose purchase gemstones and hide them in the pendant for Eugene? I remember the small silk pouch we found in the bank box. It could have been used for loose gemstones." Jablonsky remarked, looking at Coupe.

"Kate did mention that the gemstones might have been the grandmother's gift of money for his Bar Mitzvah. Annie has tracked down the jewelry store that employed Grandmother Rose. I'll see if they would have records of her buying loose stones. Creative and intriguing thinking by our amateur sleuth," remarked Antoine, complimenting Kate.

Jablonsky frowned at DeVille's praise of Dr. Chambers, whom he liked and admired, but worried over because of her lack of boundaries when it came to the civilian versus police issues and more importantly, safety.

Jablonsky decided to take Antoine along with him to the jewelry store that had employed Grandmother Rose. The store was housed in one of downtown's architecturally significant buildings, the Union Trust. An old-fashioned elevator deposited them directly into the store. They stepped onto old hardwood floors and immediately saw long, rectangular-shaped jewelry cases with polished brass fittings on the corners. There was the faint sound of Vivaldi playing in the background, and the distinctive perfume of wealth hung in the air.

"May I help you?" asked a middle-aged man outfitted in classic Brooks Brothers. Jablonsky flashed his badge, his open-sesame key for acquiring information. "Chief Detective! Is there a problem?"

"No. I'm looking for some information on one of your previous employees, Mrs. Eileen Rose, who unfortunately is now deceased. Is your manager here?"

"I am the manager. Let us go into one of the private viewing rooms." The Brooks Brother suit led them into a medium-sized room where expensive jewelry could be handled out of the range of the glances of other curious clients. The room was lined with artisan-crafted oak wainscoting, and the floors were covered with thick dark gray carpeting. A bank of windows provided a view of the busy downtown streets. The manager poured Jablonsky and Antoine some water from a crystal pitcher and excused himself to find Eileen Rose's employee file. The hushed atmosphere of the room did not invite conversation; Jablonsky and Coupe waited in silence until the manager returned.

"Eileen Rose worked for us for almost twenty years. She had her own clientele—certain customers would only deal with her for either assessing a single gemstone or an already designed piece of jewelry. She was an extremely knowledgeable gemologist; it was a loss to this business when she died so suddenly."

The manager paused, a pause that was pregnant with the unspoken question of, why are you here? Finally, he asked, "What exactly did you want to know about her employment?"

"Did you, or any other of your employees, know if she personally bought some loose gems from your dealers?" Jablonsky didn't care if he was using the correct gemology language or not.

"I didn't know of any such purchase, but that doesn't mean she didn't buy loose gems. Our New York dealers knew and liked her. She easily could have asked them to be on the lookout for certain precious or semi-precious stones, and they would have done so."

"I want to be clear—you are telling me that a purchase wouldn't have had to have gone through your store; it would have been kept between Mrs. Rose and a dealer? I'm not implying any criminal activity here; I'm just trying to discover if she did buy a few stones and who might have sold them to her."

"If there has been no impropriety, why do you want this personal information?" The manager was right to be suspicious.

Jablonsky uttered the ubiquitous answer. "It is just a line of inquiry we are pursuing in an active case. I assure you again, neither your shop nor Mrs. Rose are being accused of anything illegal."

"I will take you at your word, Chief Detective. The diamond dealer that she worked with the most is Izzy Zaideman. Let me check my contacts." The manager took out his cell phone and scrolled through his list. "Here he is. Use my name and Eileen Rose's name to introduce yourself. If you announce that you are a police detective, you may be met with hostility. Diamond brokers are sometimes accused of many things, most of which are not true."

The chief and Antoine thanked him for his time. Back at the precinct, Jablonsky made the call, mentioning the manager and Mrs. Rose first, then his title. With typical New York directness and a Yiddish accent, Mr. Zaideman immediately asked what the chief wanted.

"About ten years ago, did Eileen Rose ask you to find her a few loose gemstones that she wanted to buy for herself, not for the store?"

"Yes. I remember it well. Her grandson Eugene was having his Bar Mitzvah, and she wanted to give him gemstones instead of money. I thought it was crazy and told her so. Give the boy some cash, I said. But no, she wanted gemstones."

"Well, I agree that gemstones instead of cash is an unusual gift. Do you remember what stones she bought?" the chief asked.

"Absolutely! I'm an elephant in the memory department. It was two diamonds, one yellow and one white, for portable cash if he ever needed it. A citrine, which was Eugene's birthstone. An aquamarine, for tranquility. That's how she put it. So, I got her four good quality stones and she paid me. End of story." His tone held the punctuation mark.

"Mr. Zaideman. Would you have put the stones in a small silk pouch?" Jablonsky wanted to tie the pouch they found at the bank to Grandmother Rose's purchase.

"Now that I do not remember. It could be I gave them to her in a pouch, or she may have stored them that way."

"Do you still have the invoice?" Jablonsky knew he was really reaching with that request.

Izzy Zaideman answered him in a tone filled with contempt. "What invoice? Two old friends made a deal. I gave her the stones; she paid me. Done and done." Jablonsky thought he could hear Izzy wiping his hands together.

"You have been so very helpful. May I call again if I have more questions?"

"Of course! And, Chief Detective, you find the bastard who murdered her grandson. That's right, we heard about it, even here in New York. A very horrible business done by a very bad man."

"I agree. We will get him. You can count on it." Jablonsky ended the call thinking that if he ever needed to buy a diamond, Izzy Zaideman would be his man.

Sarah Braithwaite and Johnny wore cotton gloves as they handled the antique violin. Her skin was glowing with the sheen of excitement. She turned the violin over and over, closely examining the finish on the wood, the curl of the scroll, the nut, and the bridge.

"Is there a bow? I'd like to play it to hear its tone," she requested.

"No. Just the violin. Sorry."

"No worries, I brought one with me." Sarah took off her gloves and delicately lifted the violin and played a bit of Mozart's Violin Concerto No.4 in D major. Like the song of the Northern Mockingbird, the violin's sound was simultaneously full-bodied and heartbreakingly sweet. She and Johnny looked at each other in delight.

"It could be an Andrea Amati. I am not qualified to appraise it. You would have to go to one of the specialists at the big auction houses and in addition, have a violinist of, say, Nicola Benedetti's ability, and I might add, ear, assess it as well." Sarah gently laid the instrument on the table and stepped back. "I can't believe I'm seeing and touching it—centuries of musicians have played this violin. It is staggering to think about." Johnny excused himself for a few minutes;

when he returned, both the chief and Antoine were in the conference room, grilling Sarah.

"Is this the first time you have seen this instrument?" Jablonsky asked.

Sarah went on immediate alert. "Am I being accused of something here? Do you think I stole this?"

"Did you?" The chief locked eyes with her. "Given the situation with Zane, I'm not sure what to believe about you."

"I did not steal this violin, but I have seen others like it in Cremona. And yes, Zane was along on that trip. You are the ones who asked me to come here. Hey, do I need an attorney?"

"You have a right to one. We are just trying to find out if this violin was stolen, smuggled, or both. You study antique violins—that is why Professor McCarthy asked you here."

"If you found this violin among Zane Davies' collection, then he is the one you must speak to." Her green eyes flashed as she pulled herself up to her full height.

"Would you have known if this violin had been placed in one of your suitcases when you traveled back to the States?" The chief cocked his head to one side, indicating that he didn't trust her. Sarah's eyes filled with tears.

"I might not have known. If he bought it illegally and smuggled it out of Italy, I DIDN'T KNOW ABOUT IT. I can't help you, Chief Detective. And further, if you want to speak to me again, it will be with an attorney and my parents. Am I free to leave?" The young Sarah shook with anger, but she did not back down from defending herself from the chief's accusation

Jablonsky admired her grit and that she did not succumb to the misconception that answering more questions without an attorney would be a sign of innocence. "You are free to go, for now, Ms. Braithwaite. Don't leave the city."

Jablonsky asked the question on everyone's mind. "Do you think it is possible to trace these items to the original owner if that owner doesn't want to be found?"

"No. Private collectors are private people. They don't want transactions followed by any governing agency of any country. That's my honest opinion," answered Johnny

"What have you found in the *Catalogue Raisonné* on these artists?" Jablonsky was getting used to the lingo of the art world.

"I found nothing. These works have never been noted, even in the most comprehensive catalogs. It's a stunning find for the art world, but the whereabouts of the glass bead necklace and pendant remains unknown." Johnny threw up his hands at the mystery, then continued his cataloging work; the chief and Antoine left the room.

Jablonsky perched on the edge of Annie Lemon's desk, starring at the murder board. "Zane Davies continues to lie to us. How did he have enough money to buy canvases like the ones we've found?"

"Perhaps it was a trade—I'll give you a gem incrusted gold monstrance if you give me three Winslow Homers." Antoine was only half joking.

"I've talked with the DA. If we find even one police report on any of these art objects as being stollen, either in this country or another, we can get Zane and Joseph Davies for possessing stolen goods, antiquity theft, smuggling, and tax evasion—not to mention the international implications. Tax evasion has real teeth in terms of criminal charges. Send some officers to pick up both of them."

CHAPTER 25

JABLONSKY WAS THINKING through his interview approach to Zane and Joseph Davies when Antoine called him. "Chief! I just found out that Joseph Davies' company keeps a small jet at the old county airport. It took off about three hours ago—flight plans were filed to Miami, and from there, to Brazil. I'm at the county airport now."

"Has it landed in Miami?" In an uncharacteristic show of temper, Jablonsky slammed his hand down on the desk. Even through the cell phone, Antoine heard the sound, and knew he might be in career-ending trouble.

"Sorry, chief. The jet landed in Miami, refueled, and left for Brazil about fifteen minutes ago."

"Damn it, DeVille! How did you and the team miss this jet? I don't care if it was registered in the Pope's name, we should have had it locked down. This was a big mistake on your part. At least Brazil has extradition to the US. Who was on the plane?" Jablonsky paced around his office—did the son slip out of his grasp?

"Only Zane and a pilot. Hardly any suitcases. The necklace and pendant are small enough to fit in an overnight bag or even a pocket—if he has it, he might have taken it with him. I'm sorry, chief."

"Sorry doesn't cut it! I'll deal with you later." Jablonsky abruptly ended the call and yelled out into the bullpen.

"Lemon! Get in here!" Once she was there, he growled his accusations. "Did you know that the Davies company owned a corporate jet? You did? You knew about the jet?" Disbelief filled the chief's face.

"I found out about it early on, when we were looking at the company. It's in my report. Because you cautioned Zane and his father not to leave the city, I assumed we were covered." Lemon defended her reasoning, but at this point, she knew all the chief heard was excuses.

"Let me get this straight. You thought a suspect, which we are investigating for smuggling and possibly murder, was going to abide by my caution? The result of your naïveté is that a pilot flew Zane Davies to Miami about three hours ago, refueled, and now is on his way to Brazil. Get the Miami Chief of Detectives on the phone, right now," barked Jablonsky. Lemon was able to reach that chief without much delay, at least it was something she had gotten right.

"Thanks for taking my call, Chief Santos. A perp is using his father's private business jet to escape prosecution for smuggling and the possible murder of a young man and a priest. Yeah, that's right, a priest. Can you suggest a quick solution to nabbing him at Sao Paulo airport? You have an FBI agent who is already there on other business? That's great. Detective Lemon can give you the details of the flight—the young man's name is Zane Davies. Let's see if we can get him back here to Pittsburgh. Thanks so much. I'll wait to hear from you or your FBI contact." Lemon stood in the doorway, not shying away from the conflict.

"It takes a little over six hours non-stop direct from Miami to Sao Paolo. Chief Santos said that it is a happy coincidence that two FBI agents are in San Paolo on another assignment and would be able to board Zane's plane when it lands. If they are successful, an agent will fly back with him to Miami and then on to Pittsburgh. Zane wouldn't be here until tomorrow. Antoine just brought in the father. Mr. Davies has his attorney with him."

"Okay. Where is Coupe?"

"He's waiting in the audio-visual room." Lemon hustled out of the chief's office, glad to be out of range of fire.

Joseph Davies' attorney spoke first. "There was no reason to show up at Mr. Davies' place of business with the black and whites. He would have come here of his own accord."

"Oh really? Would that be before or after he put his son on the corporate jet to Brazil? It might interest you to know that two FBI agents will be waiting in San Paolo to turn that jet around and fly Zane back here." Jablonsky threw a gotcha look at the attorney, who obviously didn't know that Zane had left the States.

"Yeah. That's what your client has been up to." Jablonsky abruptly changed the subject. "Let's talk about the art objects that we found in those safes, shall we?"

"As my attorney told you, those safes aren't my personal ones, they belong to the business." Joseph Davies pulled down both sides of his mouth in a nasty sneer.

"These art objects are yours, all right. You must prove to me, and the District Attorney, that you purchased them, and then paid any requisite duty or any other tax, on them. If you don't prove legitimate ownership, you and your son will be prosecuted for a whole host of things related to art theft and tax evasion. That is not to mention the charge of impeding a police investigation and helping a suspect flee the jurisdiction. Let's hear it, Davies. Give me the story."

The chief watched Joseph Davies' sunburned face and neck turn almost cyanotic in color. He thought the man might have a heart attack, so tense and agitated did he look. Finally, Joseph spoke.

"If any FBI agent touches a hair on my son's head, I'll kill him!" With physical quickness that belied his age, Davies leaped out of his chair, screaming and shaking his fists at the chief. "That's right, Jablonsky, I'll kill you or anyone else that gets in the way. That's my flesh and blood you are fooling with, my only son. Two men have been murdered! Two men who knew my son and you haven't caught anyone yet. Do you think for one minute I'm going to wait until someone murders Zane over some damn piece of art?"

The attorney maneuvered himself in front of his client just as several officers rushed into the room. "Get ahold of yourself, Joe. You are threatening a chief of police, you jackass. Sit down!" The tidal wave of testosterone in the room slowly receded as Davies forced himself back into the chair. His breathing remained almost a pant—it was clear that he couldn't get ahold of himself.

"My apologies for Mr. Davies' actions and threats. He, of course, does not mean them. His son is very precious to him." The chief knew that the attorney was just doing his job, but his smarmy apology still rankled.

"Father Carlotti was precious to his mother and father, just like Eugene Rose was precious to his parents," was Jablonsky's irony-filled retort.

It was the attorney who commented. "Of course, that would be absolutely true. But my client had nothing to do with either of those men's deaths. May we move on now?"

"Does your son have a sixteenth-century glass bead necklace and pendant with him on that plane?"

"Not that I know of," Davies answered through clenched teeth.

"From whom did your son purchase the canvases and other items we found in your safe?"

"Those things do not belong to me." Joe Davies' jaw was now so tight that he sounded like a girl from New England who was named Muffy.

"Mr. Davies. Have you or any of your employees been in contact with the pilot flying Zane to Brazil in your company jet."

Joseph Davies made a sort of clucking sound. "Of course, I've been in contact with the pilot. I called him as soon as your goon squad showed up at my business." The chief could see that Davies was losing control of himself again—his eyes practically bugged out of their sockets and he leaned forward across the table.

"I don't care how many FBI agents you send; you will never find my boy! I own several fabricating plants in Brazil—those workmen will do anything for me. You are a moron, Jablonsky, you hear me? In fact, you are the gold standard for a moron. You can't even find two murderers in this city, what makes you think that you can find my son in a South American country!" Davies shouted.

The chief stood. "Mr. Davies. The first time I interviewed you, you indirectly threatened me. When Father Carlotti showed up at your home, you came out of the front door with a loaded rifle that you kept trained on him, even though the police and I had given you the command to drop it. Now today, you have threatened to kill me, which unlike your attorney, I know you are more than willing to act upon."

The attorney tried again to reframe his client's behavior, but the chief was having none of it. Jablonsky snapped his fingers into the air so the people in the media room were alerted, then officers entered the room again, and this time they handcuffed Mr. Davies.

Jablonsky gave his orders. "Take him to lock-up. The charge is that he represents a credible threat to my life and has aided and abetted a murder suspect in fleeing our jurisdiction." Jablonsky turned to the attorney. "If your client doesn't come up with sales receipts, tax receipts, and provenance for these confiscated art objects, he will be charged with the possession of stolen goods, possession of stolen antiquities, tax evasion, and then the case will be turned over to the Italian courts to decide about the violin. There is also the issue of aiding and abetting. Your client is in real trouble."

When the squad had gathered back in the bullpen, Antoine voiced the question on everyone's mind. "Why would Joseph Davies choose to send his son into exile when it was probable that the self-defense position would stand for having shot Father Carlotti?"

Jablonsky offered his analysis. "Mr. Davies is a man who wants certainty. We all agree that there was a very strong case to be made for self-defense in terms of Zane, but Davies is correct in that we still do not have Eugene's or Carlotti's murderer in custody. If Zane didn't kill either one, and he has the goods, he is in significant danger. And there was the issue of smuggling charges. I think Joe Davies fears that Zane has been lying to him all along about his art collecting business."

"Well, being exiled in South America isn't going to be any picnic, even if you are the boss' son." Antoine was relieved that the chief hadn't immediately dressed him down for having missed the fact of the corporate jet, but he knew it was coming.

"We have to wait a few more hours for the plane to land in Sao Paolo. If we can search it, perhaps we will find the neckless and pendant. Coupe, with me." Annie Lemon and the other detectives lowered their heads and swiveled their chairs around, pretending to look at computer screens, glad not to be in Antoine's shoes.

Jablonsky closed his office door. “Lemon told me that she knew about the corporate plane early on in the investigation, and that it was in her report. How is it that she knew and you didn’t? How is it that you didn’t read her notes? You are supposed to be my number one! That means you get all the perks and all the responsibilities that go with it. This is the second case lately in which you have missed an important detail. Get it together DeVille, or you’ll be back in New Orleans dodging hurricanes.”

Coupe didn’t even try to defend himself. He waited silently to see if the chief was finished with him, which he wasn’t. “I want you to go over all the material again and give me some new direction in Eugene Rose’s murder and Father Carlotti’s murder. Now, get out of my sight.”

CHAPTER 26

EARLY THE NEXT MORNING, Johnny was excitedly talking about the found art objects as he, Kate, and Bourbon Ball worked through the obstacle course at Upper Frick city park. BB did not participate in the sit-ups or push-ups, but he wagged his otter tail back and forth as a friendly greeting to the other dogs who passed by them.

"While I was working on cataloging the art from Mr. Davies' safe, here's what I overheard." Usually, it was Kate filling him in on new clues, so Johnny was rightfully proud of telling her about Zane escaping on the corporate jet. He hung from one of the high parallel bars, and hand over hand, moved from one side to the other.

Kate stopped mid-walk across the balance beam. "Why would Davies do that? At most, Zane would be prosecuted for smuggling—he believed he shot Carlotti in self-defense. It doesn't make sense. Does anyone know if he took the necklace and pendant with him?"

"No. No one knows. Do you think he has it?" Johnny swung his long body off the bars and petted BB, waiting for Kate to finish her obstacle.

"I think it is still here in Pittsburgh, which means several people remain at risk for intimidation of some sort. I worry about Mr. and Mrs. Rose's safety—I don't believe they know where it is either, but apparently, the murderer isn't privy to that information." Kate dropped down on the grass and began to do ten push-ups, in spite of the fact that Bourbon Ball positioned himself so he could lick her face on the up stroke.

"Let's finish the last obstacle. I have some advisees to see today, but before I go to the office, I want to reread Dr. Aubert's report." After the three of them raced a quarter mile to the park entrance, Bourbon Ball jumped into the back seat of Kate's SUV, and they drove the short distance to her home. "I want to focus all my attention on this report. I'm going to shower and change—will you make some coffee for us? Thank you," she said, rumpling Johnny's hair as she passed by him.

Kate printed out the appraisal, along with the multiple pictures included in the report.

She and Johnny poured over every word. Aubert did verify that the beads came from a glass artist on the island of Murano and had all the hallmarks of being a sixteenth-century piece. She also confirmed that the glass roundel opened in the back. Aubert's investigations supported Eugene's later research that it originally belonged to the La Rosa family, although she suspected the pendant was added later. She also thought the face painted on the medallion was based on Botticelli's fresco of *St. Augustine In His Study.*

Kate pushed herself away from the computer screen, sipped her coffee, then remarked, "There is no mention of any gemstones. I can only think that Grandmother Rose put them in at a later time or, that they were to accompany the gift separately."

"Aubert puts a range on what it would bring at auction; take a look at this number. It could go higher, depending on the group of people bidding on that particular day." Johnny softly whistled his appreciation of the three to five million figure.

"And," Kate added, "she refers to it as the Rose necklace and pendant. Pretty wonderful. I'm sorry, neither Eugene nor his Bubbe lived to hear it called that. The important clue is that someone else knew about its existence."

Kate called Jablonsky's private cell number and told him about Edwina Ballard and Dr. Aubert. He asked her to come to the station with the report, but to Kate's mind, he sounded distracted. She went to the university, saw her advisees, then swung over to the Fine Arts building and picked up Johnny. Since he hadn't finished evaluating the found art objects, he decided to ride down to the precinct with her. Once they arrived at the station, Kate understood why the chief had sounded distracted. The Davies' corporate jet was due to arrive at Sao Paolo anytime.

Jablonsky was on the phone with the FBI agents waiting to board the plane. He put the call on the speaker setting so everyone gathered in the bullpen could hear. Kate was surprised that the chief allowed her and Johnny to stay—she chalked it up to his preoccupation with the situation. The lead agent was speaking.

"The plane has hit the tarmac and has stopped taxiing. We are headed to it right now." The group could hear out-of-breathe running and the announcement of their presence. "This is the FBI. We are here for Zane Davies and are armed. Open the door! Open the door!" The mesmerized group could hear someone pounding on metal.

Finally, the door must have opened because the agent gave his command. "Zane Davies. You are to come with us back to the United States. Put your hands behind you. No! Stop! Do not run! We do not want to hurt you." Everyone in the bullpen heard an aggravated agent shout that Zane had catapulted himself over the railings of the portable airplane steps and apparently was running on the tarmac. "I'm firing a warning shot. Stop!"

Jablonsky looked at his detectives and shook his head in anger. "That stupid boy!"

There was the sound of gunfire, then there was silence. Finally, the agent spoke. "Chief. I'm afraid Mr. Davies tried to escape, and we had to fire at him. We made sure only to graze him. We will get him medical care and then transport him back to the States." Jablonsky took the phone off the speaker setting and spoke to the FBI agent privately. He returned to the bullpen and gave an update.

"The FBI will send us the video from the body cam later. Any thoughts?" His eyes narrowed as he looked around the room at his talented detectives. No one spoke, so Kate stepped forward.

"Would this be a good time to talk about what I have learned from Edwina Ballard and Dr. Isabelle Aubert?" A look of shock crossed everyone's face. This civilian dared to speak during this moment of heightened tension in the bullpen? Jablonsky smiled at Kate's chutzpah. "Go ahead, Kate. Fill the team in on what your good detective work unearthed." Lemon and Antoine felt the sting of Jablonsky's backhanded slap.

Kate succinctly summarized her conversation with Elise Ballard at the Corning Glass Museum, then went on to describe Dr. Aubert's appraisal. "I think this gives weight to my theory that someone knew and even saw the necklace and pendant on that day ten years ago. Whomever this person is, I believe them to be the murderer of both Eugene Rose and Carlotti."

"Why do you think the glass center didn't have the appraisal on file? Were they holding it back for some reason?" Annie Lemon asked.

"I asked Dr. Aubert the same question. She answered that it had been a private appraisal—it wasn't an appraisal for a piece of glass that the center would keep in its collection. She sent the report to Grandmother Rose but never heard from her again. I believe this appraisal answers some questions."

Lemon pursued Kate's line of reasoning. "Did Aubert mention any gemstones?" Kate shook her head no.

Jablonsky walked over to the murder board and drew an empty outline of a face. "This is who we are after. I want everyone to go through their notes again and come up with either alternatives to Dr. Chambers' theory, or a theory that builds off of it so that we can nab this perpetrator. Detectives, you are all skating on thin ice! Get your arms around the evidence. Coupe and Lemon, with me."

Once they were in his office, he continued. "Sit down, you two." Jablonsky stared out of his office window at the shower that was pelting the warm fall streets, raising a fine mist of steam; the sizzle of the water on the asphalt suited his mood. He turned and addressed his two in-the-dog-house detectives.

"Here is my theory of both murders, and here is my plan."

Antoine poured over all the reports and bits of information that had been amassed on the Rose/Carlotti murders. He knew his job was on the line, so he hunkered down and reread everything, then drove the short distance to the glass center to do two things—walk the scene again and reinterview the two people who had been working there ten years ago.

Andy Ormsby was assisting a glass artist in the hot shop. Antoine had never seen a hot glass object being made and found himself transfixed by the process. The artisan placed very thin strips of cane laid close together on a ceramic plate and then rolled them up into optic twists. It seemed an impossible task, but in the end, a very tall, exquisitely graceful pitcher with white lines curving around it from base to top had been formed. Ormsby handled the vase delicately, placing it in the annealing oven. As he wiped his sweaty face, he caught sight of DeVille.

"Detective! No one told me you were here." Ormsby swept his arms wide to indicate how exciting the activity of glassmaking was. "This is where all the creativity happens. What can I do for you?"

"Two things. I wanted to walk through this space again, particularly the area where Eugene had been working. Then, I wanted to reinterview the two older employees who were here ten years ago—if that is possible." Andy immediately showed him the oven, benches, and all the glass working tools. Cautiously and thoroughly, the detective examined everything once again. He took note of where the entrances and exits to the space were, and how someone could get at the tools unseen and leave unseen. He drew a picture of where someone could hide out of view of the students working on their pieces.

"Detective DeVille, the staffers you wanted to see, are in the conference room. I'll show you there—take your time with them."

Antoine flipped through his notes as they walked. "I have a list of ten interns, about one a year, who have come and gone from the center. I'll ask your administrators about them; you were one of the earliest of the interns, correct?"

"That's right. The center had just started the intern program. I came as a student for about twelve months and then returned to New Zealand. As I mentioned before, no student intern is privy to any of the workings of the board or the development department. Interns are just poorly paid gofers!" Ormsby chuckled at the truism.

"Did you know the other interns?"

"Only the one who was here before me and the one who came after. I met them but didn't really know them—like I said, I was here, and then I left the country. The other interns also left for different positions at other glass centers. I can't imagine what reason any of them would have to come back to Pittsburgh to murder Eugene Rose and hit me over the head." Ormsby's head wound was still quite visible, but Antoine didn't mention it. They arrived at the conference room, so Andy left Coupe to his work.

Neither of the two employees could remember any new details from the day grandmother Rose visited, although they did know who Dr. Isabelle Aubert was, but didn't know her personally. There were jokes about how several of the interns thought they were already "great artists," an attitude that made for difficulty in managing them.

"I'm going to ask an indiscreet question—how was your now boss Andy, as an intern?" Everybody connected to the situation was still a suspect, including Ormsby.

The one older woman answered right away. "He was a dream. He had that cute New Zealand accent and excellent manners. Andy was like a good nephew who came to stay for an extended vacation." While Antoine knew this was a political answer, he noted the names of the more "entitled" interns. As he wrote, there was a familiar surname—James Lupinski. Father Lupinski, James Lupinski, it can't be a coincidence. He could have kicked himself for missing this detail before.

"James Lupinski? You mention him as one of the more entitled interns. Do you remember anything else about him?"

"I do," remarked the same woman. "Talented and hardworking, and yes, a bit full of himself. After he interned here, I think he went to Washington State to the famous Pilchuck Glass School. He might still be there. I have their telephone number. Use my name, and they will be more forthcoming."

"Do you remember anything about his family? I mean, was he from Pittsburgh?" Antoine still couldn't believe that he hadn't made this connection until now.

"Sorry. I don't remember. I can chase down his application, but you'd get further by Googling him or looking on Facebook. His biography would be somewhere online."

"That's exactly what I'm going to do. Thanks, you both have been really helpful." As he wrote his notes, Coupe became distracted by the sound of police sirens. "What is that? Excuse me."

DeVille had that creepy sense that something bad was about to happen, so he ran out the front door of the building, where he saw groups of police cars speeding down Penn Avenue—the swoosh of the air as they passed made his arm hair stand in protest. In the distance, he could see a plume of black smoke filling the air and was so alarmed that he went into the small café at the center, demanding they turn on the local television channel. A "Breaking News" scroll crossed the screen; a car had exploded at the police station.

"*Sainte merde*!" he exclaimed in his New Orleans French.

Jablonsky's car was blown apart while parked in his designated spot outside the precinct. An all-hands-to-the-pump response immediately began—a hunt that would supersede the ongoing one for the murderer of Eugene Rose and Father Carlotti.

The chief was pacing back and forth in the bullpen, his broad shoulders hunched over, his fisted hand to his forehead. "This bomb is designed to slow down our search for Rose and Carlotti's killer. I know it in my bones." DeVille, who had driven back to the precinct never leaving second gear, had rarely seen the chief so visibly frustrated.

Antoine anticipated the chief's next question. "Joseph Davies is in lock-up. As far as we know, none of our officers have told him that Zane was wounded or that he is on his way back to the States. That doesn't mean he didn't get the information from the cellmate underground."

"If Davies wanted me dead, his goons would have set the bomb to explode on ignition—not just a bomb that blows up my car. This is a warning and a diversion." The chief continued to pace.

"Here is the security film from three different vantage points around your parking spot," said Lemon, starting the video. Everyone in the bullpen stopped to look at the screen, noting the smallest details. She played the video of the hours leading up to the explosion, stopping and reversing several times. Eight people had walked by, and several of the detectives recognized one or more of them. A heavy-boned man, tall and wide, wearing a knitted Steeler cap pulled down low on the face, walked past the car, and placed a bag down by the trunk as he ostensibly suffered a sneezing attack. He then walked on, minus the bag.

Annie Lemon jumped out of her seat. "That's the guy! That's Deuce Lewis, the man whom some of Davies' employees said did under-the-table jobs for Mr. Davies."

Jablonsky stated the obvious. "There was no attempt to hide the placement of the bomb—this person and his handler knew the cameras would catch his movements. Let's get a sketch of him out to everyone, including the press. Unfortunately, any perceived attempt on my life will be big news—get ready for the press to hound you." The chief turned to face Coupe and pounded one fist into the other, snarling out his command. "You and Lemon bring me Deuce Lewis!"

CHAPTER 27

THE POLICE QUIETLY ENTERED the Jumping Frog Trailer Park on foot—no cars with flashing lights, but plenty of arms. They had received information from one of their street snitches that the man who presumably planted the bomb in the chief's automobile rented a trailer on the outskirts of Oakmont, a small community on the Allegheny River. Every cop present wanted this guy and wanted him badly. If someone could get that close to Jablonsky, the everyday officer knew that they were that much more vulnerable.

A phalanx of police fanned out to surround the trailer; they could hear a man inside screaming at someone on the telephone. "You get me out of here today! You never said I was planting a bomb at the Chief of Detective's car! I would never have done that job—if I stay around here, I'm a dead man." There was silence for a minute, and then the man replied. "I'll meet you at the diner in Blawnox. Have the money and some new identification. Don't be late."

The sounds of things being thrown into a duffle bag echoed through the metal trailer, then the man moved the shabby curtains aside and peered out. All of the officers remained hidden and silent. Obviously thinking he was alone, the man stepped outside, then turned to lock the trailer door.

"Deuce Lewis, this is the police. Don't move! We have you surrounded. Throw down your weapon, put your hands in the air, and keep them there," commanded Antoine. Lemon quickly moved to Lewis and cuffed him; she picked up his gun and grabbed his cell phone.

"Don't shoot me!" pleaded Lewis in a high-pitched whiny voice. The dissonance between this big muscled-up man and his girlish voice caused Antoine and Lemon to squelch giggles.

"Okay, everyone, stand down. Let's get this scumbag to the station," commanded Antoine. The officers couldn't wait to do just that. Nabbing the perp in a high-profile manhunt always made everyone feel that, for a brief moment, there was justice in the world.

"We got him, chief. Lemon is already looking through his cell phone to see if we can trace the number he called right before we grabbed him." Antoine put the employee statements on Jablonsky's desk. "These are the most direct descriptions of Deuce Lewis' relationship to Joseph Davies. It seems that Lewis worked for Davies for years; some employees knew he did 'unofficial' jobs for the boss, but no one knew exactly what that entailed."

Lemon entered the office. "We have confirmed that Lewis spoke with one of the factory managers; that manager was picked up at a local diner in Blawnox, holding cash and new identity papers for Deuce. These guys are farm league crooks; they didn't even realize that Joe Davies was using the bombing of your car as a diversion to take the attention off of Zane and put it on looking for them."

Jablonsky liked the focus his two detectives were finally showing. "Good work. Has he been Mirandized? Okay." The chief walked into the interview room confident he had a solid case against Lewis and, through him, to Joseph Davies.

"Mr. Lewis. Several employees from the Davies Tool and Dye Company have confirmed that you routinely performed certain jobs for Joseph Davies, on the down low, that is. We also have a statement from your friend whom we nabbed at the diner that it was you who planted the bomb by my vehicle. I would like you to tell me who ordered that bomb."

Deuce Lewis was possessed of a jowly, meaty face with heavy-lidded eyes that had the stare of a rhinoceros slightly floating its head above water. His fat fingers patted his beer belly; his endomorphic body belied his reputation as someone who could get physical—could he really move that fast? Finally, in his fluty voice, Deuce responded with a single sentence.

"Who says I planted a bomb?" Just like Antoine and Lemon had been, the chief was taken aback by the sound of this bruiser's soprano voice, and like Daffy Duck, he lisped on certain words. One by one, Jablonsky placed the photos from the security camera, the signed statements from the Davies' employees, and the affidavit from the man at the diner on the table in front of Lewis.

"Come on, Deuce. We have you. We have all the evidence we need to put you in jail. Don't be stupid. Cooperate now, and things might go easier for you. Otherwise, it's at least obstruction of justice—you have a long sheet for other offenses, Deuce. Help yourself out—give me the name." Jablonsky had seen many criminals, some smart, some stupid, but this perp was winning the prize for the dopiest.

"You telling me that you arrested Jimmy James at the diner? Well, if you did, you already know who ordered the bomb. I ain't obstructing nothin'," Deuce replied, hissing the 'th' and staring at the chief from under his hooded eyelids.

"I want you to say it." Jablonsky snapped. "Say the name for the record!"

Deuce Lewis was startled by the ferocity of the chief's command. He continued to take his time considering it, slowly raising and lowering his large eyelids. "Yeah, okay, it was Joseph Davies. He was angry that you were after Zane, his son. He wanted to, you know, to make you blink, so to speak. I didn't make the bomb; I just dropped it behind your car. We knew you weren't in it. So, that's something; you're still alive, ain't ya?" Deuce's baby voice and his hissing s's made his statements cartoonish. Jablonsky lowered his head for a minute to dispel the image of Daffy.

"Planting a bomb is a serious criminal charge, Deuce, and planting one at the Chief of Detective's car will get you prison time, not just jail, but prison, whether you made the device or not. All of Joseph Davies' money won't protect you now."

"Yeah, yeah." Deuce's rhinoceros expression became one of disdain, even disinterest; he closed his heavy-lidded eyes again and snorted. He had served time before but was unaware of what awaited him in a federal prison.

The chief couldn't even muster a response to the man's ignorance of the seriousness of what he had done, how Davies had used him, and that he had been caught on camera doing it. Jablonsky gathered up the statements and the security photos.

"Write it all down, Deuce, then these officers will take you to booking." Jablonsky walked out of the room, knowing that because of the utter stupidity of this lisping perp, it was just luck that he was alive.

Zane had arrived back in Pittsburgh guarded by an FBI officer and had been taken to the hospital for observation. His wound was superficial and would heal, but he was shaken to the core that he had been shot, and more importantly, that his father was in jail. As much as Zane sometimes feared him, he also relied on him; his father had been a kind of a fixer when it came to Zane's indiscretions; *there is probably no way he can fix this,* thought the newly-minted reflective son.

Young Davies had not seen his father since he had been brought back to Pittsburgh. When DeVille and the chief sat down in his hospital room, he asked them if his father knew he was back. "No," was all the response he got.

"Does he know I was shot?"

Jablonsky shook his head.

The chief had the impression that Zane realized he was on his own, and that realization engendered a change in his attitude toward the police. He became a young man drained of the arrogant posture of an entitled know-it-all; Zane decided to tell the story of the art objects hidden at the factory safes.

"I let it be known in the art underground that I would be interested in undocumented canvases of American Expressionists and would either pay top dollar for them or make a trade. It was the way I acquired the other objects. There is a healthy business of trading in art and antiquities that is off any country's radar—I simply took advantage of it."

"Do you have a list of who the sellers were?"

"No. There was always a middleman—I never knew who the actual collectors were. I can give you the names of the go-betweens."

"How did your father pay for these items? There are no unusual bank records of large withdrawals of cash." Sitting on either side of Zane's bed, Jablonsky and DeVille both had their small paper notebooks out, taking notes.

"He can move cash around through his business. I actually don't know how he and the accountants do it—I was never privy to their maneuvers, and I don't have a head for that kind of financial detail. I just received the cash, paid the middleman, and took the goods."

"Was Sarah Braithwaite involved in helping you acquire the antique violin?" It was Antoine who asked the question, not the chief. Coupe was never convinced of her innocence.

"Not in the way you think. She took me around when she was at the violin museum in Italy. I spoke to the local antique dealers on my own and happened to hit pay dirt with someone who needed cash and was willing to part with the violin. Lots of old monied families struggle to keep their villas in repair and still pay the taxman." Zane's eyes suddenly and unexpectedly filled with tears. "Chief Jablonsky, when can I see my father?"

"We will set it up soon. I want you to write everything down, all the purchases, the amounts paid, the dates, and these middlemen. By the way, did Eugene Rose know what you were doing?"

"He figured it out and was really angry. Eugene would never do anything against the law. He confronted me about my buying and selling off the books; that's what we argued about." It was the first time that the chief heard anything resembling guilt from Zane.

"Eugene showed you the photos of the glass bead necklace and the pendant. What did you do with that information?"

"For a long time, nothing. Father Carlotti sensed that I knew about the items, so he began to pester me."

"Did Eugene know where the glass necklace and pendant were?"

"I think he suspected who had it, but he never told me. He was in the process of gathering clues."

"Zane, did you murder him?"

"No, I did not murder Eugene. I'm guilty of many things, but not that."

"Did you murder Father Carlotti?"

"No. I did not murder him. Chief, you know he's crazy." Zane paused, then, in a little boy voice, asked the essential question. "Do you think Eugene and Carlotti's search for that necklace and pendant was really why they were murdered?"

"You are well acquainted with collectors, Zane. Is there a limit to what any serious collector would do in order to acquire a one-of-a-kind, sixteenth-century Murano ruby glass necklace and pendant?" The young man dropped his head to his chest, acknowledging the truth of the chief's statement. Jablonsky had to give it to Kate Chambers when it came to motive; she was right about the collector's obsessive drive to possess.

"Father Carlotti was different from the usual rabid collector. Those items held spiritual significance for him. He felt he needed them to continue to be faithful to his vows." The chief's statement fell on deaf ears with Zane. Shifting gears, he inquired about the gemstones.

"Do you know anything about a cache of loose gemstones that Eugene might have gotten from his grandmother?"

Zane looked completely caught off guard by the question. "No, no, I didn't. Are they part of the whole La Rosa family inheritance?" Jablonsky didn't answer him.

"Do you know a man who works for your father by the name of Deuce Lewis?" Jablonsky watched Zane's face closely.

"No … No, I've never heard that name. Frankly, I rarely go to the plant or the offices. That's my father's domain—I don't fit in there. And I really don't think he wants me there, you know, the artsy gay son." A wry expression crossed Zane's face as he looked down at his delicate fingers.

Antoine, who hadn't had time to tell his boss about the Lupinski connection, spoke. "What can you tell us about

Father Lupinski?" The chief was surprised at the question but could see that Coupe had something on his mind.

"Nothing, really. He and Carlotti were long-time pals." Zane looked at a loss.

"Did Lupinski grow up here in Pittsburgh?"

"I think so. But I'm not sure. It was Carlotti who had the Italy connection. Lupinski was the kind of guy who rode shotgun for his friend. He never expressed any interest in art when I was present. I don't know anything else." Zane began to talk philosophy.

"You know how in Buddhism they teach you the theory of non-attachment? Well, I would say that in the world of collecting, you should be careful about desiring certain objects because that desire can lead you into doing things you never thought you would do. You want to possess the object, but it ends up possessing you." Zane looked at the detectives to see if they understood his point.

"The only philosophy I care about is the detective's philosophy—it's the one where I catch the murderer of two human beings. And, I'm plenty attached to that action," Jablonsky said.

Zane was a known liar and a master manipulator—mentioning the tenets of Buddhism wouldn't get him anywhere with Jablonsky. If the chief knew about cognitive dissonance, he didn't bring it up.

"We are keeping an officer on the door, so there is no chance you can attempt another run. When your physician releases you, you will be charged on numerous and serious criminal counts: fleeing the jurisdiction, tax evasion, impeding a criminal investigation, lying to the police, and possibly to the FBI—which is a federal crime—smuggling—I could go on. Zane, you will need a good criminal attorney.

The Customs Enforcement Department has already been notified about the art objects."

Back at the precinct, Antoine and Annie Lemon had researched James Lupinski online, and sure enough, there he was, a teacher at the Pilchuck School of Glass. Coupe immediately called and was able to speak directly with the man. It was an informative conversation that he shared with the chief while he made changes to the murder board. He hoped catching this detail would get him out of the doghouse.

"James Lupinski is the nephew of our Father Lupinski. He was an intern at the Pittsburgh glass center right after Andy Ormsby's year tenure. James knows Ormsby, but from his position as the head of the center rather than as a young intern. Other than this familial connection, there doesn't seem to be much else." Antoine wrote a few sentences under Father Lupinski's picture.

"How did he describe Ormsby?" The chief was curious about any backstory on Andy.

"The nephew said that he found Andy to be ambitious, but more to climb the ladder at a glass center than to become a great artist. That impression jives with what Kate said about motive and Ormsby."

Jablonsky's interest was piqued. "Have you spoken with the good father about his nephew?"

"I have. I called him about James, and he verified our information. He said he hadn't seen this particular nephew in quite a few years and had forgotten that James has had some success as a glass artist." Coupe accepted the stick of cinnamon gum the chief offered him.

"Did he say if Carlotti knew about James' interest in studio glass?" As was his annoying habit, Jablonsky began tapping his pen on Lupinski's picture.

"I did ask him that—he was adamant that he had never spoken to Carlotti about his nephew."

"This is a pretty interesting connection, a distant one, but one nevertheless. It's thought-provoking that Lupinski never mentioned this nephew when we interviewed him, considering how wrapped up in the glass necklace and pendant his friend was." Jablonsky finally stopped his tapping.

"It was my impression that Father Lupinski was telling the truth. He seemed surprised when I asked him about James. I'm just not a hundred percent about his veracity on other things." Antoine and the chief continued chewing gum and staring at the murder board.

The chief pointed to each photo. "I'm stealing Kate's favorite maxim. Everyone is lying about something all the time. All of these people are not only lying to us but lying to each other as well."

Jablonsky was satisfied they had the evidence to charge Joseph and Zane Davies with multiple criminal counts, but he still had two open murder cases. He believed he knew who murdered Eugene but wasn't sure if the same person had murdered Carlotti.

CHAPTER 28

THE INVESTIGATIVE ARM OF THE MEDIA was thrown a bone with the arrests of Joseph Davies and his son, Zane. The underground buying, selling, and smuggling of expensive art was a novel crime, and the public was fascinated by it. An additional juicy aspect was Zane's attempted escape in the corporate jet from Pittsburgh to Miami, and then the FBI involved shooting and capturing of him in Brazil. Every news outlet gave the arrests a daily segment.

Because of Kate and Johnny's involvement with the case, the chief decided to give them the insider particulars of the how, when, and why of the arrest of Zane and Joseph Davies. For Kate, however, these features were like a fast food meal—two hours later, she was hungry and dissatisfied. Like Jablonsky, Kate believed she knew who had murdered both men, but she hadn't even confided her suspicions to Johnny; she had to figure a way to draw the murderer out.

"May I ride with you to the class tonight? Joan is going to pick me up after we finish."

"Of course. What are you two doing? And where are you going to shower after class? We are absolute sweat-balls when we're done."

"She has tickets to the Manchester Craftsman's Guild Jazz Series. I can't wait. It is such an intimate setting. See this classy Louis Vuitton carry-on? Inside are my toiletries, makeup, and clothes. It's not a venue where you have to dress up, so I'm just wearing black jeans and a knit top." Kate was more relaxed before this class than she had been in several weeks.

"One of my favorite things about you is that you are always so organized. What is this?" he asked as a postcard fell out of her valise. "I recognize this building. This is a picture of The Grand Theatre in Poland—Teatr Wielki in Polish. Their national opera company is housed there. Oh, I see it is from Marco. How delicious! What's this about?" Johnny asked as he waved the postcard around like a thirteen-year-old boy torturing his sister. Kate sighed. Johnny could be so annoyingly nebby.

"It's about nothing. Joan told me he is an opera buff. He and his staff probably went to hear a performance while they were over there supervising the surgical training. He sent a postcard; that's all there is to it."

"That's all there is to it," repeated a grinning Johnny.

"Switch topics!" demanded Kate.

"After this class has ended, what are you going to do about Andy Ormsby? You know he will be calling you for a date." Kate sighed again. "I know. I guess I'll eventually have to say I'm not interested." They dropped the topic as they parked and walked into the glass center.

The small group of students were gathered in the hot shop, each placing the needed instruments at their station. Bottles of water lined the individual areas in anticipation of the thirsty and dirty work involved in shaping hot glass. Andy Ormsby was a talented glass artist but, unlike most, was also a skilled teacher. He engaged every individual student in conversation about what they wanted to achieve in the class, then finally gave the all-clear for the work to begin.

There was very little chit-chat because the work was so dangerous. Andy provided mini-lectures on the different processes and techniques. It was thrilling but muscle exhausting work. After a few hours, all of the pieces went into the annealing oven to cool down, and everyone relaxed, hydrated, and talked about the successes and failures of their attempts. Everyone, including Johnny and Kate, avoided the subject of Eugene Rose. Andy sat on a stool by them, talking and laughing; to Kate, he seemed unusually relaxed today.

"Andy. I thought I heard that there are showers somewhere in the center. I'm meeting a friend and would like not to have to go back to my house to freshen up. Would it be okay with you if I used the showers? It would be just this once."

"No problem. A few showers, lockers, sinks, and toilets have been installed for the teaching faculty and interns, so of course you can use them. After we put away all the tools, I'll show you where the showers are." The pleasure of doing a favor for Kate was written all over Ormsby's face. Johnny rolled his eyes and left for the canteen to get some iced tea.

After the other students trailed out of the hot shop, Andy called to Kate. "Follow me down to our storage area. It's not too spooky; there are plenty of lights. You can lock the door to the bathroom if you feel uncomfortable."

Like Jablonsky had done after Andy toured him around the center, Kate slowed her pace to read a few labels. "Wow. There is quite a collection here; I had no idea. Unless you want to wait, Andy, I think I can find my way back."

"Okay. I'm going to head up to my office; come look for me when you are finished."

The locker room was bright and clean. Kate stripped, wrapped a towel around her, and carried her soap and shampoo into one of the stalls. Someone had thoughtfully outfitted each stall with a teak bench and a pretty shower curtain—clearly a woman's touch. She took her time, allowing the hot water to relax her tired muscles. Finally, Kate toweled off, put on her clean undies, and dressed. A few quick touches of makeup were all that was needed.

Unlocking the door, she quietly walked down the hallway; then, since no one was around, she slowly moved through the stacks, enjoying looking at the photos on the front of each box. She stopped at one box that had a photo of a vase created using the *reticello* technique. Andy Ormsby was named as the artist, along with the date the vase was entered into the glass center's collection, a catalog number, and a few small letters, *o-p-p-i-h.*

Kate couldn't resist opening the box and taking out the vase—the crisscrossing strings of white cane formed a net around the vase and were beautifully executed. There was something in the pattern at the bottom of the vase that caught Kate's eye. At first, she thought it was the beginning of the cane work, but upon further inspection, there were several numbers discreetly worked into the thin lines of the pattern. *This is some sort of artist's message,* thought Kate.

Suddenly, she was struck by a *coup de foudre.* Her brain became like a camera shutter, rapidly taking snapshots and remembering bits of information—in that brainstorm, her suspicions about who had the mysterious missing necklace and pendant coalesced into a whole picture.

Oh, my God, Kate silently declared to herself. *He has it, and he stored it in plain sight all this time! He stored it here, in the stacks, with a piece of his own glass. But how did he get it?* Kate gingerly felt around in the box, her fingers telling her that something else was under the packing.

Sweat broke out on her brow as she realized that she was in danger, having no idea if Ormsby was still in his office or lurking in the stacks. Without finding out what was stored under the wrapping, she noiselessly returned the vase to the box, placed it back on the shelf, then backed out of the row, returning to the locker room. Pretending to just have finished her shower, she slammed the door, clomped down the hallway to the steps, and started up them.

"Hey, Ormsby! I'm done here. Where are you?" Andy appeared at the top of the stairs with what Kate thought was a strange smile on his face.

She chit-chatted with him until they entered the hot shop, which was empty—all the students and auxiliary staff had disappeared, including Johnny.

"It seemed like you took your time down there. Tell me the truth now, were you looking around in the stacks?" Kate felt a tingle go up her spine; something wasn't right. He turned to face her and declared, "It's hidden. It is hidden in with another piece of glass; you wouldn't have been able to find it."

Kate's mouth felt like cotton. She made her voice light and casual. "Find what, Andy? What are you talking about?"

"You know. I can tell by your face that you've figured it out. Yes, I have the necklace and the pendant. You are a good sleuth Kate, but unfortunately, you won't be around for any more cases."

Chief Detective Jablonsky, Antoine DeVille, and detective Lemon suddenly stepped out from behind the oven dividers. They were armed and had their weapons trained on Ormsby. Andy roughly twisted Kate's arm behind her and pulled her in front of him. He placed a piece of broken glass to her neck. The chief spoke in the voice negotiators use to talk someone out of jumping off a bridge—calm but firm.

"Andy. Don't do anything foolish. Let Kate go, and we will all walk out of here and talk at the station. No one has to get hurt." The chief lowered his gun to his side, but Antoine and Lemon kept their weapons pointed at Ormsby's head.

"Talk about what?" Andy replied, challenging the chief. Gone was the charming New Zealand accent and deferential manner.

"To talk about the murder of Father Carlotti. Andy, there are two guns trained on you in this room and more police in the hallway. You can't get away. I want you to let Kate walk over to me right now."

"No. I'm just not going to do that. This piece of glass is razor sharp—I can pierce her carotid in a second." Kate felt Andy pull her closer, pressed the glass shard against her neck, and made a small gash in her skin. A thin line of dark red blood began traveling down her neck.

"See that blood, that's just a preview of what's to come," Andy stated in a snarky, baiting tone. Kate decided to take a psychological risk.

"Andy," she said through her strained jaw. "You will still be The One who discovered the glass bead necklace and the stunning St. Augustine pendant. You will be listed in the art history books. Your name will be on the lips of private collectors and museum curators. If you don't let me go, they will shoot you, and you will miss all the accolades that are your due." The chief recognized that Kate was appealing directly to Ormsby's narcissism—smart girl. He hoped it would work.

Joan slowly walked toward the glass center. She saw Johnny standing to the side of the building—he told her what was happening inside. The chief did not want police presence on the street, so his detectives were positioned inside. Like all good surgeons, Joan was no shrinking violet; she was a confident woman, able to cut into human flesh without flinching. She and Johnny entered the building through the front door, where they were stopped by police. Joan flashed her identification and quietly lied as to why she was there.

"I'm Doctor Weisner. This is McCarthy. Chief Jablonsky wanted an ambulance on standby—we are parked out of sight. I am the surgeon on call. I'll wait over here just in case things get out of hand." With Johnny in tow, Joan moved to the side of the hallway leading to the ovens before there was any objection; she knew how to command people.

When the police returned to their positions, she and Johnny slowly made their way down the hallway, past the storage area for the tools, getting as close to the hot shop as possible. They could hear Jablonsky's voice.

She whispered to Johnny, "I'm going to create a diversion. You with me?" They grabbed some tools and, on the silent count of three, began to wack them against each other and pound them on the concrete floor. The loud noise startled everyone, allowing Kate to elbow Ormsby in the gut and run toward the chief, who pushed her behind him.

Jablonsky saw that Ormsby knew it was over; the man lifted his head and let out a wail filled with rage, frustration, and pain—the sound echoed off the concrete walls and floor. He dropped to his knees, pounding his fists on his legs. "I had it in my grasp. It was mine! It was mine!" he screamed. Antoine and Lemon grabbed his arms and cuffed him, keeping him in the kneeling position. Lemon and DeVille kept their guns pointed at Ormsby as the chief stood over him, bending his arms behind him and cuffing his wrists.

"Andy Ormsby. I am arresting you for the premeditated murder of Father Timothy Carlotti." With disgust, he turned to his detectives, "Read him his rights, and don't leave out one single word, then get him out of here."

The chief turned to face Kate, who was standing with Johnny and Joan. His continued disgust twisted his face into a scowling expression; his tone was harsh.

"That was an unbelievably dangerous thing to do. Ormsby could have slit Kate's throat!" He paused. "I could arrest you both for interfering with a police action; however, the diversion worked—I'll make my decision as to what to do with you later." Joan was already looking at Kate's wound when Jablonsky added, "Doctor Weisner, make sure our girl is okay because I'll need a word with her as well."

Kate, Johnny, and Joan gave their statements at the precinct. Jablonsky was furious over the stunt Dr. Weisner and Johnny pulled; he went back and forth about whether to charge both of them with interfering in police action. Instead, he gave them both a strong verbal warning, reiterating how close Kate came to having her throat slit. The two friends were duly chastised, but neither regretted their action.

Jablonsky looked over all three statements. He addressed Kate. "You took a huge risk, Kate, and I'm angry with you." Jablonsky's attitude was more fatherly toward her than the Chief of Detectives posture he had taken with Johnny and Joan.

"In my defense, I'd like to begin by reminding you that I had called before our class with my suspicions that Andy was in possession of the glass bead necklace and the pendant."

"Yes, and I remember telling you during that telephone call not to do anything that would communicate your suspicions to Ormsby! We knew everyone involved would be at the class, and we had our plan in place to arrest him. Okay then, tell me more about what happened when you were in the basement."

"Well, to begin with, after I emailed and then spoke with Dr. Isabelle Aubert, I knew for certain that someone else had seen the necklace. The way she described Grandmother Rose's movements the day she brought the pieces in to be evaluated made me think that, because he was an intern at the time, it was Andy who saw the items. There was, however, no way to prove my theory. Tonight, when I came out of the locker room and walked through all those unopened special storage boxes and saw a description of a glass vase that Andy had created—I couldn't resist looking at it."

"Along the bottom of the vase were five numbers intertwined in the cane pattern. I don't know what they meant. Then, on the label of the box were the small letters, o-p-p-i-h. It came to me that those letters spell Hippo backward. I remembered Johnny talking about Saint Augustine of Hippo and became convinced that Andy had kept the neckless and the pendant in the building." Kate paused to take a drink of water.

"I felt around in the box—I think there is something else in it, but I knew I had been in the stacks too long, so I just left. I didn't want to arouse Andy's suspicions. Little did I know it was already too late for that!"

Antoine interrupted. "Ormsby said he returned to New Zealand after his internship. Would he have left the necklace and pendant in the center? Someone could have opened that box."

"I don't know how long he has had it stored there. He is going to have to tell you those details. For instance, how did he get ahold of the pieces? Grandmother Rose took them with her the day she had them appraised." Kate wished she could watch the interview with Ormsby but given the stunt Joan and Johnny had just pulled, she didn't even ask.

"Ormsby refused to say anything about the stacks. Our officers are at the center now, going through the entire storage area." The chief made a few notes to himself in his tiny paper notebook.

"I can help with that—I remember where the box is—if it is okay with you, chief, I could go there right now while things are fresh in my mind." Kate looked expectantly at Jablonsky, who didn't think twice about accepting her offer to help.

"Lemon, with me," he shouted into the bullpen. "Take Kate over to the glass center. She's offered to help find the box. Call and tell them you are on your way." Kate touched the chief's sleeve, stopping him from shooing her out of his office.

"Detective Jablonsky. Before you interview him, I wanted to add one more thing. When Andy grabbed me and put that piece of broken glass to my neck, I remembered how he has gone about his life as if nothing has happened—it was as if Father Carlotti's death nor Eugene's mattered. Today, when he was threatened, I became an obstacle to achieving his plan—I wasn't a real person to him. He would have sliced my neck without a thought. He has a charming public self, but psychologically, he is an empty person incapable of human empathy. You can't appeal to any attribute we associate with a conscience—he simply doesn't have one. He is very dangerous." Kate drew out the last sentence, emphasizing her warning.

Andy Ormsby remained cuffed as he sat in the interview room. He had spent the last hours in lock-up, already fingerprinted and charged—one count of premeditated first-degree murder and theft of an antiquity, with more charges to come. Antoine and the chief watched him from the media room.

“What was the giveaway that made you sure it was him?” asked Coupe.

“First of all, he had the opportunity and the motive. The boldness of how he murdered Carlotti gave him away: dressing like a priest, carrying a little black bag, and shooting air into the IV, right under the nose of the officer sitting outside the door. The education I’ve been receiving in glassblowing showed me that it is all about planning and risk—a piece can turn out to be art, or it can smash on the floor and become nothing. Like Kate said, his private self is bold, unencumbered by a conscience.”

“To murder a priest who is struggling with his faith, I’d agree he is missing a piece of humanity,” remarked Antoine.

“Psychology aside—he’s simply a narcissistic scumbag,” replied the chief.

Jablonsky sat down across from Ormsby, keeping his expression impassive. A small drop of sweat had formed on Andy’s left eyebrow and slowly made its way down that side of his face. He lifted his cuffed hands and wiped it. “Are these really necessary?” asked a petulant Ormsby.

The chief still didn’t speak, but as it was his habit, he raised his hand and snapped his fingers. A police officer came into the room and removed the cuffs. Ormsby became his polite self and thanked the chief. “Okay, Jablonsky, let’s get on with it. What do you want to know?”

“I want to know when and how you first acquired the necklace and pendant.”

Andy leaned back in his chair, posturing as if he were a writer giving a talk in front of rapt patrons at an elite bookstore. “Now, that’s an interesting story because it was by pure chance that I saw them. Eugene’s grandmother was sitting in the conference room with Dr. Isabelle Aubert, and the glass bead necklace and medallion were on the table between them. Aubert was discussing the sixteenth-century aspects of Murano glass...."

"Cut the crap, Ormsby; I don't need a lecture on art." Jablonsky's hostile tone was like an invisible hand that reached over the table and slapped Andy across the face.

"Well, okay. I was an intern then, just a peon at the center, and I was passing by the conference room and heard them talking. I was able to look into the room without them seeing me. The glowing ruby beads touched with so much gold leaf were amazing. The roundel with the beautiful cold painted drawing of Saint Augustine—the piece was stunning. Its beauty captured me and held me in its grasp."

The chief snapped, "The only thing you were captured by was your own criminal thinking. Now, I'm asking again, how did you get the necklace and pendant?"

Unperturbed by Jablonsky's sarcasm, Ormsby continued. "This is when the story gets fascinating. When the old lady left, I followed her in my car, parked in front of her house, and sat, looking around. No one in the neighborhood came by, so I went right up to the front door and found it wasn't locked! I couldn't believe my luck. I slowly opened the door, slipped in, and heard her talking on the telephone in the kitchen. The two pieces were laid out on the dining room table. I stepped into the room and grabbed them, and left. When I got back to the car, I could hardly breathe; I was so excited. This is the first time I've ever told the story—I feel the same way right now—kinda giddy like I could rise and fly around the room."

"Okay, flyboy, get back to the story," barked the chief. *What a damn jackass* thought Jablonsky.

"Well, I was due to return to New Zealand to work at a glass center to gain administrative experience and refine my hot glass skills. I had to decide whether or not to take my treasures with me. I decided against it because I feared they might be found in my gear at the airport. Before I left, I rented a bank box and stored both pieces until I returned." Once he started into his story, Ormsby stopped sweating—to the chief, he appeared calm, like he was recounting what he did on summer vacation. Jablonsky thought, *Kate was right about his narcissism; he refers to Eugene's grandmother as the old lady, as if she were an object, like an old shoe.*

"You were in New Zealand, and the neckless and pendant remained in Pittsburgh, in a bank box. When did you transfer them to the storage area at the center?"

Once again, Ormsby preened in his chair. "When they bought one of my vases for their collection." The chief didn't feed Ormsby's need for approbation by commenting on the purchase.

"When did you meet Eugene Rose?"

"Oh, really, just recently. He took my classes here at the center. You know, it was Eugene who made the connection for me that I had his grandmother's necklace and pendant. He was quite chatty about how his grandmother had fostered his interest in glass. He would show me his book of ideas." At the mention of Eugene, nothing changed in Andy's demeanor, no hint of discomfort or guilt.

"When did you decide to kill him?" Jablonsky wanted to shatter the pedestrian atmosphere Ormsby had created.

"I didn't kill him; someone else did." Andy crossed his legs and stretched his arms, like he was sitting outside in one of the Strip District's cafés, sipping craft whisky. "Look, here's the way it went. Eugene had traced the necklace and pendant to his family. He was so excited, a true scholar and historian on the hunt. While I completely understood his drive, he couldn't be allowed to continue the search. I mean, he couldn't be allowed to think that the items were his. You understand that, don't you?" Compelled by his intensity,

Ormsby leaned toward the chief. "You see the situation I was in, don't you?"

"No. No, I don't see it. What I do see is that you decided to murder Eugene so that you could be the one who would present these rare pieces of glass to the art world. You, and your reputation, were the sole motives for murdering him and Father Carlotti."

In disgust, Ormsby spit out the name of the priest. "Carlotti. Carlotti was a mentally ill religious fanatic. He didn't care about the importance of the pieces to the art world; he thought the pendant was endowed with some sort of special power from Saint Augustine."

"It certainly had a special power over you, Ormsby," the chief pointed out, a fact that went over Andy's head. "You still claim that you didn't murder Eugene. Okay, convince me."

"I can't convince you because I don't know who murdered him." There was something in the way Ormsby looked at the chief that bespoke of confusion, almost innocence.

"You don't know who murdered Eugene?" Jablonsky repeated.

"No. I don't. He was murdered before...." Ormsby's voice trailed off.

"He was murdered before you could do it—is that your story? Really?" Jablonsky allowed a smile at Ormsby's statement. "To be clear, you didn't kill him because someone else got to him before you did?"

"Well, I wasn't planning on murdering him. I was steering him in other directions concerning the necklace's provenance and the pendant. If I had had more time with him, I could have led him down a different path altogether. He was a naive graduate student; he didn't need to be murdered. Just, well, redirected."

"Redirected?" Jablonsky's amusement turned into revulsion at the way Ormsby's self-absorption revealed itself. "In summary, then, someone else murdered Eugene Rose, but in order to protect your imaginary superstar future as the finder of the glass bead necklace and the pendant, you had to murder Father Carlotti."

"It's not imaginary! I am going to be written into the history books; you don't understand."

Jablonsky cut him off. "Give me the details of how you murdered Father Carlotti."

Ormsby let out a deep sigh as if this all was too much work. "What makes you think I murdered the priest? Where is your evidence?"

Jablonsky laid the artist's rendering taken from the police officer who had been on guard at Father Carlotti's hospital door. It was clearly Ormsby, which was why the chief and his detectives had been at the glass center waiting for him, and why Jablonsky had taken Kate's belief that it was Andy so seriously. It was just that Kate thought Andy murdered Eugene, not Carlotti.

The chief then laid the officer's statement of identification of Andy Ormsby as the man who entered Carlotti's hospital room the night he died.

"We have you, Ormsby. Why not just tell me the story of how you murdered the priest? Your confession, and perhaps a statement of regret, if you can muster it, will be to your benefit with a jury." Andy sighed again. Everyone in the room waited as he decided to speak. His desire to tell the story of his own brilliant planning and acting got the better of him.

"All right. I called Carlotti's parish to find out which hospital he was in, saying that I was a parishioner wanting to send flowers. I dressed in a black suit, found something that looked like a priest's collar, and then told the guard sitting outside the room that I was there to give Carlotti communion. I went in, injected air into his IV, and left. That was all there was to it. No glitches in the plan."

"What was in the black bag you carried into the room?"

"Well, I put some regular thin wafers in a container, and a scarf that looked like the stole priest's wear. I hid the injection tool underneath these items."

"What did you do with the gemstones?"

"Gemstones? What gemstones?" Ormsby looked positively stunned that there was a part of the drama he didn't know about. "I don't know what you are referring to."

Andy became anxious visibly—he moved around in his chair, wrung his hands, and finger-combed his hair. The droplets of sweat on his brow returned.

"Detective Jablonsky, when the auction houses and art dealers interview me, I want to assure them that the ruby glass bead necklace and the pendant are safe, just like they have been all these years. Everyone needs to know that I kept it safe for posterity."

Jablonsky had had enough. He pushed back his chair and stood. "I will report to the media that you, Andy Ormsby, murdered a priest over two pieces of glass." No one spoke. Ormsby looked down; he splayed his fingers on the tabletop. Slowly he raised his head and stared at Jablonsky with the dead eyes of a shark; the room filled with the stink of hatred.

Suddenly, like a Wall Street trader who had snorted too much cocaine, Ormsby jumped out of his chair and leaped toward the chief. Out of the corner of his eye, Jablonsky saw that he held a small, jagged piece of glass. The chief turned sideways and raised his left arm, trying to block the attack, but Ormsby was able to inflict several cuts before the officers who raced into the room could restrain him. As they finally yanked his arms around to the back and cuffed him, Ormsby spewed out a string of filthy declarations about the chief, strung together by foul expletives.

Jablonsky thought. *Kate warned me. I should have taken it more seriously.*

Antoine was one of the people who had rushed into the interview room and was now holding the chief's arm, assessing the damage. Jablonsky jerked his arm away, remarking, "These cuts aren't deep. Some peroxide and a few bandages will take care of it. He had that piece of glass all this time—how the hell was he able to keep it after being searched and patted down?"

Coupe knew that there would be a big price to pay, and rightfully so, over this breach of security. He was glad it wasn't his department.

CHAPTER 29

KATE AND ANNIE LEMON WERE TRYING to locate the glass bead necklace and the pendant when word of what had happened in the interview with Ormsby spread like wildfire. A rush of anxiety churned in her stomach; if he had tried to kill the Chief of Detectives, Andy definitely would have killed her. It was helpful that Annie Lemon was walking behind her in between the stacks of boxes. It made her feel safe.

"Here is Ormsby's vase. See the letters, *o-p-p-i-h*—I think the necklace and pendant are in with the vase." Kate reached for the box she had opened.

"Excellent catch on *o-p-p-i-h* being Hippo backward; I wouldn't have caught it."

Kate smiled at the compliment. "Should we open the box?"

"Well, we have to know if the items are inside. Here's a table we can place them on."

Kate slowly lifted Ormsby's vase out of the box; the large ruby glass necklace was swaddled in soft cloth underneath it. Kate carefully displayed the necklace on the table. Both women unconsciously stepped back. "So, this is it?" Lemon looked disappointed. "I mean, the glass beads are unusually big and pretty, but was it worth taking two lives over?"

"No," Kate responded, her eyes wet with tears thinking about Eugene. "No object is worth that. But where is the pendant?" Kate paused and then picked up Ormsby's vase and pointed to the numbers that were almost hidden in the cane work at the bottom.

"Here is an eight, a nine, two sixteens and a fifteen. What do you make of these numbers?" Kate didn't realize that Annie Lemon was known to possess a unique skill with codes. She looked at the numbers and quickly made a pronouncement.

"These are the numerical correlates to the word Hippo."

"Oh. That's true: eight for H, nine for I, two sixteens for P, and fifteen for O. I wonder if they are pointing us in the direction of where the pendant is stored." Detective Lemon and Kate began walking the storage area, turning at the numbers listed for the stacks. Finally, in aisle 16, Kate saw a large white storage box that had the title "Intern Glass Pieces" listed on it. She and Lemon lifted the box down from the stacks and placed the contents on a table. One piece, crafted in the Murrine technique, had been the work of James Lupinski, Father Lupinski's nephew. Another was the work of Ormsby. And so, it went. Underneath the six pieces in the box, they found the pendant; Kate and Annie Lemon took it back to the table with the necklace and placed them together.

They spent a few minutes admiring the fabulously gilded ruby beads and the cold-painted image of Saint Augustine; Kate took a few photographs of both pieces with her phone. She turned the pendant over and gingerly opened the back. No gemstones were enclosed.

"I wonder what will happen to it?" Kate murmured, not addressing Lemon in particular. "By rights, it belongs to Mr. and Mrs. Rose, but I'm just not sure they will want it. I think I might talk to their Rabbi and get his ideas on the future of these deadly art pieces."

"Well, the pieces have to go into evidence." Lemon left both of Ormsby's vases standing unceremoniously on the table. She placed the necklace and pendant into an evidence bag and took them back to the station.

Kate left feeling emotionally drained. From her car, she called Joan, who had been released to go home; Jablonsky didn't charge her with interference in a police action.

"Joan, I was wondering if, after some time has passed, you would go to the Rabbi's with me. I would like his counsel on how to approach the Roses. These are important art pieces that, unfortunately, have been irrevocably tainted by murder. Will you go?"

"Of course! By the way, I love you, kiddo; I'm so glad you weren't hurt!"

While the Pittsburgh airport wasn't crowded, the International travel section did buzz with activity. People stood talking in small groups, too excited over upcoming trips to foreign climes to sit down. DeVille and Lemon walked slowly along the wide aisle between the two seating sections looking like any other travelers waiting to check in for their flight. Because of their uniforms, the regular police stayed well behind the detectives; everyone's firepower was hidden. The airline worker standing behind her desk subtly indicated where the suspect was seated.

Antoine and Lemon circled around, came up behind Sarah Braithwaite, and quietly commanded her to stand up and put her hands behind her. Sarah's head swiveled like Dr. Patel's office chair.

"What are you two doing here?" she asked, remaining seated. It was as if she were meeting the detectives for 'prinks,' pre-drinks with friends before a flight or an event.

"Young lady, stand up and put your hands behind you." It was Lemon who gave the command. She motioned to the police officers to come forward. "Cuff her."

Reality set in for Ms. Braithwaite. "What are you doing? I have tickets to South Africa to see my relatives." Sarah utilized her pretty blonde looks by starting to cry and comment to the travelers around her. "I'm just a young, innocent girl. These police officers are hurting me. I'm just going home to see my family." It was a scene right out of a television series.

"Sarah Braithwaite. We are arresting you for the murder of Eugene Rose and the international smuggling of antiquities. Start walking." Antoine leaned over and grabbed the carry-on piece of luggage that was by her chair.

"Hey! That's my luggage. That bag belongs to me; you can't take it. I want an attorney." The enraged young woman was escorted out of the airport and deposited in the back of a police car. Once at the precinct, she made a call to her parents; several hours later, her parents and an attorney arrived. Sarah was Mirandized and taken to the interview room.

"Ms. Braithwaite, for such a young person, you've already become quite the accomplished criminal," stated Jablonsky, beginning the interview.

"Don't respond to that. Chief Jablonsky, is there a question here?" Her parents had hired Elise Rosen, a criminal attorney well-known to Jablonsky and the courts.

"Yes, there is a question, but first, It is show and tell time." Stefan reached under the table and brought out two violins, one wrapped in several layers of fabric. He took his time with the reveal, watching Sarah's complexion turn arctic white. Finally, he carefully laid both four-string violins side by side on the table.

"What can you tell me about these two violins?" asked the chief, his voice silky smooth. Like a cat charming his owner, he slowly blinked his eyes.

"Where did you get this?" demanded Sarah, pointing to one of the violins.

"Why, it was in your carry-on luggage at the airport. This piece of luggage, to be precise." Jablonsky held up the bag they had confiscated.

"You can't go through my things!" Indignant, Sarah turned toward Ms. Rosen. "He can't go through my bags—that's private property. Tell him!"

"You are under arrest for murder and international smuggling. He has a warrant that gives him the right to search your belongings, your residence, your parents' residence, and even your student office," replied Rosen.

"Let's start here." Jablonsky opened a laptop and clicked on a video of Sarah and Johnny at the precinct looking over the objects taken from Mr. Davies' safe. It showed Sarah picking up the violin, examining it, playing it, and then laying it back down on the table.

"Here comes the good part, Sarah." The video showed that while Johnny stepped out of the conference room for a few minutes, Sarah snatched the violin, placed it in her large fabric tote, and replaced it with a look-a-like violin. It all happened in a matter of seconds. Ms. Rosen, who hadn't seen the police video, raised her eyebrows but didn't comment.

"You were filming me? How dare you! You didn't ask my permission!" Sarah struck an indignant pose, then looked at her attorney once again, who responded with, "This is a police station Sarah, all of the interview and conference rooms have cameras. Nothing illegal was done in obtaining this video."

The chief continued. "You will remember that at the time, I asked you if you had stolen this instrument, and you lied to me."

"No, I didn't! This particular violin is from Davies collection," answered Sarah, side-stepping the issue.

Jablonsky took the other violin in hand. "This violin is a reproduction of that one. You counted on Professor McCarthy and other evaluators to be ignorant of that fact—unfortunately, you were wrong. You have been lying to everyone, Sarah. You've been lying to your parents, to Zane, and your professors here and in Italy." The chief placed the fake violin off to the side, leaving the authentic one lying between them.

Rosen looked at the chief. "Okay, Ms. Braithwaite is a liar. That doesn't make her a murderer."

Stefan slowly closed the laptop. He eyeballed Sarah and spoke in a low husky voice. "I want to know how and why you felt the need to murder your good friend Eugene Rose." Like a puff of scent emitted from a diffuser, the chief's threat was subtle, but both Sarah and Rosen took note.

Young Sarah looked to her attorney. "Do I have to continue?" There was a studied arrogance in her face but also the slightest bit of anxiety. Rosen addressed Jablonsky. "Chief Detective, so far, you only have this video that shows Ms. Braithwaite switching violins. What evidence do you have that she murdered Eugene Rose?"

"I'm going to give you the evidence. It starts with the story of three pals, three young people interested in art history, art objects, and making a name and a career for themselves. Sarah, you knew that Zane was smuggling things out of Italy. You knew he routinely made deals with private collectors that were off the books. We showed this video to Zane, and in contrast to his previous statements, he has confirmed that you knew he was both purchasing objects on the down low, and then smuggling them into the States. He had the perfect set-up—the money could be laundered through his father's manufacturing plants in Brazil." Jablonsky continued.

"You decided to get in on the action, thus, the violin. You educated Zane about which antique violins were worth money, then you struck a deal with him. He could smuggle other items in your student luggage, and you would put the violin in Eugene's suitcase, retrieving it when you arrived home. It would be stored in the safe at Zane's father's business until you were ready to go back to Italy. Because you shared a house with Eugene, you knew he could be absent-minded, giving you a chance to retrieve the violin when you both unpacked from the trip."

"This is quite an intriguing and amusing story, Jablonsky, but where is your proof?" Rosen held out her hands, palms up, symbolizing their emptiness.

Slowly, Jablonsky took several sheets of paper from a file and arranged them on the table. "Here is a signed statement from Zane Davies attesting to your arrangement with him. Here is a copy of an email that we found on Eugene Rose's laptop. And finally, here is the list of your Google searches made from your Italian professor's computer—you ordered the Belladonna while you were still in Italy." Ms. Rosen, who took her time reading the contents of each affidavit and email, slowly slid the papers over to Sarah.

Jablonsky said, "Read Eugene's email out loud, Sarah."

"She doesn't have to do that!" cried Rosen.

"Then I will. The email is addressed to Zane.

Zane, I know that you have been smuggling antiquities and now have involved Sarah in your criminal activities. I saw her take a violin from my luggage that neither she nor I had bought. Either you stop, or I will report you to the police and the chair of your department at the university. Be a man, don't involve an innocent girl in your nefarious actions. Eugene.

This is dated right after your return from Italy. Eugene thought Zane was manipulating you. He didn't realize that the two of you were in league together. Why did you murder an innocent young man who was watching out for you?"

For the first time, Sarah's facade of a sweet, dewy-eyed girl slipped—her green eyes grew narrow, and their color intensified with the knowledge that she might not be able to talk herself out of the situation. Jablonsky could see that fear was beginning to set in. Sarah looked at Elise Rosen, who nodded a go-ahead to her client. Sarah sat up straighter, and her voice gained volume as she made her case.

"You see this violin on the table between us? I love it. I adore it. I study the artists who have created this inexpressibly beautiful instrument. Look at its curves and the patina of its finish. Right now, it is mute, but without even drawing a bow over the strings, I can mentally conjure up its sweet high notes and the longing its midrange can create. There is no price one can offer that even comes close to its worth." Sarah paused in her paean to the instrument to observe Jablonsky.

"And?" responded the chief, who was intent on bringing Sarah back to the reality of her actions. "You love the violin. Okay. And how do we go from your love of antique violins to murdering one of your best friends?"

"You are such a philistine! You can't comprehend what an instrument like this violin means to someone like the musicians of the world and to me." As if she were Dorothy Parker at the Algonquin Round Table, Sarah threw down her dismissal of Jablonsky; all she needed was a martini and a cigarette.

"I may be a philistine, but you young lady, are a murderer. I ask again, what was your motive for killing Eugene?" Sarah continued to stare at the chief. Minutes passed, tension built, then, finally she spoke.

"Eugene was about to ruin my life. I couldn't let that happen. Zane showed me that threatening email—he said he would talk with Eugene and smooth things over, but I couldn't rely on him. Zane is weak. But, as you correctly surmised, I gave the violin to him to store—and yes, he was going to bring it to me when I went back to Italy—but Eugene was in the way of my plans."

"Eugene was in the way of your plans," repeated the chief. "You loved Eugene, correct?"

"Yes. I loved him, and I respected him. He was smart and funny, but—" Sarah stopped in mid-sentence.

"In the way of your plans," repeated Jablonsky again, holding a psychological mirror up to her face. Would she see herself for what she was?

Jablonsky lifted up the violin and, with ballooning anger, stated, "Eugene was a human being; this violin is an object!" As he moved the violin increasingly out of her range, its physical separation from her incited an explosive response.

"Give me that! Give me that violin, you will drop it. Give it to me!" Sarah screamed, reaching into the air to grab the instrument the chief held high above her grasping hands. Sarah became wild and out of control.

"That's enough! Sit down, Sarah! Chief Jablonsky, there is no need for these theatrics and moral platitudes." Elise Rosen tried to lower her client's accelerating hysteria. Jablonsky, on the other hand, got what he wanted—motive and means. Now, he went for her full confession.

Sarah shifted in her chair. She brushed her blonde hair away from her face, cleared her throat, then folded her hands and placed them on the table in front of her. She looked like a schoolgirl ready to recite her lessons. "I knew Eugene's habits better than anyone. I knew when he would be at the glassblowing class. The poison was easy to acquire in Italy—the Internet sells everything. I went to one of the classes with him to case the situation and discovered that in between classes at the glass center, no one is watching the area or the equipment." Sarah's voice became breathy, almost sexual. "No one stops a pretty young blonde from walking around. I was able to line his blowpipe with the poison, then leave and just wait for nature to take its course. I really did love Eugene. He was a good person, but don't you see, his goodness interfered with my plans. I couldn't let that goodness ruin my future. Really, what else could I do except murder him?"

Back in the office, Jablonsky poured a generous amount of Jameson Black into three glasses: one for himself, one for Annie Lemon, and one for Antoine. They toasted the closing of the two murder cases. Annie Lemon remarked that the world of art and art collecting was new to her, and while it was very interesting, she hoped never to be involved with it again. "Collectors seem driven by a compulsion to possess a material object to the point that they lose their minds."

"I agree on the whole, but for Father Carlotti, possessing the pendant was more about his spiritual life... although why a picture of St. Augustine, rather than therapy, would help him with his chastity issues, seems a stretch to me," remarked Jablonsky.

Antoine had the last word on motives. "Along with obsession and compulsion, I think we'd have to stir in a cup of greed and two cups of the pursuit of celebrity into our stew of motives." The three clinked glasses.

A few weeks had passed since the Rose family, the Carlotti family, and the press received the announcement of the charges against Andy Ormsby and Sarah Braithwaite. Annie Lemon was in the bullpen taking apart the murder board when Antoine walked by, heading into the chief's office. "He's here," announced Coupe.

Father Lupinski sat across from Chief Detective Jablonsky in the interview room. Stefan waited for the priest to speak, but when he didn't, he prompted him.

"You were brought here because I believe that you have something to give me. You have the gemstones that Grandmother Rose bought for her grandson, Eugene. Am I correct?"

"Yes." Lupinski laid a small black pouch that usually held rosary beads on the table. Jablonsky opened it and took out the stones. He recited Izzy Zaideman's description as he laid them on the table: "Two diamonds, one yellow and one white, in case Eugene needs money; a three-carat citrine, Eugene's birthstone; and a four-carat aquamarine stone, for tranquility. How did you acquire these?" Jablonsky touched each stone lightly with his fingertip.

"I stole them," replied Lupinski quietly.

"You stole them. Well, Father, I think you'd better tell me the whole story." Jablonsky settled back in his chair.

"When Father Carlotti hired Bogey Johnson to toss Eugene and Sarah Braithwaite's house for the flash drive, he didn't find the drive, but he found these gemstones in a freezer bag under some frozen vegetables at the bottom of the freezer drawer. Apparently, Eugene's grandmother had given them to him before his Bar Mitzvah, with a note about their meaning. I'm not sure anyone except Eugene knew about them, not his parents or even the girl. It was just luck that Bogey stumbled across them." Lupinski stopped and drank deeply from a water bottle that had been placed in front of him.

"Did Sloppy Bogey ask for payment for the gemstones?" Jablonsky couldn't believe that Bogey didn't confess to finding the gems; the chief had to accept that he might have misjudged the grifter's moxie.

"Absolutely. I'm not sure how they settled the transaction, but it had something to do with one part cash and one part identification of rich men at the club who were open to betting. One evening Carlotti showed me the stones—he didn't know what to do with them. He was totally fixated on getting the pendant. I advised him to hold onto the gemstones and just wait to see what happened."

"You didn't advise him to go to the police? You and Carlotti were quite a priestly duo. It seems like you both have an unusual understanding of the ten commandments. What happened next?" Jablonsky tried to rein in his moralism—he hated hypocrisy and crime so much.

"When Father Carlotti was murdered, I went to his bedroom and took the pouch with the gemstones, which he had hidden in his sock drawer," Lupinski snickered over the hiding place. "I know you think of him as a criminal, but he wasn't much of one. Father Carlotti wasn't motivated by money. He really didn't care about the gemstones—he believed the pendant was a true religious relic, that it had been blessed with the spiritual powers of Saint Augustine, and that those powers would help him stay true to his vows."

"How does this story end, Lupinski? What were you planning to do with the gemstones?" The chief was starting to get annoyed.

"To tell you the truth, I don't know. I've been thinking about leaving the priesthood because of the current zeitgeist, and I thought the gems would provide me with some money to start a new life. Then again, I thought about giving them back to the Rose family, who, of course, are the proper owners and deserve to have them. I also thought about trading them for cash to feed the poor in our community." Lupinski drew in a deep breath and slowly let it out. "I don't know what to do." Jablonsky knew that the priest wasn't appealing to him to help make a decision, so he sat quietly, the gemstones glittering on the table.

"Since you didn't turn over these gemstones of your own accord, you will have to be processed for possessing stolen goods and impeding a police investigation. You should think about the seriousness of having a police record, no matter what kind of life you choose going forward."

Jablonsky stood, delicately securing the stones in the small black pouch, then placing it inside an evidence bag. Lupinski also stood, and when an officer came into the interview room to take him to booking, the priest said nothing; he just touched his hand to his forehead and nodded to the chief as they left.

CHAPTER 30

KATE AND JOHNNY SAT WITH JOAN, watching her favorite Pirate pitcher, Cheeks Malouskas. Joan was on her feet, shouting something at the catcher, who was used to the lady surgeon's belief that she knew better than he, whether it was a strike, a ball, or an out. Joan's season ticket seats were right behind home plate, so her voice could be heard by the Pirate catcher and the umpires.

It was the end of the season and the team had a chance at post-season play; the crowd was noisy and eager, and the clear, unobstructed view of the city skyline from PNC Park filled everyone with pride. Arguably, it was the most beautifully designed baseball park in the whole country.

Joan had purchased black Pirate tee shirts with the big gold P on the front for her two friends, who wore them tonight, along with comfortable jeans. She had called Johnny saying that she had the tickets, admonishing him to help Kate with her grief over Eddie Fitzroy by doing something normal, like going to a baseball game.

Kate filled them in on the gemstones and light-fingered Father Lupinski. In the end, he had decided to return the gems to the Roses, who then decided to use them to start a scholarship fund in Eugene's name.

They stood for the seventh inning stretch, linked arms, and belted out the lyrics to "Take Me Out to the Ballgame."

After their rowdy rendition, Joan asked Kate, "Whatever happened to the necklace and pendant?"

"Ada and Sam have given permission to Johnny to give a yearly lecture on Grandmother Rose's glass collection, which now will include the glass bead necklace and the pendant. It will officially be named the Rose Collection and will become part of the Carnegie Art Museum's permanent collection. I'm thrilled for everyone because it honors Eugene and his grandmother in such fine style. However, Sam Rose said that he never wants to see those pieces again. Who can blame him?"

Another inning began, and the three friends concentrated on watching Cheeks Malouskas end it without giving away any hits; the stadium rocked with appreciation, and everyone stood chanting, "*Cheeks, Cheeks, Cheeks.*"

Johnny washed down the last of his kielbasa sandwich with some cold beer. Standing close to Kate, he spied another postcard tucked into her purse. As he slowly lifted it out, Joan caught sight of it. "What's that?"

The professor answered for Kate. "Marco Rossetti is sending Kate postcards from Europe. This one is from Italy—a picture of the La Scala Opera House in Milan."

"Really? That Leopard loves his opera!" Johnny hadn't heard Marco's nickname before and jokingly kept repeating it. "The Leopard. The lone Leopard. The leaping Leopard. Well, that's a fabulous nickname. We could relentlessly tease Marco about this name for months."

"Oh, shut up. You know, it's been fun getting actual mail. I look forward to going to my box and finding these little picture cards. All he ever writes is what opera he is seeing—but it's strangely very cool and fun."

Another inning began, and the three friends concentrated on watching Cheeks fire in pitches that clocked at over ninety-five miles per hour. Kate and Johnny hung on each other, howling with laughter at Joan's animated involvement with the calls. "What are you—blind? That's a strike! Your eyeballs need laser treatments!"

During a lull in the game action, Joan became serious, asking Kate if she was thinking about curbing her sleuthing. "I thought I had lost you at the glass center. It unnerved me, and I'm not scared by much. Katie girl, you are my soulmate friend. I can't do without you."

"You know that because of my parents, I'm a bit obsessed, not with art, but justice." replied a smiling Kate, who embraced the idea that certain friends are your real soulmates. "The reality is that I'm not constantly involved in murder cases; I do have a regular job. I've only been in lethal situations because of other people's bad choices. Besides, who would want to hurt me?"

THE END

ACKNOWLEDGMENTS

CHIEF DETECTIVE STEFAN JABLONSKY and amateur sleuth Kate Chambers are two characters that are smart, quirky, and committed to justice. Torchflame Books has recognized their universal appeal and have published this second novel in the Pittsburgh Murder Mystery Series. Thanks to Wally and Betty Turnbull for continuing to represent the best in the business of independent publishing; they are a pleasure to work with.

Thanks also go to Jori Hanna, both my publicist at Torchflame and the development editor for Broken Glass. I appreciated her insightful character suggestions and also the fact that she caught a few errors in who knew what and when did they know it.

Dr. Kathleen D'Appolonia, my friend and official civilian reader, who returned as the clue monitor and good grammarian, turned in another excellent job on this second manuscript. Thanks to my brother Jeffrey, and my sister Lorelei, for cheering me on; our relationship is living proof of the validity of my theory of the Kaleidoscope Effect, presented in The Healing Process: Stories of Ordinary People Working Through Grief.

Finally, thanks to my husband David, who provides the day-to-day support necessary for any writer to do their job, and to my two dogs, who always look like they understand when I talk out loud to them about plot twists and poisons.

ABOUT THE AUTHOR

REBECCA A. MILES (STEPEK) was raised, educated, and established her career in the city of Pittsburgh, Pennsylvania. From her work as a psychologist specializing in Behavioral Medicine in Oncology, she became a recognized expert and presenter on grief, the grieving process, and the psychology of dealing with loss.

She believes that all forms of criminality are about loss—the loss of the rule of law and its subsequent effect on the community, the loss of privacy and security in one's home, the loss of control over one's body, the loss related to the death of dear friends and family due to criminal acts, or the loss of meaningful family possessions.

Chief Detective Stefan Jablonsky and amateur sleuth Kate Chambers return in *Broken Glass*, book two in the *Pittsburgh Murder Mystery Series*, working together once again to pursue the murderer of a young man who was searching for a valuable family antiquity. In this meditation on obsession, Jablonsky and Kate enter the underground world of collecting fine art, particularly blown glass, and must confront the question of whether there is any limit to what certain collectors will do in order to possess a desired object.

Rebecca A. Miles received her doctorate in psychology from Duquesne University.

Connect with and follow Rebecca:

rebeccaamilesmysterywriter.com
twitter.com/RMmysteries
goodreads.com/author/show/5028437.Rebecca_Miles
amazon.com/Rebecca-Miles/e/B06Y4ZJPJ2

GROUND TRUTH

WHEN TWO SKELETONS ARE DISCOVERED in Pittsburgh and Kate Chambers believes that she has insider information about the crime, she joins Chief Detective Stefan Jablonsky in his investigation.

It doesn't take long to identify the victims: two siblings who had gone missing twenty years ago. As Kate digs into the neighborhood and Jablonsky starts chasing down leads, the list of suspects grows.

With the cold case reopened and witnesses dying soon after coming forward, it's clear that someone has a lot to lose. Kate and Jablonsky must work together to unravel the mysteries and make sure that whoever killed the siblings doesn't get away with murder a second time.

Lightning Source UK Ltd.
Milton Keynes UK
UKHW012121020223
416402UK00009B/98